island tempest

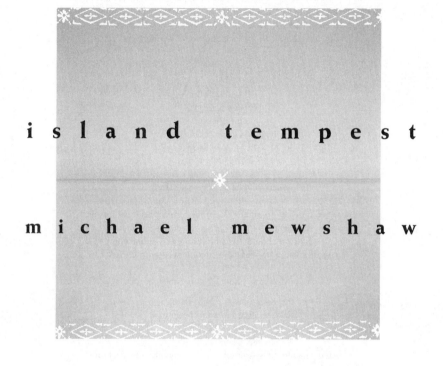

island tempest

michael mewshaw

G. P. PUTNAM'S SONS

New York

G. P. Putnam's Sons
Publishers Since 1838
a member of
Penguin Group (USA) Inc.
375 Hudson Street
New York, NY 10014

Library of Congress Cataloging-in-Publication Data

Mewshaw, Michael, date.
Island tempest / Michael Mewshaw.
p.   cm.
ISBN 0-399-15221-0
1. Gated communities—Fiction.   2. Community life—Fiction.
3. Neighborhood—Fiction.   4. Revenge—Fiction.   5. Crime—Fiction.
I. Title.
PS3563.E87185   2004   2004044709
813'.54—dc22

Printed in the United States of America
1   3   5   7   9   10   8   6   4   2

This book is printed on acid-free paper. ∞

Book design by Stephanie Huntwork

In memory of Robert and Barbara Kirby

Why is it there is so little about old people in books? . . . I suppose it's because old people aren't able to write themselves and
young ones don't take any interest in them. No one's interested
in an old man. . . . And yet there are a great many curious things
that might be said about them.

—ANDRÉ GIDE
The Counterfeiters

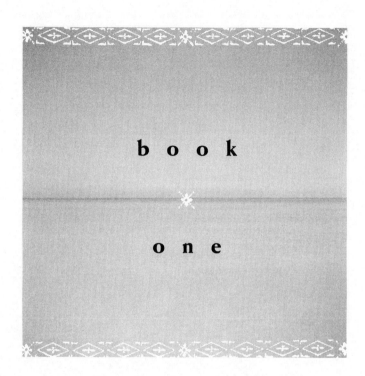

book

one

1

It was evening on the island of Eden, that hour when the wind diminishes and noise carries for miles. The muted surge of the ocean, the spritz of golf course sprinklers, a dog barking in a house across the street (or was it across the strait on the mainland?), the dull whine of insects against the mesh screen. At such moments, Florida felt profoundly ahistorical and tidal flux was the lone measure of time in the Empire of Amnesia. Yet Frank Pritchard remembered. He remembered more than he liked to. And less.

In a corner of his canopied patio, he sat smoking and musing. Beside him, a small TV broadcast a basketball game—the Miami Heat versus the L.A. Lakers. Frank watched it and, at the same time, declined to pay strict attention. This was a feat of mental gymnastics he frequently performed these days—balancing two things in mind at once. Not so much multitasking as avoiding one thought with another.

It was January, little more than a year since his wife died, little more than a week since his daughter's visit for the holidays. Because it pained him to think about Dorothy, he concentrated on Willow and how much he treasured her company, how he wished she had stayed longer, how tempted he had been to beg. But Dorothy and he had always been determined to make their only child emotionally and financially independent. In that they had succeeded beyond all expectations and almost beyond Frank's tolerance. Willow was now thirty, unmarried and childless. She lived in Italy. An artist, she insisted on going where the light was good—as if Eden were an area of darkness.

When it became uncomfortable to think about Willow, Frank dipped back into the basketball game. The Lakers led by ten. Then slowly he segued into wistful reveries about a grandchild. If pressed, he would have conceded that this was a displaced wish that Willow were young again and he had a second chance to prove how much he loved her.

Kids! On Eden, as in so many enclaves of its kind, the word "kids" had an incantatory ring. "The kids are coming for Thanksgiving," people started boasting in September. "They'll be back at Christmas," parents preened in their good luck. "The kids are bringing their kids for Easter." This was the status equivalent of claiming, "I was there for the IPO and got in on the seed round." Or, "I bailed out of the market before the crash." Suddenly, every man's self-worth seemed bound up in whether he had been, and still was, a good father.

Not that Frank Pritchard had been such a bad one, but he had traveled a lot during his corporate career, and when he was home, he had had to catch up on his rest, review his investments, reacquaint himself with Dorothy, and prepare for the next business trip. Only on overnight flights to Europe and Asia had he ever enjoyed the leisure— and the extra glass of wine in the first-class cabin—to indulge in introspection and contemplate his daughter's bright future and regret that he hadn't spent more time with her. He had always meant to make it up to Willow. But then it was too late, and she was the busy one—with boys, school, her own travel, and now art.

To salve his conscience, he used to bring her souvenirs from airport duty-free shops. T-shirts that said, "My Father Went to Hong Kong and All I Got Was This Lousy . . ." Dolls in international dress. Key chains with famous landmarks in miniature. As his income grew, and Willow got older, he splurged on perfume and jewelry. Once, in Amsterdam, he bought her a diamond bracelet.

It dawned on Frank that Willow now apologized for her absence in much the same fashion as he had. Rather than give him grandkids, she sent him souvenirs, photos of herself in celebrated spots, and trinkets and brainteasers. Rubik's Cube, a puzzle ring from Istanbul, MENSA quizzes, conundrums from the *Scientific American*, a subscription to the *Manchester Guardian*, whose crossword puzzle was reputed to be the world's most difficult. These had been his mind diet before his gray matter began to feed on itself.

Frank swung his gaze around to the fairway, where the last foursomes were bundling into their carts and heading for the clubhouse. A grainy veil distorted the green on the thirteenth hole. This might have been mistaken for a symptom of macular degeneration, but it was a visual effect produced by the mesh that tented the pool and patio, screening out insects, animals, and shanked balls. As the golfers retreated, dog walkers invaded the rough, each with a plastic sack in hand, poised to stoop down and clean up after his pooch.

The scene looked timeless and immutable, and Eden might have passed for the authentic original that nouveau riche resorts imitated. But that was an illusion Frank had had a hand in creating. The island had been developed in the past decade by the real estate division of the corporation Pritchard used to run. With the exception of its fringes of mangrove forest, nothing, especially not its winter population, was indigenous to the place. The perennially blooming flowers, the trellised vines and topiary shrubs, the palms and royal poincianas, the Bermuda grass on the fairways and close-grained turf of the greens, everything had been imported. Even the sand for the golf course traps and the beach coves had been brought over by the boatload from the Bahamas.

But certain Florida life forms had swarmed in on their own cold-blooded steam. Fish and manatees thronged the coastal canals, and birds by the thousands, not to mention insects by the millions, drifted ashore on tidal currents and trade winds. To the astonishment of home buyers who arrived before landscapers finished off the last touches, artificial lakes were no sooner bulldozed out of coral bedrock than they filled with tea-colored water, then slimy weeds, then the beady eyes and corrugated backs of submerged monsters. Alligators were given free rein of Eden as long as they didn't frighten golfers or gobble up pets. When they did become obstreperous, uniformed teams of trained animal handlers trapped the gators and transported them to the Everglades.

Just recently, a couple of power walkers striding across the golf course in the clement air and blissful peace of dawn claimed to have spotted a panther. Though the alleged sighting upset some folks, it excited many others. Nothing could have delighted them more than the idea that an endangered species—the same perky-eared, gimlet-eyed cat pictured on Florida license plates—shared the island, living in the shadows of their townhouses, condos, and villas. But in the opinion of the animal handlers, such a huge, warm-blooded predator couldn't possibly hide on Eden.

In the still air, Frank heard a sliding glass panel squeal open. His neighbor's door needed grease. A man in a wheelchair rolled out onto the patio of the house next to Pritchard's. He was a muscular, swarthy fellow, a source of curiosity for several months. The crippled man made it a point to keep to himself. No one on the island had met him.

Although Pritchard might have gone over and introduced himself, he felt too deeply mired in his own predicament to intrude on someone else's. So he gazed on from a distance, much as he stared absently at the darkened pigment on the backs of his hands and wondered, When did this happen?

The man was in bathing trunks, his upper torso a meaty inverted triangle from which atrophied legs extended like unrealized afterthoughts. Frank had often watched him unstrap belts from his waist and knees, and tumble into the pool and swim. But this evening he stayed put in his chair and peered out at the fairway, where the last of the sun backlit the dog walkers. Then he groped under his seat cushion and extracted something that gleamed in his hand.

Frank picked up a pair of binoculars and took a closer look. Adjusting the lenses, he attempted to zoom in on the object, but was balked by the light. He could only make out what appeared to be a length of polished steel, perhaps a tool to tighten the wheels of the wheelchair. The man lifted it at arm's length, as if to measure the space that separated him from the dog walkers.

Abruptly the timed pool lamps winked on next door, and in their shimmering blue glow, Frank saw that the guy had a gun. It looked like he was debating whether to take a potshot at a dog or its walker. Before Frank could cry out, "Stop!" the cripple thrust the gun barrel into his own mouth, sampling the taste of something bitter and mysterious.

Pritchard sprang to his feet. The legs of his wrought-iron chair rasped against concrete. The binoculars slipped out of focus. With naked eyes, he watched the man wheel around toward his house. Had he heard the commotion? Or just changed his mind? Frozen in place, Frank waited for an answer in the form of a pistol shot.

A minute passed. Then another. Still there was no noise, not even of the sliding door slamming shut. Pritchard sagged back into his chair. In silence and slo-mo, Shaq threw down a thunderous dunk. The Lakers were leading by twenty. The dog walkers retreated, toting their warm plastic sacks. Frank listened to the trill of frogs and crickets that had clicked on as if they were controlled by a timer.

He could have called the police. He might have raced over and made sure his neighbor was alive. But he was a private person himself, well acquainted with melancholy, a husband who had watched his wife endure a slow death and believed that a quick one was preferable. He lit a cigarette and remained in his corner until halftime, then went inside to fix a Lean Cuisine.

The next morning, in a routine that hadn't varied since his retirement, Frank showered, shaved, and slapped his cheeks with cologne. Then he slipped into his magician's robe. A gift from Willow, the robe swirled with astrological signs that made him feel silly. But it kept him warm in the early hours when he resumed his station out on the patio. His office. That's what Dorothy had dubbed that corner, with its table and chair and TV. Now that she was gone, he manned his post there every day doing . . . doing nothing much.

On TV the stock market tickertape slithered along the lower lip of the screen, beneath a larger crawl that reported events in Iraq. The Dow, the S&P, and the NASDAQ had suffered another nosedive. Frank muted the audio and watched the commentators mouth their cockamamie wisdom about price/earnings ratios. He had never expected to become one of those former CEOs who sat on their asses monitoring their assets. He was tempted to switch off the set. But that seemed like pulling the plug on a terminal loved one, and Pritchard felt he couldn't afford to cut any connection to life.

The light at this hour, on a winter A.M., had an opalescent sheen that suggested that nothing too serious, nothing with sufficient weight to cause trouble, could befall him. Yet the sun rained down on Pritchard like razor blades, and at the corner of his left eye, a hairy-legged spider scampered about. He recognized it as an eye floater. The ophthalmologist had advised him not to worry, there was nothing to be done about it. So Frank ignored it as he would any minor annoyance. Above all he wanted everybody to believe he was fine.

To steady his nerves—he hadn't slept well for worrying about his neighbor—he read *The Worst-Case Scenario Survival Handbook* and smoked. He could have done the same thing indoors, but he had never smoked in the house while Dorothy was alive. She hated cigarettes and complained that their foul smell insinuated itself into everything from the kitchen curtains to her cotton underpants. For him to light up a Camel in the kitchen or living room would have been a desecration of her memory.

From *The Worst-Case Scenario*, he learned how to survive a train wreck, an airplane crash, a snakebite, and a bear attack. He read on, hoping to discover something of relevance to his situation. But nothing applied.

Two women were on the patio with him. One sat in a chair beside him, squinting through the binoculars at the pool next door. The other was in Frank's pool, swimming laps.

"You seem unhappy," said Randi Dickson, holding the binoculars a fraction of an inch from her mascaraed eyes. "Why? You have so much to look forward to."

Unconvinced of his life's coming attractions and wanting to spare Randi more complaints, he glanced at the mercury smudge of his swimming pool. Barely roiling the water, creating less than a whisper of disturbance, a lean woman in a red Speedo maillot sharked from end to end, executing effortless flips, and breaststroking against her gentle wake. Ariel Murphy was the nurse/companion/physiotherapist who had treated Dorothy during the last months of her life, and

Pritchard would no more have let her go than he would have smoked in the house.

Randi sighed. "What are we going to do about you, Frank? Why don't you refill the hummingbird feeder? Remember how they used to flit around? So tiny and colorful. You enjoyed that."

Indeed, he had. When Dorothy first bought the binoculars and a book about bird life in Florida, they both spent many a pleasant hour logging onto the computer a list of the specimens they had spotted. They had had good times together, Dorothy and he, and had planned to have more. Now he seldom picked up the binoculars except to do what Randi was doing—spy on his neighbor. As for the hummingbirds, they had proved to be a big disappointment.

Initially they had descended on the feeder in flashing metallic droves. As they fluttered to and fro in relentless waves, one hummingbird, no bigger, yet far greedier and more thuggish, began to dive-bomb the rest of them. Before long, it chased off the flock and arrogated the drip bottle of sugar water to itself. When it wasn't poking its needle beak into the jackpot, it perched for hours on the feeder, a threatening sentinel.

It infuriated Frank to have a bully cheat the others out of a share. And it bothered him almost as much what the little lout was doing to itself. Free as a bird—that's what it should have been. Instead, it might as well have been in a cage. When he couldn't shoo it away, Pritchard quit refilling the feeder.

With Randi lost in contemplation of the neighbor's pool, he took the opportunity to stare at her. A handsome, stylish woman. An ash blonde with a lustrous tan and a taut body that she toned up at the island fitness center. In her early fifties, a dozen years Frank's junior, she looked far younger. She was a trophy wife currently between husbands, and provoked wariness and malice among Eden's matrons. Although Dorothy hadn't been given to gossip or jealousy, she agreed that Randi must have had her eyes done, her tummy tucked, her dewlaps lifted.

This had never struck Pritchard as a fatal flaw. Whatever Randi was doing, it worked. Just speaking objectively, she was damned attractive. Or at least she had seemed so before Dorothy got sick. Ever since the funeral, Randi had vowed "to be there" for Frank. And "there" meant here on the patio. She dropped by once, sometimes twice, a day, and kept him company watching the stock market. But he missed his wife too much to pay Randi personal attention.

"There he is," Randi whispered.

The man in the wheelchair rolled out of his house.

"Who do you think he is?" she asked.

"His name's Barlow, the postman told me. Cal Barlow."

"I know his name. I mean, who *is* he? What's wrong with him?"

"Maybe he was born crippled. The way he moves around, he looks like he's been handicapped a long time."

"Not 'crippled,' not 'handicapped.' You're supposed to call them 'differently abled.'"

In this guy's case, Pritchard had to admit, it wouldn't be political correctness to call him "amazingly abled." Thick through the chest, each vein and sinew of his arms as neatly defined as a diagram in an anatomy textbook, he wheeled over to the pool. He wore one of those ball-crushing slingshot-size swimsuits that Frank associated with the European resorts where Willow did watercolors. After releasing his seat belts, Barlow leaned forward and let gravity suck him out of the chair and into the chlorinated water. He porpoised to the surface in a silver spray and rowed forward with his arms while his lifeless legs trailed behind. Unlike Ariel, who eeled along as gracefully as an otter, this guy had the grumbling power and churning push of a tugboat.

"Isn't he something?" Randi said. "That body, those biceps. It shows what you can do."

"What can you do?" Frank asked.

"Whatever you want. It's mind over matter. That's why I'm always after you to join the fitness center or come for a walk with me."

"Ask Barlow to keep you company at the fitness center. By the looks of him, he could be your personal trainer."

"You said it. What a hunk. Freddy tells me he plays tennis." Freddy was her son and Eden's assistant teaching pro. "Freddy says he's good. He scoots around the court in his chair like the Energizer Bunny. Didn't you play in college, Frank? You should take it up again."

"Bad as my back is, I'd wind up in a wheelchair myself."

"Some girls in my art class, they think Barlow must have been wounded in the war."

"Vietnam?"

"That was thirty years ago. He'd have been about five back then." She lowered the binoculars to her lap. "My hunch is he was wounded in the Golf War."

The Golf War? No, of course, she meant the Gulf War. Still the idea of a gory skirmish on the fairways appealed to Frank. An outbreak of violence between players in carts and those who carried their own bags. Mangled corpses identifiable only by their white shoes and plaid pants. Greens oozing red. Where could he sign up?

"Or he might have been a policeman or a fireman," Randi went on. "A hero at the World Trade Center. He sure looks like one."

"A cop?"

"A hero. He looks so brave and vital, he doesn't let you feel sorry for him."

Pritchard thought it wise not to mention that he had seen Barlow with a gun barrel between his teeth. He didn't want to disappoint Randi. Then, too, there was a chance he had misread what he saw, imposing his own mindset on the man's innocent actions.

While Ariel continued her nearly effortless progress in his pool,

Pritchard had the sense that the suntanned mesomorph and the freckled ectomorph were competing. Then Barlow began to struggle. His heavy arms slapped the water in slower, arrhythmic lurches until at last he grabbed the side of the pool and rested his head on his crossed wrists. After he caught his breath, he planted his palms and flexed his shoulders, heaving himself up onto the patio, and grappled hand over fist across the concrete. His dead legs left snail tracks to his wheelchair.

His climb into the chair was a prodigious feat of athleticism. Gripping the armrests, he knelt for an instant like a priest at a prie-dieu. Then he transformed himself from a priest into a gymnast mounting parallel bars. With a swivel of his hips, he swung his butt around and plunked it onto the seat cushion. He buckled the belt at his waist. Bending down, he disentangled his legs, which had looped around each other like noodles in a saucepan, and attached the belt over his knees. Once his feet were in their stirrups, he tilted the chair back and whirled in a circle. He might have been drying his hair or practicing his balance or simply indulging in the pleasure of the spin. Then again, Pritchard thought, he resembled an animal circling its cage to make sure it was safe.

"I can't imagine what it's like to be paralyzed," Randi said.

Frank thought he could, but he didn't say so. After all, no matter how bad he felt, he wasn't in a wheelchair.

"It makes you reflect," Randi said as Barlow rolled back into his house, "on the advantages you have and take for granted. You could lose it all overnight."

"Don't I know it."

"Better enjoy it while you can. Because who knows how long we have left?"

Pritchard didn't care for this line of conversation. His every third thought was already of death and his every fourth was of homicide.

"I've been thinking," Randi said. "To be honest, I've been doing more than thinking. I've been researching the subject." She set the binoculars on the table, which was littered with bank statements, proxy forms, annual reports, and solicitations. "You need a vacation."

"From what? I'm already in Florida doing nothing."

"Time to do something different! Have you considered a cruise?"

"A bunch of folks in tuxedos and ball gowns worrying about catching the Norwalk flu? No, thanks."

"I don't mean that kind of cruise. I mean one that combines learning and adventure, in a sumptuous environment, with like-minded, outward-looking people." This had the ring of a line from a travel brochure, but Randi delivered it with a passion that smacked of originality. She dragged her chair closer to his. The metal legs twanged.

"Can I share my fantasy with you, Frank?" She clamped a hand, a nice one, nubby with rings, the nails handsomely polished, to his knee.

What could he say except, "Of course." The problem was where to fix his eyes as she spoke. He assumed the guise of a doctor who concentrates on the ceiling as he checks a patient's pulse and palpates a belly.

"There's a cruise out of Mazatlán," she started.

"You remember how I am about Mexican food."

"It's a Norwegian line. First-class in every category. Four-star food and accommodations. You sail up the coast to the Bay of California, which is absolutely swarming with marine life. Whales spawn there. That's the great attraction. You motor out in dinghies to the pod. You dive in and swim with them. Can you imagine?"

Unfortunately he could. Frank regarded whales as dumber, bloated dolphins. And dolphins, for all the terrific press they got, had begun to bore him. He was tired of hearing how intelligent they were, so much smarter than human beings and more sensitive too. You almost expected them to spout poetry rather than water. When was the last time, he wanted to ask, you saw a dolphin train a man in an aquarium?

He switched his eyes to Ariel, still swimming laps. The freckled shoulders, the flare of her rump, that surprisingly fleshy buttress to her rail-thin figure. A manic runner, a marathoner, she jogged to Eden from the mainland, miles away, then hopped into the pool to cool off. Where did she find the energy? Pritchard figured it must have had to do with her upbringing in South Africa.

"After a morning with the whales, you return to the boat for a shower and a nap," Randi said. "You should see the cabins. How cute and cozy they are. Trust me, you won't have any trouble sleeping." She squeezed his leg for emphasis. "Not after I'm finished with you."

Frank cut his eyes from Ariel to Randi, who mimed innocence. "Being out on the water is exhausting," she explained. "Plus there are all the activities aboard ship. It's not just drinks and dinner and dancing and shuffleboard. There are lectures and films about wildlife."

Her mention of "wildlife" brought to Pritchard's mind his classic 1966 Jaguar XKE. Randi resembled the car. Hand-rubbed enamel, sculpted lines, kid leather upholstery, everything, to all appearances, in prime condition. But under the hood, the engine required constant tinkering and frequent infusions of oil, cash, and other lubricants.

Such a temperamental engine, with a hair-trigger clutch, left him longing for a lower-maintenance model, a more elemental wildlife. Those people who claimed to have spotted a panther on Eden, he hoped they weren't hallucinating. Better yet, he hoped to see the big cat himself. He had no fear that it would turn on him and tear him apart. To the contrary, he believed such an encounter might pull him together again.

"What's your fantasy, Frank?" Randi asked.

Before he could answer, Ariel coasted over to the aluminum ladder and climbed from the pool. Holding her long strawberry-blond hair

in both hands, she wrung it like a towel, squeezing out braids of water. Rivulets ran down her arms. Cut high in the leg, the Speedo maillot exposed the points of her hips and the paler flesh, faintly marbled
with bluish veins, that stretched to her pelvis. The suit clung like a
second skin. No, it seemed to be skin itself, soft and dusted with
down like a baby's head. Frank had difficulty believing that Ariel had
a child herself. He imagined her taste, and a memory from his adolescence flooded in—a vanilla milkshake swimming through a straw,
coating his tongue in sweetness.

"Do you need me for anything?" Ariel called.

"No," he lied and watched her walk into the refrigerated air of the
house.

"How long do you plan to keep her around?" Randi's voice had
minute serrated teeth like the curved knife Frank used to section his
morning grapefruit.

"As long as possible."

"To do what? I admit she has a lovely face. Very decorative. But
she's got the body of a ten-year-old boy. And as far as I can tell, she
does nothing."

"She reminds me of Dorothy."

That brought Randi up short. It also brought a soft, dewy expression to her eyes. Her feelings for Frank, she always insisted, were
an extension of her friendship with his deceased wife. She moved
her hand from his knee to his thigh. "You were about to tell me your
fantasy."

"You don't want to hear it."

"Yes I do."

"No you don't."

"I wouldn't have asked if I wasn't interested."

He might have said something about the panther, how eager he
was to see it. But the discussion about Barlow and Frank's determina-

tion not to mention the crippled man's pistol somehow stirred a deep-buried obsession. "If I had a gun, if I had the guts, I'd take it to the club tonight, and if I thought—"

"You're not thinking right, honey."

"If I thought I could get away with it—I don't mean legally, just get away with it long enough to shoot everybody on my list—"

"Frank, that's not funny."

"I'm not joking."

"If I didn't know you better, you'd scare me." Her hand left his leg. "You still haven't recovered from Dorothy's death. You have a lot more grief work to do before you reach closure."

"Tell you what I'd like to closure. I'd like to closure my hands around their throats."

"Stop it, Frank. Dorothy had cancer. I know it was horrible. It was a tragedy for the two of you. Nobody would argue with that. But you can't blame people."

"Yes I can."

"The doctors did their best. So did you. I remember the days, the weeks, that you spent at her bedside. Think of Dorothy's example. She stayed positive and upbeat till the end."

"Yes, she was a saint. But the whole time she was dying, my friends and fellow board members were plotting to kick me out and disman-tle everything I had built."

"I agree it was terrible timing on their part. They should have been sensitive to your situation."

"They did it on purpose," Pritchard said. "I know how they think. I was distracted and they blindsided me."

"Honey, you should see a doctor and have him prescribe those pills."

"To hell with that. Leave them to Bob Dole."

"Not *those* pills. I'm talking about antidepressants."

"I'm not depressed," he protested with a vehemence at odds with the vacant distraction of his eyes. He gave the impression of an actor in a poorly dubbed foreign film, one where the picture didn't match the sound track.

"Of course you are," she insisted. "It's chemical. Nothing to be ashamed of."

"I'm not ashamed. I'm . . . I'm angry."

"You're mad because you don't want to deal with your sadness."

"No, I'm mad because they packed the board and destroyed the company. We had a reputation. A century of brand-name recognition. They jettisoned that and spun off every unit except the entertainment division."

"Well, it was the one that had the healthiest numbers."

"Now that's all the company produces—good numbers and lousy television. I didn't work forty years to leave behind a bunch of god-damn game shows and sitcoms and shopping channels."

"That's not your legacy, Frank. You know that and so does everybody else. You created a corporation that was sound in its fundamentals. That's why it was such an attractive takeover target."

"Whatever their target was, the ones they hit were employees in the manufacturing sector. They lost their jobs, their pensions, everything! Meanwhile, the board pocketed millions in stock options and bonuses. They robbed the people blind."

"You're overdoing it," she said soothingly. "They didn't steal. And you can't deny you made out pretty well in the reorganization."

"I don't give a damn about the money. What am I going to do with it? I couldn't spend it all in my lifetime if I tried."

"Oh, Frank, let me help you."

"Help me what? Spend my money?"

"That's not nice." She drew down the corners of her mouth in an unhappy face. "I'm worried about you. I'd like to put some joy back into your life."

"Sorry. I'm grateful, but . . ." He couldn't finish. He felt like a fool. He had done exactly what he dreaded—revealed that he wasn't, in fact, fine.

"Honey." She caressed his neck. "You're confusing the personal and the professional. Your grief with business. That's something no CEO can afford to do—get emotionally involved. You might as well blame Dorothy's death on Bush or the War on Terror or Iraq or Enron."

Frank didn't find this consoling. He felt everything was connected—the economy, his career, corruption, national policy, Dorothy's death. But how could he explain this to Randi?

"It's time for you to look after yourself, Frank, and leave the big picture to somebody else. Thank God you've got Willow. Thank God you've got your health and friends. Thank God we've got each other." Randi stood up, a sportive woman in white slacks and a blue linen blouse. "Now I need to go home. I'll pick you up for the party tonight."

"I've got a few things to do here." He flicked a hand at the papers on the table.

"Business first. That's more like the man I remember." She leaned down as if to offer an air kiss, brushing her mouth in vague proximity to his cheek. But she zeroed in and laid her lips against his. "Love you," she said.

2

It was that fading, in-between hour, Cal Barlow's least favorite time of day, when he couldn't fathom where the afternoon had gone or guess how he would survive the night. Though he was seldom in physical pain any longer, the ache of these empty intervals reminded him of his months in rehab, especially in the beginning, when he had worn a halo. An ungainly metal device bolted around his skull, screwed into the bone, and braced by struts to his shoulders, the halo had been like having a birdcage over his head. His own private prison with bars in front of his face.

He had arrived in Florida during the tail end of hurricane season, and every day he stationed himself at a window and watched afternoon thunderheads boil up at the horizon. Purple and brooding as men-of-war, they crackled with lightning, then split open for an hour or two. As one tropical depression slashed the island to ribbons, the sand traps and water hazards on the fairway seemed to play leapfrog.

The ponds filled up with silt and the bunkers became hip-deep wallows. Dazed alligators scuttled back and forth, bewildered about where they belonged.

Barlow didn't blame them. He was bewildered too. He spent so much time watching the rain drill what might have been solid steel rods into the Bermuda grass, he began to see the rods even when the sun was out. Along with making him fear that he needed glasses, they left him feeling stir-crazy and disconcerted.

In autumn, the earth exuded the cloying scent of flowers, as if from a hundred-dollar wreath at a wake. Then the wind changed and dry air blew in like an astringent cologne. Where the advent of winter up north was announced by wood smoke, here it sailed in on a bracing scent of citrus. But in every season there was the sound of air conditioners, whose ceaseless thrum reminded Barlow of ventilators in the intensive-care unit, pumping oxygen to patients too far gone to breathe on their own. The worst of them, the quadriplegics, were little more than heads on pillows. Barlow thanked God—he really did view it as divine intervention—that he hadn't wound up like that.

Above the waist he was intact, and intensive therapy had restored some sensation to his lower extremities and allowed him to control his bowels. No bags or catheters for him. No trailing smell of urine or worse. A high-functioning paraplegic, he had, everyone agreed, made remarkable strides.

Still, there were limits. Unlike so many spinal cord cases, he refused to spend the remainder of his life praying for a cure or searching for a reason. He recognized why and how he had been crippled, and he had pressing problems that didn't permit him the luxury of fretting over things he couldn't change.

Barlow forced himself into action. It was always better to be busy. Inertia was the enemy, and so was wasted effort. He planned every move like a chess master and systematically eliminated repetitive motion. Another lesson from rehab. Do things right the first time.

Wheeling out of the bedroom, he crossed toward the kitchen. His house was a spacious Spanish-y hacienda, the kind Cal associated with big shots and high rollers in Las Vegas. Laid out on one floor and paved with terra-cotta tiles. Terrific for a smooth ride, but terrible whenever he fell. The rooms were sparsely furnished and arranged for wheelchair access. By the time he moved in, special fixtures had been installed in the bathroom. A low sink, a roll-in shower stall, a toilet with grab bars that helped him transfer from the chair to the commode and back again.

The kitchen appliances could be operated from a seated position. The sink, the stove, the slate drainboard—everything was within easy reach. He didn't need to cook for himself. He could have ordered out. Name your cuisine and Eden had catering services that delivered it to your door. One crew, a kind of Meals-on-Wheels for the rich, had cornered the market on gourmet dishes. Alert them a few hours in advance and they'd prepare a four-course sit-down banquet for fifty. For an extra fee, they'd throw in flowers, balloons, and confetti. But Cal liked to fix his own food.

It was a talent his grandmother had handed down to him. A short, black-shawled woman from Calabria, she had taught him to make pasta as a little boy. Not that he did Italian dishes these days. The smell of garlic and oregano overwhelmed him with nostalgia, and nothing he prepared tasted half as good as Nonna's cooking. So he stuck to basic American fare.

While a hamburger sizzled in the skillet, he emptied a plastic bag of salad greens into a wooden bowl, tossed in a fistful of cherry tomatoes, and drizzled on ranch dressing. After melting a slice of cheddar on the burger, he pried open a bun and let it soak up grease from the skillet. Another unsettling reminder of rehab. In the early going, when he couldn't roll over on his own, therapists muscled him around in bed, moving him every few hours to prevent pressure sores. When they wanted to turn him over, they tucked him into a padded apparatus and flipped him like a hamburger in a bun.

For days after what the doctors referred to as "the incident," pins and needles, pitchforks and knives, bolts of lightning and storms of static electricity assaulted him nonstop. With its wiring out of whack and its circuitry misfiring, his body suffered prolonged seizures of hyperesthesia. The exact opposite of anesthesia. Pain pulsed through his wrecked nervous system and left him morbidly sensitive to the lightest touch. The weight and weave of a sheet felt like cinderblocks. He howled for the nurse to lift the abrasive cotton from his skin.

Once the agony subsided and numbness set in, Barlow was laid out on a tilt board, strapped down like a convicted killer on a gurney. But instead of a lethal injection, he was subjected to something almost as awful—a gauntlet of motion and flexibility, extension and rotation tests. In one exercise, "assisted coughing," the physio helped him clear his lungs of mucus. What could be easier than coughing and spitting? But after those sessions he felt like a cyclist finishing a grade-six mountain ascent, dizzy and quivering with exhaustion.

When the hamburger was medium rare, Cal dished up his food. Water glass, salt and pepper shaker, plates and cutlery—he set them in their accustomed places in the accustomed order on a tray. Do it right the first time, the same way every time, and you didn't have to make half a dozen return trips.

With the tray securely fixed on his lap, he wheeled into the living room and positioned himself in front of the television. He selected a program as carefully as he had prepared his dinner. At all costs, he wanted to avoid movies starring Christopher Reeve, telethons for crippled tykes, footage from the Special Olympics, and the new season of *The Sopranos*. He also abhorred reality TV—*Big Brother, Brave New World, Survivor,* and their knockoffs. It was worse than being in jail to watch a bunch of punks picking their noses around the clock. What sort of asshole invited constant surveillance? At least in the joint you got locked down at night and had a bit of privacy.

Cal tuned into Animal Planet. A show about cougars in the backwoods of the American West. The big cats resembled Florida panthers. But unlike the panther, an endangered species down to a last few dozen stragglers skulking in the boondocks of the state, the western cougar had mounted a comeback. Eighty thousand of them were on the loose, the commentator claimed, more than when Columbus discovered America.

Barlow shivered in excitement. Goosebumps spilled down both his arms. In his condition, he had to satisfy his deepest cravings vicariously. Chaos in the Middle East, catastrophic blizzards on the Weather Channel, color-coded terrorist alerts on CNN, a panther on the prowl in the sleepy precincts of Eden. It pleased him to imagine the world on edge, teetering on the brink of a precipice.

God, they were beautiful beasts. As hunters on Animal Planet closed in on a treed cougar, Cal wished it would pounce and claw a couple of its tormentors. Leave them a bloody souvenir to remember it by. But no such luck. A fat dork lugging a rifle with a telescopic sight zapped the cat with a tranquilizer dart, and it fell in what appeared to be slow motion, bouncing from branch to branch, pawing futilely at pine cones, landing softly on hard ground, saved by the cushion of its ample pelt. Barlow had watched guys at Allenwood take tumbles like that. Zonkers on 'ludes. They collapsed section by section, scrabbling at the wall, smacking facedown on the floor, and never felt a thing.

It turned out the hunters had tracked the cougar not because it had killed anybody or attacked livestock. It hadn't done anything

wrong at all. They just wanted to study it. Trucking it off to an ex-
perimental enclosure, a kind of wired island several miles in diameter
and deep in the forest, they fitted it with an electroconvulsive collar
and set it . . . no, not free. They let it out on work release, on an in-
visible leash, while cameras scanned it around the clock. Whenever it
hit the boundaries of its range, it got a shock that goosed it into a
frenzy and infuriated Barlow. How could they do that to such a fine,
fully fanged creature—reduce it to a helpless house cat without its
even knowing it?

He flicked off the TV and carried his tray to the kitchen, cleaned
the plates, and left them to dry on the drainboard. Then he filled a
tall glass with water and tossed down his pills. Every day he dosed
himself against the spasticity that shivered his legs, and the abdomi-
nal cramps and urinary tract infections that were a constant worry.
Because of diminished blood flow to his legs, he also had fragile skin.
The smallest scratch could fester into an ulcer. So he wore soft, loose-
fitting clothes, easy to put on and pull off, and since a wrinkle could
cause sores, he was careful to keep them from bunching up. Sweat
suits were popular with paraplegics, but not in Florida's heat. Cal had
a wardrobe of thin baggy trousers and T-shirts.

With the air cooling and an aura of benign narcosis descending
over Eden, he decided to go for a spin. As long as he varied the time
and the course of his rambles, he thought it was safe to venture outdoors. He slathered on mosquito repellent, then checked his pistol, a
9-mm Beretta Parabellum with a fifteen-round clip. He shoved it under the wheelchair's seat cushion, out of sight but within reach. After
arming the security alarm, he bumped over the front doorsill and
locked up behind himself.

It was often said of upscale American communities that after dark
nobody walks and anyone on the street is apt to be frisked by cops.
But not on Eden. Here the paved hike-and-bike paths teemed with

joggers, bikers, skaters, and scooter pushers, all zipping along with their ears plugged by Walkman headsets. These people looked like the big cat in its enclosure, wired and electronically tracked, and in their wake, they trailed the sound of hornets trapped in a Coke can.

The posted speed limit on the island was 17 mph. The theory behind the odd number was that motorists would notice it and pay heed. This encouraged citizens to park their cars. Why drive when you could walk or pedal almost as fast?

Barlow joined the crowd. With everybody maintaining regular speed and respectful distance, they might have been targets on a conveyor belt in a shooting gallery. But amid this gaggle of potential witnesses, he figured he was unlikely to get whacked.

Not your usual SMOPs, the Slow-Moving Old People, the shrunken, sun-crusted peanuts who plugged the arteries of the rest of Florida, Edenites looked sharper and dressed smarter. Even the ones that tootled along in golf carts appeared healthy and bustling.

You saw them everywhere, those E-Z-GO vehicles. When not in service, they were plugged into electrical outlets to recharge their batteries. Outside the post office and bank, in front of the clubhouse, and down at the marina, they stood like horses tethered to hitching posts.

Cal didn't tarry. His chair had canted wheels, and he sat assertively upright, powering it along with callused palms. There were no handles at the back of the chair; it wasn't meant to be pushed. This was a high-performance sports model. The occasional curb or step presented no problem. He was trained to deal with a whole flight of stairs.

When you thought about it in a certain way—which was how Cal preferred to think about it—he was no more impaired than plenty of these folks. He felt equal to any man who was seated. If only he could convince everybody to sit down!

Blue-rinse ladies with no hips or asses ambled along indefatigably on skinny pins mapped with varicose veins. Spry geezers in shoes like earth pads, thick-soled and double-wide, looked like they couldn't be toppled by anything short of a dumdum bullet. Yet Barlow had seen them conked out beside the path, with oxygen masks over their mugs and a medical emergency team rushing to haul them away before the other wrinklies went hysterical and commenced hyperventilating.

They could have been Cal's mother or father. The thought sent him into a shallow trough of sadness that he feared might tilt him into something deeper if he didn't slide out the other side damn quick. He couldn't afford to go sloppy and sentimental. He had to keep his guard up. Just because they had white hair didn't mean they couldn't hurt you. The guy next door, for instance, the one eyeballing him through binoculars—Barlow wondered what his game was. He had half a mind to drop a dime on the snoop. Or maybe something ten tons heavier.

3

After Randi left, Frank lit a cigarette, stared into space, and let space stare into him. He shoved aside the piles of paper on the table. Each day's mail brought a raft of charitable appeals, preapproved lines of credit, deferred compensation, and stock options. As a CEO, he had had to delegate responsibilities, but he had always attended to financial matters himself. Now he no longer bothered to open any envelope with a cellophane window on it. Since sympathy notes about Dorothy's death had stopped arriving, he rarely received personal letters and could muster no enthusiasm for professional correspondence.

He turned, as he inevitably did in times of duress, to *The Worst-Case Scenario Survival Handbook*. How to Perform a Tracheotomy, How to Use a Defibrillator to Restore a Heartbeat, How to Escape from a Sinking Car. Many entries seemed aimed at the specific requirements of Florida residents. How to Escape from Quicksand, How to Fend Off a Shark, How to Wrestle Free from an Alligator.

Because a panther had been sighted, he reviewed How to Escape from a Mountain Lion. The key was not to run or crouch down. You wanted to make yourself bigger, more menacing, by waving your arms or flaring your shirttails. Playing dead might trick a grizzly bear, but it wouldn't fool a big cat. You had to show it you weren't prey, you weren't dead meat begging to be devoured. You'd fight back.

This last factoid resonated deeply with Frank. Part of his problem was that he had begun to resemble prey, carrion ripe for the picking. He had to remind people, himself included, that he was dangerous, not dead. But how?

Lighting another cigarette, he lingered in the darkness and found himself musing about his late father. He knew he took after his old man. So it troubled him to recall how remote his father became as he aged. Had Frank inherited his emotional detachment? Not that he wished to blame his father for his faults. If he blamed anything, it was life itself, the black humorous force that knocked you flat in the name of teaching you a lesson. In that Punch and Judy show that passed for education, he considered his father a classmate.

It was time to go inside and eat. Because he had no appetite, Frank prepared his meals by the numbers. Six o'clock signaled that he should refuel. He dined the way Weight Watchers dieted. In dead earnest, he portioned out food and consumed just enough to maintain vital functions. Though the kitchen, Dorothy's high-tech heaven of culinary worship, boasted restaurant-quality appliances—a Wolf range, a Sub-Zero refrigerator—and a larder of gourmet supplies, he cracked an aluminum tray of Lean Cuisine out of the arctic of the freezer and slapped it into the maw of the microwave.

He set the timer, and as the machine ticked off its incandescent minutes, he stepped out of the line of irradiating fire and ventured as a transient through the slow, mysterious rooms of his once familiar house. He knew he wasn't alone. He sensed Ariel's presence and advanced under the soaring ambition of the cathedral ceiling searching for her.

Furnished with odds and ends that Dorothy had shipped to Eden when they sold their home up north, the living room had an eclectic décor, a hodgepodge of designs that had been popular over the past forty years. Dansk tables, an Eames chair, a red leather Bibendum chair, an Eero Saarinen tulip table. And on every flat surface, there were the awards, tributes, plaques, trophies, and framed photographs that Frank had coveted during his career.

These mismatched furnishings and mementos were as dispiriting to him as a mausoleum. They might as well have been fossils. True, each item carried a history, a subtext, of a former house, a family event, a personal milestone. But now they all seemed pointless and as bogus as the ceremonial sword that had been bestowed upon him by the Japanese minister of economics. When Dorothy had it appraised for insurance purposes, she discovered it had been manufactured on Taiwan and had a value of eighty dollars.

A ping alerted him that the Lean Cuisine had been waved to optimum warmth. He backtracked to the kitchen, where Ariel was at the chopping block ladling chicken Marsala onto a plate. She passed the meal to Frank, then perched on one foot, propping the instep of her other foot against her knee like a Masai warrior. She had pulled on a pair of khaki shorts and a white T-shirt, a neutral backdrop for the freckles spangling her bare arms and legs.

To Frank's astonishment, hunger, something near starvation, seized him. At first it had no object. Or none he would acknowledge. He was simply suffused with an emotion that for a man his age seemed as superfluous as an appendix. A vestigial organ that might burst and cause septicemia. Then when it dawned on him what he wanted, he exclaimed, "Ariel, the egret," with a sort of gruff, off-putting bonhomie.

"I wish I never told you my nickname. Nobody but the blacks on my father's farm call me that."

"Why haven't you gone home?" he asked.

"I hung around to talk to you. I've been mulling things over in my mind." Her accent carried the hard consonants and flattened vowels of Cape Province.

"Sit down." He sat at the breakfast bar.

She remained on her feet—or rather on one foot. At a distance, her slight build and fair coloring could be mistaken for those of a young girl, but up close she showed signs of age and weather and sun. She was in her late thirties, he supposed. Maybe her early forties.

"I think it's time I gave notice," she said.

"Of what?" He steadied himself. Still in his flamboyant magician's robe, he wished he had on a pin-striped suit and was behind a polished desk, armor-plated against bad news.

"I feel bloody useless here. I come. I swim. I goof around for a few hours and then bugger off home. How much can that be worth to you?"

"Look, if it's the money, if you're not satisfied—"

"No, I'm embarrassed to get paid. It'd be different if you let me do anything." She switched from one foot to the other.

"I value your company."

"You've got Mrs. Dickson's company."

He tried to digest this, process it. The plate of chicken Marsala had stopped steaming and started to congeal. What could he tell her—that he was a saner, less irascible person with her around?

"I'm a board-certified physio," Ariel said. "A qualified masseuse. An expert personal trainer. I have a lot to offer. You're not taking advantage of my skills."

"I realize I must look badly out of shape," he said.

"It's not how you look. It's what you do—lay about all day smoking. You don't move from that chair. How can that be healthy?"

"You're right. I should get active and go to the fitness center."

"That'd be a start," she said. "You need interests, a hobby, maybe a dog."

"That's what Willow tells me." He didn't mention what he told Willow: he didn't see himself scooping crap into a plastic bag.

"Unless you know something I don't," Ariel said, "I don't believe there's anything I can do for you."

"That's not true."

"Yes, it is. You won't even let me stretch you or give you a massage." She pronounced it *mah*-sage.

The idea of her laying hands on his body was almost as disturbing to Pritchard as her leaving him.

"I could finish the rest of the week," she said. "But if you don't mind, I'd rather start looking for a new job."

"Whatever you like," he mumbled, swallowing the urge to plead, to bleat that he'd double her pay. He'd get fit, start simulated Delta Force training. He'd become combat-qualified. But he feared making a fool of himself. A bigger one.

"I hate to do this." Her voice softened. "I realize you've been through a lot. But you don't give me much choice."

"I'll be fine." In full dismissive executive mode, he plunked the chicken Marsala down on the drainboard and shook her hand.

"Well . . ." Finally both of Ariel's feet were on the floor. "I guess it's cheerio, then."

He scraped his plate into the sink and switched on the tap. Frothing water washed his dinner down the garbage disposal. When he buried his face in his hands, there was so much give to his flesh, such looseness of skin from bone, his face seemed to pour into his cupped palms. But he could maintain this abject pose only so long. A Zen master might quietly meditate; Western tradition decreed that in these circumstances a soul should set itself on fire, go ballistic, go batshit.

Frank pitched out of the kitchen and into the living room. It was so much easier to be mad than sad. You just had to lift a fluted Steuben vase from the mantelpiece and let it drop. Glass of that quality created little noise. It landed with a discreet thunk, quietly shattered, and spread glittering shards in a pattern like a controlled break on a billiard table. By contrast, Baccarat crystal exploded with a sharp report, its fragments describing an arabesque that couldn't be equaled except on the most expensive Persian carpet.

After peppering the floor with glass slivers, he threw in some Meissen and Wedgwood for variety. Costly ceramics disintegrated into beige sand. One massive ashtray, however, accelerated at the invariable rate of thirty-two feet per second, cracked the terra-cotta, and remained intact. To obtain pyrotechnic results, Pritchard had to impart a savage wrist snap to the ashtray, hurling it down with added speed. That cratered the tiles and unleashed a Roman candle–like eruption.

Frank had been educated as an engineer and hadn't forgotten his physics, his grasp of everything from Newtonian mechanics to nuclear fission, quarks, and black holes. But on the event horizon he inhabited at the moment, he gloried in mindless innumeracy. It was a thrill to break things, especially your own belongings. A child could have told him that. Every manufactured object ached to fall apart, every human construct was dying to be deconstructed. Beyond the alchemist's dream of transmuting dross into gold lurked the atavistic nightmare of precious possessions turning into trash. Since in the end we are condemned to molder into an inanimate essence, why not do some tonic damage en route?

He grabbed an antique ormolu clock, a commemorative gift from the people of the Czech Republic, and flung it against the fireplace.

Behind its arbitrary arms and specious numbers, it was nothing but a roach nest of springs and sprockets. In Brownian movement, they bounced around the room for an arithmetically predictable period before subsiding into inertia.

Frank's hands closed on the Japanese ceremonial sword. Worthless though it was, it had a keen cutting edge, good for smashing plaques and trophies and framed photographs. It knocked chunks out of the marble mantelpiece and mutilated the imitation logs in the fireplace. Dragging him along, the sword cleaved open the Bibendum chair, decapitated the tulip table, eviscerated the Eames chair, described cryptograms on the upholstery and dented the tubular chrome frame of a Knoll couch.

Finished in the living room, he marched through the house like a drum major waving a baton. He banged at lightbulbs, cut down a coatrack, and scored the dining room table with blade marks that might have been made by a butcher disarticulating a pig. Then in the kitchen he rested.

Behind him lay a horde of destructions. Ahead of him stretched an expanse of appliances ready to be razed. Although the Wolf range and Sub-Zero refrigerator looked impregnable, he was confident he could crush the cabinets and the crockery they contained, mangle the microwave, and circumcise the sink spigot. But for the moment he had done enough damage. He felt in top form, deeply endorphinized. The next time he slumped, he knew exactly what to do.

The sword had endured nobly. A few scratches and nicks. Nothing a whetstone couldn't repair. Frank laid it on the stove and went to dress for the night's party.

4

On the hike-and-bike trail Cal Barlow was boxed in by two power-walking women. "The chemo worked like a miracle," one of them said.

"Does the little darling have hair?" asked an elbow-swinging mama.

"Yes. He's in complete remission."

"It's a wonder what they can do with brain tumors."

"Yes. His blood work is perfect. We're bringing him home to-morrow."

"Want to borrow my travel cage?"

"No, the vet's going to lend me one. I can't wait."

Barlow couldn't either. Shouting, "Excuse me," he squeezed through. An island policeman passed him in the opposite direction. Plump and sun-pinkened, the rent-a-cop puttered along in a gray golf cart, wearing a lettuce-green uniform that made him look like a booth attendant at an amusement park. Probably a retiree from the mainland earning a few bucks to stretch his benefits.

Second to cleanliness, security was Eden's obsession. Gatehouses manned by armed guards blocked both ends of the causeway, and everyone employed on the island—legions of maids, gardeners, golf pros, pool cleaners, and harbormasters—had to undergo a thorough background check. Each dim cul-de-sac was illuminated by "crime lights" that resembled old-fashioned streetlamps on steroids, and closed-circuit cameras sprouted like strange fruit from strategically spaced trees.

Cal had heard locals boast that Eden was like a Caribbean resort, only without the poverty, dodgy politics, and truculent natives. Still, he didn't share the general assumption that the community was safe. It wasn't just the feeble senior security force that puzzled him. He had done some reconnoitering and discovered an odd detail about the CCTV cameras. Skulking around one of the guard shacks, he had chewed the fat with an old guy monitoring the video screens and noticed that they didn't cover the interior of the island, only its coastal perimeter. The inland cameras were fake.

That was the ultimate luxury big money could buy, he supposed, protection from outsiders and privacy for insiders. Nobody in a position to clock the peccadilloes of property owners except the powerless little brown, yellow, and black people who mowed the lawns, mixed the drinks, and Hoovered up the messes.

Still, Barlow believed it stood to reason that with so many categories and subsets of Hispanics, Asians, and West Indians on Eden, somebody had to be dealing. Or should have been. Even these oldsters had disposable income and appetites, and there was a younger group of Europeans and South Americans, all prime prospects. What a ready-made market, virgin territory, for a man with balls and connections!

In his last life, this would have set his mouth watering and his dick twitching. But in present circumstances, he needed to keep a clear head and clean hands. As for his dick, he didn't like to dwell on it unless or until he learned how to use it again. Baby steps. That's what they preached in rehab. You had to think of yourself as an infant given a second chance to grow up.

As he struggled to focus on the future and shake off the past, Barlow had difficulty locating his place in the present. He didn't feature himself in the themed residential units of Tahiti Townhouses and Portofino Grove, the beachfront villas of Bali or the enormous McMansions of Acapulco Villas. Glass-and-chrome high-rises housed the condos of corporate execs and wheeler-dealers who owned businesses up north but maintained Florida residence to escape state taxes. Then there were two stark towers where the terminally ill were stashed until they hit the end of the road—a hospice, a crematorium, and a memorial chapel huddled under one roof.

Cal didn't care to go there. Breaking away from the pack, he cut across the golf course, where no one ventured at night after the panther sighting. Miniature flags fluttered near the tee markers and larger ones flew at the greens. A committee of patriots had replaced the normal bright markers with the Stars and Stripes. In the unending War Against Terror, nothing was too good for the boys at the front and no opportunity was missed to raise morale at home.

In their carts, players never fully appreciated the contours of the land, the mounds that the course architect had bulldozed out of coral flats. But Barlow felt them in his arms and in the sweat that dripped down between his pecs. He gloried in the aerobic buzz—enough to stimulate thought, not so much that he had to stop to catch his breath.

No matter how he revolved the wheel of possibilities, he couldn't guess why the Justice Department had beached him here. When the feds fabricated his new identity and palmed him off on the Witness Protection Program, he hadn't expected to land in clover, much less Paradise. Periodically, agents dropped by unannounced, but they asked all the questions, they didn't answer them. So he had had to cobble together his own theories. Dubious about Uncle Sam's generosity to stoolpigeons, he speculated that the feds hadn't bought the house— it must have been worth a million bucks—and renovated it specially for him. More likely they had seized it in a drug bust from some crippled narco. Then rather than auction it off, they slotted Cal into it.

At times, he toyed with the possibility of a bored, fat-ass bureaucrat in Washington playing a wicked joke on the locals. Like one of those psychos that release piranhas into swimming pools. Just for the hell of it. Just to see how much havoc he could wreak.

But by nature and experience, Cal had no feel for gratuitous acts. He was a percentage player, adept at numbers; he didn't believe anybody did something for nothing. Sure, they fucked up, but more often they fucked you over. So he wondered whether his life of luxury was a test. Maybe the feds counted on him dipping his fingers into Eden's unprotected pie. Sooner or later, they must have thought, he'd take a shot at turning the island into his personal cash spigot, and when he did, they'd toss him out of the program and onto the street. The equivalent of capital punishment. The mob would whack him in a matter of weeks.

Or were the feds trolling him as bait? Watching him around the clock? Did they hope the mob would track him here and they'd collar the hit man, then climb link by link up the chain until they nabbed the guys at the summit of the shit heap?

Barlow had coughed up the names he knew—the bastard that shanked him on the cell block, the wise guys he did business with back home, his so-called friends who doubted he'd hold up in prison and feared he'd roll over on them to get his sentence reduced. But behind the foot soldiers, there was always a man with a plan, a whole cadre of kingpins Cal had never met, only heard referred to by nicknames.

Because he had brains, because he worked behind a desk, not out in the neighborhood breaking legs, there had from the beginning been questions about Cal's toughness. After his conviction, no matter how vociferously he swore he'd do his time straight up, somebody decided why take a chance? Cheaper and safer to hire some geek to sink a blade in his back. They never considered the knife might hit a vertebra and cripple him, not kill him. After that, Barlow had no compunctions about spilling his guts.

Illuminated by stars and a full moon, the fairway undulated around him. As he whizzed past sand traps and ponds, frogs quit croaking and alligators slid into the water with the sound of a sled plowing over slushy snow. The greens, which from his patio looked pancake flat, had ripples and cross-grains. How the hell did players ever knock a ball into the hole?

Clumps of vegetation dotted the course, shady bowers for overheated foursomes. The exotic shapes of sable palms, Shiva-armed banyans, and jacarandas didn't look real to Cal. This time of year he still expected to see the bare limbs of oaks and maples.

The chair coasted along, ghosted along. He wasn't tired. His pulse rate and heartbeat remained within the comfort zone. But a rotten stench smacked him in the kisser and slowed him down. The halitosis of trees, the fetor of life and death and subtle gradations in between. Like so many things, it brought back Allenwood, where the stink possessed the solidity of an object, the weight and stomach-turning texture of a bag of baby ape shit.

Then at the highest point on the island—twelve feet above sea level—he caught a different scent. Distinct from the briny tang of the ocean and the odor of algae around exposed mangrove roots, there was what might have been the pungency of fur, of animal musk. He slipped the Beretta from under the seat cushion. The hair on his arms stiffened into antennae. From the crest of the knoll, his squinting gaze took in a pond and on its weedy shore, a low-slung shape. It might have been a gator. He blinked and strained his eyes, his streaky vision.

No, it was a big cat down in a crouch drinking water. Cal realized that he shouldn't, he couldn't, shoot it. To kill such a rare beast was unspeakable. If the panther attacked, he'd fire in the air and scare it away. Then he'd haul ass out of here himself. If he got caught with a gun, he'd be busted for parole violation.

He wanted a clearer view. He wished he had glasses. He'd never have a better chance to glimpse a panther in the wild. Once-in-a-lifetime luck. Ripe as the air was, the cat wouldn't catch a whiff of him. Holding the pistol in his lap with one hand, palming a wheel with the other, he advanced slowly. The tension provoked sympathetic trembling in his feet. His toes twitched in their stirrups. This mild spasticity had the side effect of heightening his concentration. He pulled his finger from the trigger housing to guard against reflex firing.

Transfixed by its reflection in the water, the panther hadn't budged. Through the narrowed slits of his own eyes, Cal watched and waited for it to do something. Anything. Hell, maybe he'd have to squeeze off a round to stir some action.

Then as he rolled closer, the cat changed shape, acquired greater clarity. It was beige and bigger than he thought, with a shiny coat and snub-nosed muzzle. Its tail . . . It didn't have one. Barlow retraced its sleek lines and realized that the panther . . . the panther was a golf cart.

He felt like shooting it. A fucking E-Z-GO. A customized job with a Rolls-Royce grille bolted to the front end of a standard model.

How the hell had he mistaken it for an animal? Probably its battery was on the blink and the owner had abandoned it and waddled back to the clubhouse for a beer.

Barlow reversed up the hill. Crestfallen, he halted there with that jailhouse BO in his nostrils, the squeezed cheese of a thousand cons crammed into a space built for a hundred. The sweaty fear and feral stench. No monkey house in a Mexican zoo smelled worse.

Yet even at Allenwood, at his lowest and most self-loathing, he had been a man, a husband, a father, a son. Now who was he? The right pocket litter—a driver's license, credit cards, and a Social Security number under his fake identity—didn't make him somebody. Uprooted from the self he had constructed since childhood, he had let the government assemble a spindly, unconvincing person like a model airplane that came in a kit.

He couldn't say what had knocked him flatter—losing his legs? or losing Phyllis and his son Sammy? The feds offered to take the three of them into protection, but Phyllis nixed that and wouldn't hear of letting him keep the boy. The cops warned her she wasn't safe. There'd be a contract out on her and Sammy. But she knew better and so did Barlow. Her family was mobbed up, and she was safer with them than with him. The thing he wondered was whether she had been in on the hit or had known about it in advance. Though he didn't like to think so, he didn't kid himself. By now, he bet, she had hooked up with somebody else and told Sammy to call the bastard Dad. Dead. He was as dead to them as his central nervous system was dead to his legs.

There came a ragged, skirling roar, louder than a cougar. Barlow's hand closed on the Beretta. A man, to all appearances deranged, rammed his shoulder against the golf cart, rocking it back and forth. The tires skidded on the greasy bank, and the E-Z-GO rolled into the pond. The Rolls-Royce grille nosedived, dragging the rest of the cart down after it. As it disappeared with a burbling gulp, the man roared again, triumphant.

Then he charged uphill toward the wheelchair. Cal recognized his next-door neighbor, the nosy white-haired spy. At the same time, he heard footsteps behind him. Panicked to have people closing in from two directions, he shot a look over his shoulder and saw somebody in black bearing down on him. He damn near popped a cap into the shadowy figure. But at the last second, the black-clad form spotted the other man, veered off the path onto the fairway, and vanished. Swinging around to the hard charger in front of him, Barlow took no chances. He aimed the Beretta and shouted, "Stop right where you are."

A red stain streamed down Frank Pritchard's pants. He appeared to have been Bobbitted and to be bleeding to death.

5

Where Randi Dickson grew up, the way she grew up, poverty was a full-time occupation. It didn't leave you much energy for anything else. In that corner of Kentucky, the mountains had been honey-combed, stripped, and flattened to unearth the last seams of coal. Then the mines shut down and the big companies shoved off and folks had to work 24/7 to keep nostrils above water. If you weren't willing to kick your feet and flail your arms, you went under. Simple as that.

As a young girl, she dreamed that wealth and leisure were syn-onymous. If she made enough money, she imagined she could cruise through life like a surfer. Sure, she'd encounter occasional patches of rough water and the odd lull and trough, but she wouldn't sink. Big bucks would buoy her up and she'd ride out the doldrums until she caught the next wave.

Since there was nobody rich in her holler, she vowed to mosey along and find a millionaire to marry. She had found three of them, but while she rebounded from each divorce with a healthier bank balance, she had no sense even now that she could coast. It was hard work managing money; the more you had, the more hours you spent on the job. There was always a new investment scheme to analyze or a scam to guard against. Her phone rang at all hours with brokers updating her about currency fluctuations and first-mover advantages. Then there were the pitchmen, no better than carnival barkers, who finagled her unlisted phone number and warned that she'd better get into futures. Yesterday was dead and she had to catch the train for tomorrow. They recommended derivatives, hedges, dark swaps, costless collars, and bundled energy.

The vocabulary alone wore her out and left her whimpering in confusion. She appealed to Frank for advice. She had read that she should apply Vabastram to every potential market position. To Randi, Vabastram sounded like a feminine hygiene product. Frank explained that it was an executive planning tool, an acronym for "value-based strategic management." But he refused to go further and take a hands-on approach to her portfolio.

Look at Martha Stewart, he said. A few tips from influential friends and the feds cracked down with felony charges. Look at Enron, Tyco, Global Crossing, and Qwest. These days, you didn't just have to worry about picking a winner. You had to wonder whether you'd go to jail. "Damned if I'm spending my golden years in the clink," he told her.

His golden years! The poor puppy. His golden years had turned to tarnished brass. Randi sympathized about Dorothy, his ouster from the board, the blow to his self-esteem. He really had been treated shabbily, and she knew he was one of those principled men who didn't feel better just because he came away with thirty or forty million dollars. He needed solace. He needed someone to share his grief and guide him back onto the right track. Whatever he had intended to do with Dorothy after retirement, he could do with her. He would never find a more cheerful traveling companion or ingratiating hostess. Why was he holding out?

Maybe that skinny-ninny Ariel distracted him, swanning around in her swimsuit. Obviously she had her eye on Frank. Her freckles brightened whenever he spoke. And why not? He was a wealthy, well-preserved, handsome man. If he weren't sunk so deep into himself, he would have pounced on her by now. Randi's problem was to wake him up, without alerting him to Ariel's availability.

There were men she might have mentioned who didn't have Frank's reluctance to get involved. They pleaded with Randi to open her portfolio to them in return for access to theirs. Willing to discuss wins as well as losses, they understood a woman's desire for intimacy, and dared to strip financially naked on the assumption that she would do the same. It was all part of foreplay for people of their age and stage. Whether they actually went to bed together was irrelevant.

At least it was to Randi. As a rule, she didn't get much of a rush from sex. That's why she was so good at it. She regarded lovemaking as another aspect of the hard labor of staying rich and never expected pleasure for herself. She concentrated on giving it.

That Pritchard had thus far been indifferent didn't discourage her. She had developed the habit, with an assist from self-help books, of viewing her defeats as temporary delays on the road to victory, her frustrations as valuable lessons in a lifelong course of education. And who better to teach her than Frank, whose intelligence proved that old adage about the brain being the sexiest organ? She conceived of his mind as resembling the Turkish puzzle ring that Willow had given him—a chaos of concentric circles and doodads that only a genius or an idiot savant could fit together.

But if she had a lot to learn from Frank, she believed she also had things to teach him, especially in the area of sociability and party skills. That's why she insisted he come along tonight. He needed to practice enjoying himself.

Dressing as a panther in a pair of black tights and a leotard, she attached a long slinky tail to her butt—arguably her best feature. Then, certain that Pritchard would forget that it was a costume party, she searched the closet for something he might wear. Years earlier, after a political benefit, she had brought home plastic caricature masks of Al Gore and George W. Bush. The masks still lay on a shelf side by side, like classical effigies of comedy and tragedy. Only in this instance both men looked like clowns. She scooped up the two masks. Let Frank choose between them.

Along with the masks, she lugged a week's worth of newspapers out to the garage to the recycle bin next to her metallic champagne Mercedes 230 SLK. Like everyone on Eden, she worried about the environment, global warming, and the wetlands, and agreed that it was imperative to protect the mangrove forest. Where recycled cans, bottles, and newspapers came into the equation she didn't entirely understand. Still, she knew that if pollution killed the mangroves and aerosol sprays depleted the ozone layer and greenhouse gases heated up the atmosphere, the polar caps would melt and Eden would be among the first places submerged.

The mere idea of this made Randi feel faint. She slid behind the steering wheel, arranged the Gore and Bush masks on the passenger seat, then had to heave a sigh and take a brief time-out. These days there was so much stress—crime, terrorism, anthrax, snipers—and now with the war in Iraq, there was talk of reinstating the draft. It petrified her that they'd ship Freddy over to fight in the desert. Her son who couldn't abide sand in his shoes or starch in his collars.

But then she remembered that Freddy was too old to be drafted. Rather than relieve her, this added to Randi's woes. How old did that make her?

With a remote control, she scrolled up the garage door. Bougainvillea blossoms littered the driveway. She hated to drive over them,
crushing the beautiful flowers beneath her tires. Nature was so fragile.
But what choice did she have? The life cycle was cruel and relentless.
There was no magic cream or potion. She had tried them all. You
could only postpone the inevitable.

Again she attempted to imagine a world without Eden and without her in it. But her brain went blank. It was like when her lawyer
talked about generation-skipping trusts and *per stirpes* provisions. How
could she reckon the needs of kids unborn to a woman her son hadn't
even met yet? Randi was a down-to-earth gal. Mention *per stirpes* and
there popped into her mind an image of her up in the stirrups on an
examining table, legs akimbo and a gynecologist poking at her pri-
vates. That was something tangible. But descendants decades from
now? Herself dead? She couldn't deal with that. She had too much to
do first—find another husband for herself and a wife for Freddy, then
travel and relax at last.

When she discussed estate planning with Frank, he laughed and
said, "Let me introduce you to my lawyer. He's made a lot of money
for dead people and for ones that haven't been born yet."

She didn't find that funny. Why couldn't he simply tell her how
much he had willed his daughter and her lineal descendants? Better
yet, tell Randi she was too young to fret about such matters.

A glance into the rearview mirror reassured her that she didn't
look her age. Not even close. She'd have estimated forty-five at the
outside. She lavished care on her skin, never stepped outdoors without sunblock, and was treated by an excellent dermatologist. Each
spring before they migrated north, all his patients had their precan-
cerous lesions zapped off. It was a ritual event on the island, like
burning winter brush before planting fresh crops.

Then every few years Randi flew to South Africa for a facelift and a safari. The Mount Nelson Hotel offered a terrific package deal. With the rand–dollar exchange rate weighted in her favor, cosmetic surgery was a bargain, and afterward a game park was an ideal spot to convalesce. She loved the animals and the landscape, even if she did have to look at them through puffy eye slits.

Although she couldn't see him having plastic surgery, she hoped Frank would travel to Africa with her. First, however, she had to coax him onto Prozac. And that, she knew, was a cure that carried its own disease, a pill that sometimes replaced one dysfunction with another. Her third husband had lapsed into despondency, and after months of zombie-like denial, he started antidepressants. In short order, they leveled him out and left him totally limp.

Come to think of it, her second husband hadn't been altogether firm either. A self-described romantic, he revealed that his notion of spooning invariably involved knifing and forking. Too many evenings consisted of a monstrous meal, a couple of bottles of wine, a gooey dessert, and cognac. Then he flopped into bed and snored as Randi lay awake watching the soft pudding of his belly shake.

At this remove in time, she had fuzzy recall of her first husband. She only remembered his hair, the dark brambles on his chest and back. In the beginning, he had appealed to her as a big cuddly bear. But once they lived together, she confronted the gorge-raising reality that he shed. The bathroom floor, the shower stall, the living room rug, and worst of all the bed were furred with his leavings.

A spunky girl and a good sport, Randi bought a Dustbuster and vacuumed the sheets every morning. The instant her husband exited the bathroom, she attacked it with a wet mop. In the end, he filed for divorce, accusing her of obsessive-compulsive cleaning.

By comparison, Frank Pritchard was well groomed and tidy, with what people called "a shock of white hair." He didn't call it that. He insisted it was no shock. It was a predictability. He said the same about his cheekbones, noble chin, and compassionate gray eyes. All purely genetic, he pointed out. He took no credit for his good looks and dismissed it as ridiculous when his photograph dominated the annual report and cropped up regularly in *The Wall Street Journal* and *The New York Times*. It was only after Dorothy died that he began wearing a frown like a clothespin that prevented his face from falling off.

As she swung the Mercedes up the driveway to his house, Frank was cooling his heels under the porte cochere, his hands in the pockets of his tan gabardines. Of course he had forgotten to wear a costume. Unless in a blue blazer, white shirt, and striped tie he intended to impersonate the CEO he used to be.

He leaned close to a light fixture next to the front door. Inside the globe, a batch of anole lizards pressed themselves to the glass. Each pad of their suction-cup paws, every internal organ of their minute bodies, was visible through transparent skin. By the time Randi and Frank returned from the party, the lizards would be cooked to crisps and curled like bacon bits in a dish at a salad bar. Tomorrow the gardener would unscrew the glass, sweep out the corpses, and reseal the light fixture. But by nightfall new anoles would appear on the griddle.

"Frank," she called.

"How do you suppose they sneak in there?" he plaintively asked.

"Frank, we'll be late."

"How can we save them from cooking? Maybe I should—" He unlocked the front door and switched off the outside lights. "At least these won't roast."

He was so tenderhearted, she hated to be impatient with him. As he walked around to the passenger side of the car, she said, "Don't squash the masks."

"What's this?" He held Gore in his right hand, Bush in his left.

"Gush and Bore," she jollied him. "It's a costume party. Take your pick."

"A pregnant chad and a dangler," he went along with the joke. "How do you tell them apart?"

"Do you like me as a pussycat?"

"You look great. Better than these guys." He brandished Gore's bland plastic mask. "He should never have shaved his beard. He should have let it grow down to his chest, like Fidel Castro, and refused to concede the election."

"I didn't know you voted Democrat." She sped down the driveway, then slowed on the street.

"Why fight like hell to get elected, then surrender and make nice? He won the popular vote. Why concede?"

Randi laughed, hoping there was a punch line on the way. No matter how oddly he behaved, she assumed he was joking. No matter how low his spirits plummeted, she believed she could perk him up if he'd let her.

"Just once," he said, "wouldn't you love to have a politician take to the warpath? Call for a general uprising. Go underground. Start urban resistance and a rebellion in the mountains."

"Do you think Bush is doing such a bad job?"

He ignored the question and glanced at the Bush mask. "Thanks for bringing these. Which one should I wear?"

"You choose."

"I like them both." He clamped the Bush face to the back of his head. "I saw a show on TV. Indian woodcutters wear masks like this to scare tigers from attacking from behind."

"No tigers on Eden," she said.

"What about the panther?"

"You mean me?" She fished the tail from under her rump and gave it a provocative shake.

"The one on the golf course."

"You don't believe in that, do you?"

"I'd like to think something's out there."

"Yeah, a lot of lost golf balls."

"And you accuse me of being cynical."

He pushed Bush to one side of his head and strapped Gore to the other side. He might have been wearing earmuffs with his face sandwiched between them. Randi didn't know where to look, especially when, as they snailed along at 17 mph, a breeze vibrated the masks. The warbling sound reminded her of stroke victims in Assisted Living, their sad attempts to control a slack tongue in the saliva pool of a gaping mouth. She shut the windows.

As they overtook a passel of exercisers on the hike-and-bike trail, Frank said, "Day and night, it never stops."

"What?"

"The race against free radicals." After a moment he added, "I can't smoke at the club. I'll need Nicorette."

She knew not to argue. Better to save her breath and persuade him not to attend the party disguised as a triple-faced totem pole.

Road signs and house numbers on Eden were so small and unobtrusive, newcomers had difficulty locating addresses. Even commercial establishments placed a premium on discretion that approached outright secrecy. Randi had lived a month on the island before she learned she didn't have to travel to the mainland to shop. Concealed in a grove of royal palms, a climatized mall housed restaurants and boutiques, a bookstore, a community center, and a gourmet deli. Randi swung in at the neon-lit oasis of gas pumps.

"I'll fill up," she said, "while you buy your gum. Leave the masks with me."

"Damned if I will." He winged the door open with his shoulder. "No woman'll pump gas while I'm healthy."

"Thanks, honey. I'll get the Nicorette. Why not take off the masks?"

He wasn't listening. Amid wavery high-octane fumes, he extracted the nozzle and thrust the black snake of the fuel hose into her tank. The gas station attendant, locked in his Mylar box, eyed Frank and his masks as if unsure whether to offer help or heave a net over him.

Flicking her cat tail, Randi escaped to the polar air of the deli, which broadcast Bach rather than Muzak. The establishment was like one of those posh airport gift shops that promise duty-free prices but charge a fortune. Wine racks cradled imported vintages from France, Italy, and South Africa. The takeaway counter flaunted foie gras, caviar, Brie, croissants, and brioches. At the cash register, where chain stores hawked the *National Enquirer,* there were the Sunday London *Times, Le Monde, Corriere della Sera,* and *Die Welt.* Nicorette gum set her back just slightly less than what she found Frank paying for a tank of gas.

"Outrageous," he said.

"It's only money." She gentled him by the elbow back into the Mercedes. He let himself be led but continued to fume.

"It's not the money," he said. "It's this damn outsourcing."

"What outsourcing?" She ground the gears in her eagerness to get away.

"If I wanted to spend my life pumping gas, I wouldn't have gone to college. I wouldn't have headed up a Fortune Five Hundred company. I'd have cut to the chase as a teenager and become a grease monkey."

"It doesn't hurt you to have a little exercise and do things for yourself."

"These days, the paying public has to do everything for itself. Forget about service, forget about the customer's always right. We're expected to do their jobs, then shell out for the privilege. You eat a meal and have to bus your own table. You hop a plane and have to pack your lunch. You're lucky you don't have to travel with your own toilet paper."

"It's cost-efficient, Frank. You know that."

"Yeah, it saves companies money. Not you."

Lord, what was he nattering about? After hours of dead-ahead, drone-zone staring, why did Frank have to wake up with these bees in his bonnet? Fortunately, the club was nearby. As Randi handed over the car keys to the valet, she decided not to mention the masks and rile Pritchard further. If he wanted to wear them both, so be it.

While the architecture of the rest of Eden chose as its template the world's exotic ports of call, the clubhouse was constructed in imitation of Monticello. Under its dome, the island's aristocracy—everybody except the South Americans and the Europeans—admired one another's costumes. Some had pillaged the wardrobe of the little theater, decking themselves out as Auntie Mame, the Man of La Mancha, and Gilbert and Sullivan characters. A few women who could get away with it dressed as grass-skirted hula dancers or gals from *Sex and the City*, and they complimented friends who had cobbled together disappointing outfits from their closets. The men in particular had made uninspired choices. Randi couldn't count the number that showed up as slovenly ships' captains and crusty fishermen. They looked the same way they looked every day at the marina.

Initially, Frank's masks prompted no nasty comments. A few good-natured partygoers observed that he was a living allegory of the 2000 election when the candidates had been two sides of the same coin and Florida had voted Bush into office by a margin no wider than Pritchard's head. But as the evening progressed with only canapés to dilute the alcohol, a tipsy woman insisted that the third face, Frank's, was that pinko campaign spoiler, Ralph Nader. Then a fellow costumed as a ceiling fan blew air up Al Gore's nose, and a guy in a firefighter's uniform sprayed seltzer into Bush's mouth.

To Randi's relief, Frank didn't react angrily. He didn't react at all. While she wouldn't have claimed that he looked happy, at least he wasn't haranguing anybody about politics or corporate thievery. But then Bob Emery, who had been the prime mover in ousting Pritchard and had replaced him on the board of directors, sidled over as if they were boon companions who had long since put business disagreements behind them. Draped in a white smock—was he supposed to be a butcher or an ER doctor?—Emery held out his hand. Pritchard ignored it.

Emery's florid face darkened. He gestured to the masks. "Well, Frank, you may have lost your manners, but I see you haven't lost your sense of humor."

"I don't have a clue what you're talking about."

"If the masks aren't a joke, maybe it's your marbles you lost."

"I don't have a clue what you're talking about," Pritchard tonelessly repeated.

"Oh, I get it now. You've decided a split personality is better than no personality at all."

After the savage fantasies Frank had described, Randi feared swift and brutal retribution. But to her astonishment he smiled. Or maybe not so much smiled as wrenched his mouth into a rictus every bit as grotesque as Bush's and Gore's. "No, Bob. I figured since you're two-faced, I'd better have three. That gives me more eyes to make sure your hands aren't in my pockets."

Reaching out his glass of red wine, Emery said, "Let me top up your drink. Put you in a better mood." He poured without looking, missed Pritchard's glass by a yard, and doused his tan pants with what looked like a bloodstain.

"Son of a bitch," Frank shouted. He went for Emery's jugular vein.

Randi squeezed between them and got smashed. It required the combined strength of a peacemaking Renaissance courtier and an Arabian sheik to pry Emery and Pritchard apart.

"A misunderstanding, a mistake," Emery said jovially once he was at a safe remove.

"Sprinkle salt on your trousers," the courtier advised. "Or should it be soda water?"

"It'll rinse out in the wash," Randi promised. "No permanent damage."

Pritchard yanked the masks from his head, flung them to the floor, and crunched a foot into each face. Then he stalked off to the bathroom.

6

The bathroom reeked of cigarettes. Regressing to high school, a contingent of retirees had hidden here to smoke. When Pritchard burst in among them, the men reacted as if caught by a teacher. Some tossed their butts into the hissing urinals. Others skittered into the stalls. All of them begged him not to tell their wives.

Frank waved that they needn't worry. Jawing on a plug of Nicorette, he stood at the sink and examined the damage to his pants. On the drainboard, between a jar of combs bathed in alcohol and a flask of aftershave lotion, there was a basket of hand towels. He grabbed one and dabbed at the wine stain. That made it worse.

It came to him in slow increments that that might be what he wanted. The thought entered his mind wavering and tentative as a shoelace guided by a shaky hand. It took him two or three attempts to tease it through the eyelet, but at last he got it straight. He would have to make things much worse if he wanted them to get better.

Leaving the cindery limbo of the men's room, he found Randi in the hall, fingering her cat tail as if it were worry beads. "Are you okay?" she asked.

"I've had it here. I'm going home."

"I'll drive you. You can change your pants and—"

"I'd rather walk."

"Don't do that, Frank."

"Why not? You always say I need exercise. I'll cut across the golf course."

"It's dangerous."

"You make it sound like Central Park."

"But the alligators. The panther."

"The mood I'm in, they won't mess with me."

She slipped her arm through his. "I'll walk with you."

"No, stay. I need to be alone for a while."

"Oh, Frank, promise me you're all right."

"I'll be a new man tomorrow."

Out on the parking lot, he prowled among the ranks of cars. Those polished hunks of imported steel, the extravagant flukes and formidable fenders. The sleek pride of Ferraris and Lamborghinis, sedate Infinitis and Audis, smug Beamers and Mercedeses and Porsches. Battalions of SUVs waiting to be summoned to battle, paramilitary toys for boys, symbolic support for the troops. Take back the streets and kick the rest of the world to the curb. One Humvee H2 had the vanity plates MRY-BORD—puerile shorthand for Bob Emery, chairman of the board.

Holding his house key at thigh level, Pritchard circled Emery's Hummer, as though admiring its macho tank massiveness, but in fact scoring its length and width with an uninterrupted gouge. Strips of paint fell to the pavement, crinkly as tinsel.

Job done, he strode out onto the moonlit moors of the fairway, past rippling water hazards and the wide white eyes of sand traps. It stunned Frank how good he felt. Maybe he wouldn't bother having his gabardines dry-cleaned. He'd unfurl them from the tallest palm tree on his property as the flag of his newfound assertiveness. This was the drug, he guessed, that addicted criminals. A chemical riot, a synaptic explosion, it put you in high spirits and prompted you to search for the next target.

Almost at once he spotted it. Near the ninth green, next to a weedy pond croaking with frogs and humming with bugs, a golf cart gleamed like a gift from God. Or was it devilish, not divine, fortune that placed it in his path? He recognized the Rolls-Royce grille and the MRY-BORD plate. Without a pause to consider the legal consequences, his chances of being caught, or the condition of his temperamental sacroiliac, Pritchard lowered his shoulder and shoved. He relished the strain, the purifying difficulty. Pouring everything he had into the effort, he rocked the E-Z-GO back and forth until it rolled into the water and sank.

Frogs and insects fell silent, and in that abrupt absence of outer noise, he became hyper-aware of the clamor of his heart, the bang of blood at his temples and wrists. To bring his body up to speed with his frantic inner organs, he felt he had better run. Wild-assed with exaltation, he charged up the knoll. He might have dashed a record mile to his doorstep had a harsh voice not commanded, "Stop right where you are!"

The cops! Somebody—the parking valet, a passerby—must have seen him keying Bob Emery's car and called security. He broke out in a cold sweat, clammy as the cabernet sauvignon. Far more than being arrested and booked, he hated the ignominy of getting caught like this.

"What the fuck do you think you're doing?" the voice demanded.

The officer, it shocked him to see, was crouched in a shooter's stance, aiming at Pritchard's chest. Frank's ribs, right where he expected the bullet to strike, puckered with gooseflesh.

"Put your hands up and come closer," the cop said. Strangely, he was in a chair. How long had he been sitting here? How had he known Frank would follow this route?

Then he recognized his next-door neighbor drawing a bead on him from the wheelchair. He let his hands drop.

"Keep them up," Barlow ordered.

"I can explain."

"This I gotta hear." He didn't lower the pistol.

"I was coming home from the club when I saw a friend's golf cart and—" And what? To his own ears he sounded as sniveling and guilty as those guys sneaking a cigarette in the can. "I thought I'd push it back up onto the path."

Barlow hooted. "Pull that bullshit defense in court and you'd go down quicker than the cart did."

"No, honestly, once it was rolling, it got away from me."

"Hey, I'm crippled, not blind. I saw you shove it into the water."

A flash of defiance shot through Pritchard. He dropped his hands a second time. He had dealt with presidents, Middle Eastern potentates, tinhorn dictators. He wasn't about to be bullied by somebody in a wheelchair. "What do you want me to say?"

"Just the facts, ma'am. Just the facts."

"The fact is it's a practical joke."

"Pretty expensive giggle. What's a cart like that go for? A couple grand?"

"Depends."

"I guess you got the money, you're free to have fun any fucking way you want."

"Right." Frank kept it terse. "Mind pointing that somewhere else before we both wind up sorry?"

"You ask me"—Barlow set the Beretta in his lap—"the one's going to be sorry is the guy that owns the cart. Then he's going to do his damnedest to make you sorry."

"Why's he need to know?"

"What are you saying? Half the kick of a good joke is the secret?"

"Precisely." Emboldened, Pritchard walked up beside the chair, as if the two of them were out for a friendly stroll.

"My hunch—correct me if I'm wrong," Barlow said. "This has something to do with what's leaking down your legs. Looks like you got your dick caught in a fan."

Frank had an inspiration that the truth—a short version of it—might serve him better than lies. "The guy that owns the cart spilled a glass of wine on me. Ruined a two-hundred-dollar pair of trousers."

"So it's payback."

"That's it."

"Now you're even."

"Not by a long shot." Anxious to quit this place and this line of conversation, he nodded for them to head home.

Barlow tilted his chair and heeled around. "Doesn't sound like Eden—people throwing wine. What's the deal?"

From annual stockholders' meetings, Frank had mastered the art of the *non sequitur* response. "You know, we're neighbors."

"Yeah, I've noticed you over there spying on me through binoculars."

"I'm a birdwatcher."

"And I'm a blue-crested boobie." Barlow's callused palms grated like sandpaper as he shoved the rubber wheels. His smiling tanned face gleamed full of teeth.

Frank's instinct was to apologize, but still in a feisty mood, he said, "If I watched you, it's because I was worried."

"About what?"

"Put yourself in my shoes. A man's in a wheelchair, and he has a gun. Some days he sticks it in his mouth. Some days he throws himself headfirst into the pool. What am I supposed to think?"

The smile wavered. "You tell me."

"I was afraid you intended to kill yourself."

Barlow coughed up a laugh. "Not my style. You saw the gun near my mouth, I must have been blowing dust off the barrel."

For a while, there was only the whisper of the chair on the path, the tremolo of bugs resuming their nightsong back in the barbered plots of jungle. "You don't mind"—Barlow broke the silence—"I'll make you a deal. You don't mention I got a gun and I'll keep my trap shut about the golf cart."

"I'd be glad to do that if I knew why you had it."

"I'm—how do you call it?—physically challenged. Okay, let's call a spade a spade. I'm a fucking crip. I need protection."

"Eden is probably the safest place in the continental United States."

"But not completely crime-free. We got a category of offender on the island, senile delinquents, out playing trick-or-treat at night."

Frank laughed along with him and assumed they had an agreement. Mutual silence. *Omertà*, as gangster movies put it.

"Tell me," Barlow said, "about this guy you'd like to get even with."

"It's not just one. There's a whole crew." At the far side of the fairway, Frank spotted their houses, the pool lights a blur behind the bug mesh, the interior lights controlled by timers that switched them on in random patterns. A breeze carried the scent of chlorine and jasmine, the purr of pool filters and air conditioners. Before he could catch himself and question the wisdom of what he was doing, he asked, "Like to come in for a drink?"

"Better my place." Barlow wedged the Beretta under his seat cushion. "It's set up for the chair."

"You sure? I don't want to intrude."

"Sure I'm sure. I'd like to hear about these people that pissed you off."

"They're not all that interesting."

"Revenge is always interesting. You know the old saying. It's the best way to live."

"You've got it backwards. The saying is 'Living well is the best revenge.'"

"Never looked at it like that myself."

They passed from the golf course onto the paved hike-and-bike trail. In front of Barlow's house, instead of a lawn, there was a low-maintenance swath of bleached gravel, cactus, and coral chunks. Cal unbolted his door, bumped up over the sill, and hurried to punch in the code on the alarm. This puzzled Frank. Most Edenites, all rich, theoretically on cordial terms, depended on the guarded gates and didn't bother installing home security systems.

Because it was sparsely furnished, Barlow's home looked larger than his and as impersonal as a motel, utterly devoid of photographs and souvenirs. In the living room, there was only a television and a La-Z-Boy upholstered in nubby material threaded with shiny fibers.

"I've got Scotch, gin, and vodka," Barlow said. "Not much for mixers."

"I'll take Scotch neat."

Barlow poured them both a healthy dollop of J&B. "Just a child's portion to help us sleep."

They sat and silently toasted each other. Cal encouraged him to prop his feet up, lean back, and relax. Frank preferred to remain upright, his polished wingtips, flecked with blades of grass, planted on the tile floor. It occurred to him that Barlow probably didn't have a license to carry a concealed weapon and that's why he was so eager that they keep each other's secret.

"That E-Z-GO you deep-sixed," Cal said, "when they fish it out, I'll bet there's nothing to link it to you. People'll think it was an accident."

"In some ways I wish they wouldn't." Frank sipped the whiskey, facing Barlow, but trying not to stare at him. His upper torso resembled the Michelin man's; his lower body looked deflated, boneless.

"What are you saying? You want to get caught?"

"I'd like them to know someone's after them."

"You really got a hard-on to punish them, don't you, Frank? Hey, you don't mind we're on a first-name basis, do you?"

He shook his head that he didn't.

"You can call me Cal. Tell me what they did to you."

Pritchard figured, why not? Why not call him Cal and why not tell him some version of the sad, infuriating story? New to Eden, isolated in the extreme, Barlow had no familiarity with the principals involved and no motive to spread gossip. Not unless he was a major stockholder and decided to alert the board of directors about the contempt they already knew Frank bore them.

So he unburdened himself. Holding it to half-throttle at first, then gradually stepping on the gas, he described his underhanded fellow executives, how they shouldered him aside and drove the company into a radical reorganization.

"You accusing them of criminal malfeasance?" Barlow asked. "Cooking the books? Fudging the numbers? Skimming the profits offshore?"

"No. What they did wasn't illegal, strictly speaking. It was just wrong. Unethical. Immoral."

"Immoral?" The word was an awkward fit in Barlow's mouth. Reaching out the bottle, he gave Pritchard's glass another gulp of J&B.

"Our company started over a hundred years ago as a family business," Frank explained. "Even after it went public, it kept that family feel. In small towns where we owned factories, jobs passed from generation

to generation. Fathers and sons, mothers and daughters worked together. I used to visit those plants. I knew the people and their kids.
It was personal. They sent me birth announcements and wedding
invitations."

"Jesus, this sounds like *It's a Wonderful Life.*"

"It *was* a wonderful life until the greed pigs broke up the company
and spun off its parts. All they cared about was showing a huge short-
term profit and inflating their bonuses. They put entire towns out
of work. They threw thousands of people into the welfare line. They
stopped funding pensions and health benefits. These were folks I
cared about, Cal. They trusted me."

"Hey, don't blame yourself. What could you have done?"

"You hear the cliché, what man on his deathbed ever wished he
spent more hours at the office? Well, I do. I wish I had spent as long
as it took to fight those sharks."

"You talking about the fella that spilled wine on you?"

"He's the biggest shark, but he's not alone. They're all into feeding
and basking."

"So why didn't you fight to keep control of the company?"

Frank sighed and sensed something inside him begin to disintegrate.
He feared he might weep and blab to this stranger about Dorothy's last
days in intensive care. That's where he had been when Emery and his
pals closed in for the kill. By Christmas week she had shrunk to a skeleton, just scattered bones under a sheet. Unplugged from life support,
she had had only a morphine drip to ease her pain as she lay in bed on
her back. Frank pleaded with the doctors. Dorothy always slept on her
side. It gave her nightmares to sleep on her back. No wonder she
wouldn't, she couldn't, stay still. Gasping, she fumbled to rip the oxygen mask from her face. But her wrists had been tied by gauze to the
bed rails and the struggle bruised her arms purple.

Ariel was on one side of the bed, mopping Dorothy's brow with

Kleenex. Frank was on the other side, holding her hand, trying to soothe her. ICU nurses had decked the halls with holly and mistletoe, and they bustled in and out of the room wearing Santa Claus caps and reindeer antlers. Pritchard wanted to throttle them. Thankfully, Ariel chased them away, and the two of them resumed their vigil until Dorothy drew one last breath and simply didn't take another.

Because he couldn't bear to reveal any of this to Barlow, Frank repeated what he had told Randi. "If I had a gun, if I thought I could get away with it, I—"

"Whoa! Whoa, man!" Barlow rolled over and clamped a hand to Pritchard's arm. His grip had the power to crack bones. "Don't talk guns," he whispered. "You never know who's listening."

"You don't understand how I feel."

"'Course I do. The business I used to be in, when we had problems with disloyalty, we believed in severe punishment for anybody that broke ranks."

"You were what? A soldier?"

Barlow grinned. "In whose army? Kidding aside, I'm not exactly military material."

"I thought you might have been wounded in action."

"I'd like to lie to you, but my problem was . . . was more in the nature of an industrial accident. But you, getting back to that, listen to my advice and stay away from guns." He was still speaking in a whisper.

"You've got one."

"Strictly self-defense. You want to go on offense against those guys, you're better off flying under the radar, sticking to misdemeanors."

"That trivializes it."

"Not true."

"You said it yourself. What I did to Emery's cart might not even register."

Barlow gave Frank a reappraising glance. "Excuse me, I didn't real-ize you're dead set on making a point that nobody can ignore."

"That's exactly what I'd like to do."

"Then you better get ready to spend a stretch behind bars. This is Florida. Proud home of the Hurricanes, the Seminoles, and lethal in-jection. You whack one of your former colleagues, you'll wind up on death row."

Pritchard's gaze slid down the incline of his paunch to the wine stain on his trousers. Angry though he was, he doubted he had it in him to shoot somebody. He felt foolish for running off his mouth. He must have sounded nuts, a candidate for the loony bin.

Barlow, however, didn't appear to be horrified by what he had heard. And he didn't recommend exercise, medication, talk therapy, or religion. He suggested down-and-dirty vindictiveness. "A turd in the punch bowl, a stink bomb in an elevator can be more effective than nuclear weapons, Frank. What those bastards did was disrespect you. For that you don't commit a felony and risk a hard fall. You dis them back. Think Vietcong. Classic guerrilla tactics. You hit and run and hide. You belittle them, demean them, and it drives them nuts be-cause they can't catch you. The cops on Eden, they couldn't find their asses with both hands. They're too busy watching for trouble from the mainland. Meanwhile you're free to have a ball."

It did sound like fun, something Frank had had very little of in the last year. If nothing else, it would get him out of his head, which wasn't a great neighborhood to visit these days. He recalled the giddy thrill of vandalizing Emery's Hummer, then sinking his golf cart. Half a dozen board members, plus cadres of their craven lawyers and sycophantic accountants, owned property on the island. Sud-denly he could see a busy season ahead of him.

But he mentioned none of this to Barlow. His old self again, Pritchard adopted the poker face that had served him well during hostile takeovers. "How rude of me to accept your hospitality," he said, "and drink your whiskey and spend the whole time talking about myself. Tell me, Cal, what business were you in?"

"Nothing that'd impress a guy of your caliber."

"That's not how it strikes me. You sound like a man who knows his way around the block. Where was it you worked?"

"New York, New Jersey, that area. Nickel-and-dime stuff."

"You must have made a killing. I mean to be living in Eden at your age."

"Well, of course"—he patted the wheels of his chair—"after the accident, there was compensation. You know, benefits and so forth."

"Didn't mean to pry."

"No problema. That's all in the past. I'm looking ahead. Now that I'm settled, what I might do—I'm seriously considering it—I might join some of these activities they have on the island."

"Good. I know the right people. Anytime you'd like an introduction, just gimme a ring."

"Don't suppose you play tennis, do you?"

"Used to. Not anymore. My back quit on me."

"A shame. Maybe we could get you in a wheelchair and hit a few balls."

"There's an idea." Frank laughed as he stood up. He expected a crick in his spine, a stab in his hips and knees, but despite the night's gallivanting, he felt spry. "I promise not to watch you through the binoculars, Cal. But I do look forward to seeing you again soon."

"Same here, Frank." Barlow coasted along beside him to the door. "Those two women I see with you on the patio, I meant to ask, which one's your wife?"

"My wife's dead."

"Sorry, man."

"Randi and Ariel, they just help out."

"Well, we need all the help we can get, don't we?" Barlow winked and let Frank pass in front of him. "Meanwhile your secret's safe. And don't worry about me. I'm not the self-destructive type."

Back at his house, Pritchard was astonished by the state of the place. What kind of madman would attack a lifetime's keepsakes with a ceremonial sword? Tiptoeing from room to room, he almost expected to bump into the culprit, some drug-addled hooligan. But then he caught sight of the guilty party in the antique hallway mirror and realized he couldn't let Randi or even a hired charwoman see the appalling aftermath of his meltdown. What the hell had been on his mind?

He took vigorous broom swipes at the apocalyptic mess, and within minutes was awash with sweat and hot-wired with lower back pain. He removed his blazer and loosened his tie. The largest chunks of wood and glass he bagged in double bin liners. Then he swept up the sand from the shattered Meissen and Wedgwood. The grating sound of it under his shoes, the sight of it trickling from the dustpan into the wastebasket, reminded him of cremains. Willow had carried Dorothy's urn to Europe, abiding by her mother's dying wish that her ashes be sprinkled over her favorite places. All of which Dorothy had traveled to with Frank. All of which they had planned to visit again.

7

In bed that night, stretched out on his back to prevent his ligaments from shortening, his spine from curving, and his legs from shriveling, Cal Barlow questioned the truth of what he had told Pritchard. As some might see it, everything he had done in the past few hours was self-destructive.

Just owning a gun risked getting him expelled from the program and slammed back into the joint. But to break out the Beretta and wave it in Pritchard's face, that was sheer shit for brains. Then to admit he kept the piece for protection? Why not announce he was hiding from the mob? Better yet, spell out his real name, previous address, and prison serial number?

Too many mistakes. Now, how did he undo them? Play on Pritchard's sympathy? Suggest he was suicidal after all? Complain of sleeplessness, depression, despair? Let Frank see him again trying the Beretta for size in his mouth? To be honest, the temptation was always there. The thought had crossed his mind. As a last resort, the ultimate loophole, he could shoot himself.

But Barlow wasn't about to own up to any of this. That was the kind of punk behavior that got you bent over a sink with the whole cellblock cracking on you. When you had your back to the wall, you needed to be aggressive. There were buttons he could push. Remind Frank he appreciated his appetite for revenge. Churn his anger and encourage him to confide. In his own Waspy, tight-assed way, Pritchard had the brains to understand balance of power. Mutual assured destruction. MAD.

It was almost funny to picture the old guy becoming a gutter fighter. School, sports, the corporate ethic, everything had taught him to play fair. In his prime, it never would have occurred to Pritchard that a low blow or a sucker punch was sometimes the best way to make your point. But now that he had lost his juice, he needed to learn a new game. Like a turtle without a shell, he still had a snappish bite, but no natural protection.

Fate was always throwing these switcheroos. Never before having had a reason to cheat, Frank suddenly had no choice if he wanted to get even. Meanwhile, Cal, crooked as a stick, had been forced onto the straight and narrow by a stab in the back. This might have amused him—if he hadn't been dead from the waist down. If he hadn't been alone in bed, computing as he often did at Allenwood exactly how long it had been since anybody had touched him with tenderness.

During that time, nobody touched him at all unless it was a guard frisking him or some freak picking a fight. Then magically—no, it was the opposite of magic—he landed in intensive care with doctors and nurses touching him around the clock. But he couldn't feel this laying on of hands, and even when the drugs let him sleep, and he lucked into an erotic dream, there were no pneumatic babes, no piledriving sex, just a wish to be cradled in someone's arms.

. . .

The next morning, Frank phoned to invite him to eat with a bunch of his friends. The Breakfast Club, he called it. An affinity group of old-sters that met every week at a restaurant on the mainland.

"The thing of it is," Cal temporized, not caring to be stuck with these guys if they bored him, "I have an appointment later on. I bet-ter drive my car."

"You drive?"

"What about the words 'differently abled' don't you understand?" he said, to yank Pritchard's chain.

"I'll go with you and catch a ride back with one of the fellows."

"You just wanna see how crips drive."

"If you're shy, I'll take my own car."

"No, I like to show off."

In a clean pair of tan pants and a white shirt with the collar un-buttoned, Pritchard tarried in the shade of the overhang that jutted out from his own house. It was an impressive porch with columns like you'd see in a Cadillac or Mercedes ad. That's what belonged in the driveway, a high-tab model, not Cal's modified VW Golf.

Frank had his face close to a light fixture, like he was watching TV. Barlow rolled down a window. "What's on? Katie Couric or Regis Philbin?"

"Anoles. Three of them. Dead." Frank slumped into the passen-ger seat.

"Personal friends?" Cal asked.

"I left the light off last night. I thought they'd survive."

"Why take it so hard? It's just lizards. Lots of them around."

"I'd like to save them. They eat bugs."

"Everything eats something." Barlow glided down the driveway.

"How's this thing operate?" Frank asked.

"It's got automatic transmission and a hand brake. No pedals. You speed up and slow down by pushing or pulling on the steering wheel."

"Very logical. Is it as easy to drive as you make it sound?"

"Yeah, once you have the hang of it."

In the cool morning air, the streets were empty of cars, but exercisers thronged the hike-and-bike trail. Most carried cell phones. Some wore hands-free sets, with wires swinging from their ears and lips like spittle from the mouth of a stroke victim.

"What do you suppose they have to talk about?" Pritchard seemed as perplexed as he had when he lamented the fried lizards. Here was a guy, Cal guessed, who no longer received many calls and seldom made any. Barlow could relate to that.

"During my lifetime," Frank said, "every technical innovation that was supposed to revolutionize communications has turned into a toy. Part of the total entertainment package. You're probably too young to remember when photocopiers came in."

Actually, Cal remembered from family lore that his uncle had stolen a Xerox prototype and got five years for trying to counterfeit twenty-dollar bills.

"Know what happened when we bought early-stage Xerox machines for our headquarters?" Pritchard asked.

Cal shook his head that he didn't.

"Guess."

"They broke."

"Nosiree bob. Right off the bat, our employees—I'm speaking of otherwise responsible people—pulled down their underpants and sat on them. Copying their own asses."

Barlow erupted in laughter; his hands shook the wheel. The VW sped up and erratically slowed down.

"You think that's funny?"

"Sure! Forbidden games! Folks love them."

"Not me."

"Come on, last night, rolling that cart into the pond, you got your rocks off."

A blush encrimsoned Frank's face right up to his widow's peak of white hair. They rode in silence at 17 mph. At the causeway gate, the geriatric guards had created a bottleneck in both directions, bidding every outbound vehicle a warm goodbye and scouring the trunks of the hired help to ensure that no major appliances left the island with the trash. As for inbound motorists, those without resident tags underwent a polite interrogation. If they didn't have legitimate business on Eden, they were turned away. But residents, visitors, and rejectees alike were accorded one courtesy in common—a dousing from a high-pressure hose.

The first time this sudsy jet hit his windshield, Barlow thought it was disinfectant—the kind of fumigating shower that cons passed through in prison. But it was a quick spray to wash off the salt crust that cars acquired driving over from the mainland.

While Cal and Frank waited in line, they watched a barefoot old coot sweep the beach with a metal detector. Hooked up to earphones, this sad sack patrolled the shore every day searching for loose change.

"What do you figure?" Cal asked. "He lives on Eden. He has to be rich. What's he hope to find? A silver dollar?"

"Just killing time," Frank said. "Killing it before it kills him."

This, Barlow thought, sounded like the jaded wisdom of a lifer, not the happy-face Hallmark-card sentiment of an island bumper sticker. I BRAKE FOR ANIMALS. MY GRANDCHILD IS AN HONOR STUDENT. ONE HUMAN FAMILY. That sort of horseshit. No doubt about it, Pritchard was a different breed of cat.

Once past the gate, they gathered speed, tires humming on the segmented concrete. Railed-in catwalks on either side kept fishermen from getting a fanny full of fenders. At low tide, the ocean was glassy smooth, its shallows glinting turquoise and aquamarine. Long-legged birds pecked at minnows, oblivious to the WaveRunners that zoomed around them and the paraskiers that hovered overhead. Barlow would have loved to scooter over the Atlantic or float from parachute silks.

Signs warned boaters to watch out for manatees. Cal had once spotted a pale oblong of lard lolling near the ducts of a sewage-treatment plant and couldn't believe old-time sailors ever mistook manatees for mermaids. Even a man as desperate for sex as he was wouldn't be turned on by a doughball with fins and a blubbery back filigreed with propeller scars.

At the far end of the causeway, they entered a scruffy satellite community such as might exist cheek by jowl with a military base. A service hub, a commercial grid, an ant farm of frantic activity, it answered those needs that were aesthetically incompatible with Eden. Islanders and their employees traveled here to shop for big-ticket items—cars, boats, household supplies in bulk—and to drop things off for repair.

The air throbbed with power tools, the earth was polluted with axle grease and bilge water, and a pitiless light sluiced through the shabby vegetation. Yet more often than anyone except Cal might suspect, Edenites gravitated to these potholed streets to indulge in a little slumming, a grubby glimpse at the lives of those less fortunate. Few of them would admit that they frequented the fast-food outlets, the porn video rental, or the massage parlors where for the right tip you could score a localized rubdown.

Draining away from the coast to inland swamps, side roads were lined by trailers and low, flat-roofed cinderblock houses. Here, surrounded by chicken feathers and fur balls from rabbit hutches, lived the gardeners, pool cleaners, and maids who commuted to the island each morning.

On aimless rambles Barlow had followed these streets until they dead-ended at hummocks of saw grass and leather fern. Steaming mud sprouted plants armed with teeth, and strangler figs that competed with pines for air and light. One road opened out onto a flat, dry expanse, crisscrossed by tire ruts and skid marks. Cal surmised the field was an airstrip for drug smugglers. That didn't surprise him. What did was the burial ground of electrical appliances at the edge of the Everglades. Weathered by sun and rain, loosely threaded together by wires and vines, the TVs, washing machines, and refrigerators were topped by a sprinkling of computer terminals that squinted at the sky, baffled at being forsaken here. Not even broken—just old-fashioned, and therefore valueless.

Pritchard directed him north on a dual-lane highway, through a thicket of strip malls. The din of war and drumroll of patriotism hadn't diminished since 9/11. Stars and Stripes fluttered. "These Colors Don't Run" was the boast of many a billboard. "United We Stand." "God Bless America Vacancy," read a motel sign. "Stop Terrorism. Kill Osama. Barbeque on Our Terrace," a restaurant advertised.

"You say you never served?" Frank asked.

"Not in the military I didn't."

"Then you missed something. The army sent me to Italy, France, and Germany."

"World War Two?"

"How old do I look? This was after Korea, before Vietnam."

"Peacetime," Cal said.

"Cold War," Pritchard corrected him.

Amid the walk-in clinics for coronary emergencies, kidney dialysis, and other infirmities of the aged, there was one for family planning and pregnancy. In this corner of Florida, it was difficult to believe that people still had babies—or were trying not to. It gladdened Cal to be off the island, if for no other reason than to remember that life continued here much as it did in the town where he grew up.

Frank had him stop at a diner that might have been a greasy spoon in New Jersey, a trucker's home-away-from-home, a joint with leather-ette booths, a jukebox, and waitresses with thirty-six-inch waists and forty-six-inch bustlines. Only one detail undercut the retro authenticity—the flotilla of luxury foreign cars on the parking lot.

He waited until Frank climbed out of the VW before he wrestled his folded wheelchair from the back seat, shaking it open as he would a canvas deck chair. As soon as he attached the wheels and inserted the cotter pins, he was ready to roll. Pritchard offered a hand, but Barlow ignored it and swung from the car, completing the transfer with an agility that amazed customers at the windows of the diner.

Inside, the Breakfast Club had commandeered a round table. Members immediately made room for him. The youngest had a good thirty years on Barlow, but because of his handicap, he supposed he qualified as an honorary oldster. Or maybe at their age they accepted everybody on equal terms.

Pritchard dealt with the introductions in an offhand fashion. Lon-nie, Seb, Steve, Tony, and Adrian. No last names. No fuss about ca-reer highlights or professional titles. They all lived on Eden and had golfer's tans. Every inch of exposed skin was braised the color of well-done steak. Below their open collars and above the drooping elbow-length sleeves of their polo shirts, Cal noticed cobwebby white flesh.

To connect names and faces, he focused on who had hair, how much and where. Lonnie and Steve wore elaborate comb-overs. Seb was bald, with leopard splotches of pigmentation on his scalp. Much of Adrian's and Tony's hair appeared to have migrated to their ears. When did that begin? Cal wondered. Something else to look forward to. Whom the gods would destroy, they first redistributed their hair.

"If you want to belong to the Breakfast Club," Lonnie said, fingering a spot on his chest, "we have four rules. First, no bitching about wives."

"Gotcha," Barlow agreed.

"Girlfriends, or women you have your eyes on, are fair game for comment." Lonnie kept fretting at his sternum as if fiddling with a radio dial. "Rule number two: no bragging what a big shot you were before we met you."

"Fine by me."

"Three, no lying about your golf score."

The moment the words left his mouth, Lonnie, it was clear, regretted mentioning the game to a cripple. Pritchard said, "Cal's too young for golf. He plays tennis with Freddy."

"No kidding?"

"I'd like to come out and watch you guys golf," Cal said.

"Anytime," Adrian said. "The joke is the game's a good walk ruined. But riding in a cart's always fun."

"You hear about Bob Emery's cart?"

"Tell him the fourth rule." Pritchard spoke over Seb.

"Number four, nothing's sacred, nothing's outa bounds. Everybody razzes everybody. Getting mad is an expellable offense." Lonnie nudged Barlow. "You know why God invented golf?"

Cal shook his head that he didn't.

"So white guys get a chance to dress like Italians."

Barlow laughed and kept it up until the rest of them joined him. "What's on the list of approved topics?" he asked.

"The cosmic verities," said Adrian, an owlish guy with glasses so thick they distorted the shape of his eyes. "Sports, politics, and sex."

"Look who's bragging," Tony broke in. "Adrian hasn't had sex since the Eisenhower administration."

"Speak for yourself," Adrian shot back.

"The older the buck," Seb said, "the harder the horn."

"Damn right," Steve said. "Look at Frank."

They all, including Cal, did exactly that. Looked at Frank, who blushed as he had in the VW when Barlow accused him of getting his rocks off by rolling the cart into the pond.

"Hell," Steve ran on, "he has a regular harem at his house. There's that young freckle-faced gal and—"

"She's a physical therapist," Frank insisted.

"Yeah, with an emphasis on the physical. And there's Randi Dickson, with an emphasis on—"

"Money and older men," Adrian piped up.

"Nothing wrong with paying for it," Lonnie said. "Whether you're shelling out for dinner or diamonds, it amounts to the same thing."

"Yeah, it all costs," Tony agreed. "Even Viagra's not cheap. Unless you're loaded like Frank."

"Thought the rule was no talking about money," Pritchard objected.

"Business and the market are off limits. Money *per se* is okay."

"That sounds like a distinction without a difference."

"No, what it sounds like," Lonnie teased, "is you're afraid to discuss Viagra."

"I've got no basis to discuss it."

"If you've got a dick, you've got a basis. No rule at the Breakfast Club against talking about erectile trouble."

"Rectal trouble?" Swiveling from speaker to speaker, Seb was a beat behind the conversation. "Been there, done that, got the T-shirt." He yanked up his polo shirt and showed Cal what he wore underneath—a T-shirt with the logo "Freedom from Cancún." No, when he smoothed the material, it read, "Freedom from Cancer."

"I'm a survivor," he told Barlow. "Had it in my colon and survived the operation. Survived seizures, a heart attack, a stroke, two wives, one of my kids." He seemed positively giddy, as if he hadn't just post-poned death but cheated it altogether. "Now it's my prostate. But I'll whip it too."

This prompted debate about PSA scores. Frank had accumulated a storehouse of information about the human prostate, its ills and treat-ments, and he cautioned club members against false positive and false negative test results.

"Know what I figure?" Adrian interrupted. "Frank's got the oppo-site of Alzheimer's. He doesn't forget a thing. Statistics, phone num-bers, names of birds and plants and fish, they're on his brain tape forever."

Gradually it came to Barlow that these affable and rambunctious Breakfast Clubbers were like former major leaguers, full of beans and reminiscences, gathering for the annual Old-Timers' Day game. Only instead of strutting their rusty pitching and batting skills, they got together for the express purpose of demonstrating that they still had their marbles. Sure, some of them had lost a step or two, and the con-versation sometimes had a canned quality. But they were determined to show they could still play the game.

In some respects, they played it better than Barlow, and it relieved him when they quit ribbing one another about erectile troubles. For a second he had feared they might work their way around the table and ask him about foreplay on wheels, legless love, pain without sex. Rule or no rule, there was a roof on how much razzing he could stand.

"I don't know about you guys," said Tony, a roly-poly fellow. "But I don't attend club meetings for the talk. I come to eat. I want a piece of that pee-can pie."

"It's pronounced pa-*khan*," Adrian prissily insisted. "A pee can is a truck driver's boot."

"I come to smoke, drink coffee, and eat cream chipped beef." Seb caught up with Tony. "All the things my wife won't let me do at home."

"Let's not go into what your wife won't let you do," said the waitress, plucking a pencil out of her hairnet. "You boys deserve to have your mouths washed out with Lysol. Now how many of y'all want shit-on-a-shingle this morning?"

8

The first one to finish eating, Barlow excused himself, claiming he had an appointment. The Breakfast Clubbers followed him out of the diner, shaking the pins and needles from their feet and plucking at the seats of their Sansabelt slacks. Pritchard lingered at the VW as Cal disassembled his wheelchair. He knew better than to offer help; Barlow prized his independence. He admired the guy's grit and the nonchalance with which he negotiated a path through a world of obstacles. Watching him sling the folded chair into the back seat, Frank was ashamed of his own bouts of self-pity.

"You fit right in," he said. "The boys liked you."

"I got a kick out of them too." Cal inserted the key in the ignition and revved up the AC. But Pritchard stood in the way of his closing the door. Frank thought there was something more he should say. He couldn't decide what. The heat on the parking lot had the power to drive ideas out of his head, down his notched spine, like a hurricane lowering the barometric pressure.

"Look," Barlow said, "I can run you back to Eden. I'm not in any hurry."

"No, thanks. Lonnie'll give me a lift."

"It's no trouble. It's not a set appointment I have. I just need a massage. You know, for my legs."

"You go ahead. I hope you had fun."

"Absolutely. Catch you later." And off he sped, pressing the steering wheel and plunging into the river of traffic that slurped through the highway's heat mirages.

Lonnie waited in the chilled capsule of his Infiniti sedan. With one hand he adjusted the vents, redirecting the flow of air. With the other, he fingered his chest where a pacemaker caused phantom twinges. "You say he's your neighbor?"

"Yeah," Frank said. "I thought he'd like an outing."

"Glad to have him join." Lonnie splashed out onto the highway. "What do you figure he did for a living?"

"Some type of business up north. Said he hurt himself in an industrial accident."

"Damn shame. A fella his age."

Lonnie glanced into the rearview mirror. He spent a lot of time in his car, Pritchard had noticed, studying the road behind him. Let drivers in front fend for themselves. Lonnie's worry was what might be gaining on him. "Hell of a build on him," Lonnie said. "And quite a head of hair and that tan. Think maybe he's Jewish?"

"What's it matter? There's no property covenant on Eden."

"Just wondering." Wondering and busily watching the road unfurl in their wake. Frank braced for a head-on.

"I'd guess he's Italian," Pritchard said, "and they anglicized the family name at Ellis Island."

"Well, he wasn't offended when I joked about golfers dressing like wops. My experience, you don't find many Italians, not that young, with all that muscle and hair, in corporate boardrooms."

"Maybe he was in business for himself."

"He must have made out like a bandit to afford Eden."

"I like him." Frank was telling Lonnie the truth—which was more than he had told Barlow when he invited him to the Breakfast Club. Having tipped too much of his hand last night, Pritchard decided this morning it would be wise to stay in Cal's good graces. But the dumbfounding fact was that he did admire the guy and enjoyed his company and his capacity for fun. These days that was often as close as Frank came to enjoyment—seeing somebody else have a ball. He recognized a good time when he noticed other people having one.

"Hey, isn't that your girlfriend?" For once, Lonnie was looking at the road ahead, where through the gimcrackery of discount outlets, marine supply depots, and bail bondsmen's offices Ariel raced at breathtaking speed.

"How does she do it?" Lonnie marveled. "This heat's a killer."

"She's in great shape."

Beautiful amid the scrub brush, broken bottles, and wind-tossed trash, she seemed so frail she might have been blown off course in the backwash of traffic. Frank was about to suggest they offer her a ride when Lonnie wisecracked, "She's so skinny I bet she hums in the wind. She's the kind should wear a sign, 'In case of sex, this side up.'"

"That's not funny. She was a saint with Dorothy."

"Sorry."

Now it was Pritchard who stared at her bouncing ponytail of strawberry-blond hair, her shapely legs. He couldn't bear it that she had abandoned Eden. He had to bring her back. The strength of this conviction verged so close to desperation that he didn't recognize it was desire. At such moments, his body and emotions no longer seemed to cohere. It was nothing so simple as his legs and arms slipping out of sync. His organs floated free of their moorings—his head in his heart, his stomach in his feet. To complete the sensation of corporal estrangement, his eye spider parachuted into view.

Across the causeway, past the guards, through the gratuitous hose-shower, the two men rode in silence, lost in the head fever of their private regrets. Lonnie dropped him on the driveway and had no sooner vanished into heat vapor than Pritchard went into the garage, not the house. In the past few months he had driven his lemon-drop-yellow XKE so infrequently he had no faith it would start, and he didn't have the patience to search for the jumper cables or to wait for a mechanic. A dead battery would kill his plans.

The Jag had been a retirement project. Once he had had it restored at larcenous cost, he had competed in rallies and motorcrosses, tooling at high speed around the state. Dorothy served as his navigator, snugged into the seat beside him, reading a map. But ever since she got sick, and especially since her death, it frequently slipped his mind that he had a means of transport.

Today the XKE grumbled to fitful life, and Frank aimed it back where he had just been. Screwing up his nerve, he drove 20 mph in the 17 mph zone. Eden's meridional light, tropical foliage, and effusions of chlorophyll tired his eyes and wearied his soul. Confronted by such excess, such gushing exuberance, he felt a question come to him: Am I dying? Or is it the world? But as he cruised to the mainland, that sad bad feeling fell away.

When he didn't spot Ariel in the commercial grid, he doglegged up and down side streets. The area was poor, the vegetation sinfully rich. Sapodilla and West Indian mahogany trees shaded sidewalks where blades of grass cracked the concrete, a sight as unsettling to Frank as hair spiking up through a helmet. On a corner, men drinking beer lounged under a tree with fallen blossoms spread out on the ground in front of them like a picnic for lotus eaters.

He caught up with Ariel on Gumbo-Limbo Lane. She was running at a brisk clip, her T-shirt drenched, her ponytail limp and russet-colored with sweat. Hugged by Lycra bicycle shorts, her bottom barely shook.

As the Jag pulled abreast of her, she didn't slow down or glance at it. Maybe she was accustomed to being pestered by motorists. Maybe, Pritchard feared, she was determined not to give him the time of day. He lowered the window.

"Ariel, it's me."

"Wot?" She was startled.

"Who'd you think it was? Some guy hitting on you?"

"It does happen, you know." She stooped down to look in at him. "What are you doing here, Mr. Pritchard?"

"Climb in and I'll explain."

"I'm too grotty. I'll bugger up the upholstery."

"Don't worry about it."

"No, it's leather. There's no mistaking that smell. I set my bum on it and you'll have to reupholster it."

"I'd like to talk to you."

"My house is a little farther along. Let's talk there."

She sprinted off, and he nosed along behind her, the XKE sleek as a barracuda at her heels. It struck him as unseemly to stare at her butt. Like Lonnie, he focused on the rearview mirror, thinking this argued for his noble intentions.

Her house was a trailer, the sort, Pritchard feared, that turned turtle in hurricanes. Over it arched the crazily bent branches of the gumbo-limbo tree that gave the lane its name. Loblolly pines, straight as cell bars, walled in the property, and on a patch of crabgrass a beach umbrella tilted from a wood-plank table. Seated at the table, a teenage girl watched over a little boy in an inflated wading pool.

"Thanks, Carla. I'll pay you Wednesday," Ariel told the girl, who had a glinting rivet in her exposed belly button.

Pritchard was heaving himself out of the Jag when Carla strolled by. "Nice ride," she said.

The little boy in the pool was naked, and his fair skin appeared soft and fresh enough to smear. Sun had bleached his bowl-cut hair a shade of blond one step removed from white. No expert in these matters, Frank estimated his age at four.

"Say hello to Mr. Pritchard," Ariel said. "You've heard me talk about him. I worked with his wife."

"The one that died?" The kid didn't have his mother's accent, but he didn't speak like a local either.

"Yes, Mrs. Pritchard was very sick."

"That's sad."

"He remembers how weepy I was," Ariel explained to Frank. The boy clambered over the side of the pool, and his mother oiled his chest with Coppertone. "This is Nicholas," she said.

"Nice to meet you." Pritchard didn't know whether to shake his hand or ruffle his hair. So he settled for saying, "Aren't you a big guy." Since direct sunlight had a tendency to yellow his own hair, Frank moved under the umbrella. Randi maintained it was cigarettes that caused the discoloration, and he didn't care to give her another excuse to badger him to quit smoking.

"Time for you to be in the shade too, Nicholas. Sit at the table with Mr. Pritchard, while I bring your toys from the pool."

Nicholas crawled up onto the bench, undaunted by the prospect of splinters in his bare rump. "Do you have kids?"

"A daughter." It amazed him how comfortable the little boy was around adults and how much he sounded like one.

"Can she play with me?"

"She's grown up and lives a long way from here."

"Too bad. Is she the only one?"

"The only one."

"You must be lonely."

"You bet I am."

Balancing a plastic tea service of miniature pots, saucers, and cups, Ariel walked over and arranged them in front of Nicholas. "Like something to drink?" she asked Frank. "There's iced tea and lemonade in the fridge."

He gazed at her angular face, its laugh lines and well-exercised smile muscles. She wasn't the type for Botox and that blankness of expression that suggested a clock without numbers or hands. "Lemonade sounds good," he told her.

With Ariel in the trailer, Nicholas poured pool water into a cup, pretended to sip it, and smacked his lips. "That's dee-licious." Then he asked, "Do you like tea?" and poured Frank a cup.

The boy's body radiated heat and his hair smelled like Ivory Snow. Memory of Willow as a baby shot through Pritchard, painful as an arrow. "I love tea," Pritchard said. He lifted the cup near his lips.

"Dee-licious?"

"No, ugh. It's atrocious."

Nicholas let out a belly laugh, shaking layers of baby fat. "Aatrocious," he said in perfect imitation.

Delighted by the little guy's antics, Frank nevertheless held his happiness in check. Life for him had become a series of stomach-churning dips and rises. When the roller coaster hit a rare high spot, he instinctively girded himself against the next dive. He glanced away from Nicholas and studied the gumbo-limbo tree, its massive trunk coarse as the hide of a dying elephant. Beyond the fence, the crushed shell road was as white as bonemeal. In the grass, a gazillion ants carted off a dead beetle. Things in this climate fell apart. The center, the circumference, nothing held together. On Eden evidence of decay was disguised, but here you couldn't avoid it.

How, Frank wondered, had this lovable kid and his lovely mother landed in a trailer on a dead-end lane? What kind of lout would let them down? Who with an iota of sense wouldn't appreciate their inestimable worth? Pritchard had witnessed this sort of insanity in business. Fools who undervalued their assets and sold out, believing that something better awaited them down the road.

From conversations overheard between Ariel and Dorothy, he recalled talk of a husband or boyfriend. A beer-guzzling lunk she met in college. A guy with a motorcycle and a bass guitar who harbored illusions of a record contract. Ariel, he remembered, referred to him as somebody "who couldn't organize a piss-up in a brewery." When she stopped complaining, Frank presumed the jerk had split or she had thrown him out. That she had ever linked up with a loser in the first place mystified him.

Surveying this meager setting, he imagined how easily he might alter everything. In a bank out on the highway, housed in a modular structure no more substantial than this trailer, Frank had a checking account for miscellaneous expenses that contained one million three hundred thirty-six thousand dollars, drawing next to no interest. If he shifted as little as a tenth of that to Ariel's pocket, he could free her from the stockade of pines and offer Nicholas and her a new life.

But he knew she wouldn't permit it. He'd be lucky to talk her into returning to Eden.

Ariel had showered and put on a tank top and a pair of baggy shorts with patch pockets. Carrying a tall glass silvery with condensation and clinking with ice cubes, she crossed the yard in bare feet.

"Careful of the ants," Frank warned. "They'll chew your toes off."

"My feet are too tough for them. I never wear shoes when I don't have to. Back home I ran track meets barefoot."

"I don't believe you."

"Haven't you heard of Zola Budd? Masses of South Africans run without shoes."

"I notice you wear them here when you jog."

"The macadam's too bloody hot."

Frank sipped the lemonade and puckered his lips at its tartness. It was homemade, not from a can or a carton. "Have you found a job yet?"

"Still looking." She sat opposite him and Nicholas, who was preoccupied with his teacups and saucers. "There's every prospect I'll have one by next week."

"Doing what?"

"Any number of possibilities."

He couldn't decide how to sneak up on the subject. So he simply blurted, "I wish you'd come back to Eden."

Ariel paused as if to edit her words and spare his feelings. "I can't. There's nothing for me to do there."

"You do plenty for me. I miss . . . I miss . . ." What could he reasonably admit to? "I miss your company."

"Yes, it gets to be a habit, doesn't it, having a person around. I don't deny I miss things too. But there comes a time to move on."

"I agree. Wholeheartedly. I'm moving on, and that's why I need you."

"I don't mean to be stroppy, Mr. Pritchard, but what's changed?"

"Since our conversation, I've made up my mind to start exercising. I want to hire a personal trainer to teach me the breaststroke and the butterfly."

"This is a bit sudden. Why not stick with it a few weeks and make sure the wheels don't fall off. Then decide whether you want coaching."

"It's more than coaching. I need tips on nutrition and general health."

"The fitness center'll cover that for you."

"It's not just for me," he said, sensing this was either an inspiration or a great mistake. "My neighbor, the crippled fellow next door, he needs help too. His legs get knotted up. He's out searching right now for someone to rub them down."

"He won't find anybody that's qualified."

"Of course not. Not a masseuse with credentials like yours."

She fixed her blue eyes on Frank in a blunt stare that he found simultaneously disconcerting and stimulating. Like a lawyer who never asks a question whose answer he doesn't know in advance, he had made it a career principle never to broach a subject he hadn't thought through. But now he was flying blind.

"He's a great guy," Frank said. "I admire him. His attitude, his tenacity, his *joie de vivre*. You'll like him too."

"How'd you get to know him overnight?"

"He joined a club I belong to."

"That's good for you." She couldn't conceal her delight. "To get out and about and have friends."

"And good for him," Frank said. "I thought since you complained there's not enough to keep you busy at my place, the two of us together might make it worth your while. Naturally, there'd be more money in it for you."

Ariel sighed and rubbed her arms as though freezing in Florida's heat. It took willpower for him not to reach over and warm her up.

"I don't want to hurt your feelings, Mr. Pritchard, but I find Eden depressing."

He was tempted to confess that he did too. "Because of Dorothy?" he asked.

"That's part of it. I cared for her. We were close and we talked a lot. And I can't forget how she suffered at the end."

"I haven't forgotten either. And I can't ever thank you enough."

"You don't have to thank me. It was . . ." As Ariel hesitated, he prayed she wouldn't say it was a job. "It was an important experience for me."

A signal seemed to pass from Ariel to Nicholas. He climbed down from the bench and toddled back to the wading pool. "It's hard for me being on Eden, not just hard because of Mrs. Pritchard," she said. "It reminds me of South Africa."

"I understand. You miss home."

She shook her head. Her damp hair whipped from side to side. "I'm afraid it's not the good bits the island brings to mind. It's the old days of apartheid. Eden has that same deadness. The rules, the guards, the gates, all the security. You might as well be in bloody Johannesburg, with everybody behind walls and barbed wire. You never see any blacks or coloreds unless they're workers. Then at the end of the day, they hurry off. I might as well be coming home to the Cape Flats."

"There's plenty of room at my place. You could quit commuting and move in." Instantly he recognized his mistake—rushing things, scaring her.

"That's a daft idea," she said. "What am I supposed to do with Nicholas? There are no nursery schools, no facilities on the island for children. Anyway, since I don't like it, why would I want to live there full-time with a lot of rich people who've lost the plot? No offense to you personally."

"None taken," he assured her, backtracking and retrenching. "It might interest you that I'm not crazy about Eden either and I'm making plans, really I am, to change it, shake it up. I don't expect you to live there. That was just a . . ." What was it? A wet dream? ". . . a thought. If you don't mind the commute, you can stay here and set your own hours."

"That still leaves Nicholas." She combed her fingers through her hair, separating strands. "I don't have reliable day care. I have to depend on neighborhood teenagers and they're in school most of the time."

"Bring him with you. There's the pool and all the room in the world to play in." He glanced over at the wading pool and shouted, "Wouldn't it be atrocious to visit me every day, Nicholas?"

"Dee-licious," he exclaimed.

"I'm sorry to sound like an American, Mr. Pritchard, but I don't like him to be around people who smoke."

This caused him to reconsider. How many extravagant promises was he prepared to make? "Tell you what, I'll hide the cigarettes when he's around."

"And the ashtrays?"

"Them too."

As she hesitated, apparently toting up the pluses and minuses, Pritchard had the feeling he was enduring an IRS audit.

"Okay," she said, "I'll try it."

"And you'll look after Barlow?"

"I'll do what I can. I'll review his medical records. He may require specialized therapy."

"That's all I ask. Consult and decide what's best." Her willingness to be persuaded surprised him almost as much as it pleased him.

"If you're serious about my bringing Nicholas—I'm thinking out loud now—I may buy one of those three-wheel strollers. The ones with bicycle tires. They're built for speed. I could strap him in and push it when I run to the island."

"That sounds exhausting."

"No worse than running with ankle and wrist weights."

"What are you training for? The triathlon?"

"I'm not training *for* anything. I'm training against getting fat and sloppy."

"But it's dangerous to run on these roads."

"Not really. I'll wear a bright vest. Once on the causeway, there's the hike-and-bike path, and on Eden it's as safe as a—"

She didn't finish. "Tomb" was the word that popped into Frank's mind. People often remarked that they felt that they had died and gone to heaven there. It sounded good to them, even if it did suggest they had kicked the bucket.

"Please, don't run after dark," he said.

"Why not?"

"The panther."

She giggled. "Don't be silly, Mr. Pritchard."

"I'm serious."

"That's a load of bollocks. I'm not afraid of animals. I've been around them all my life. I walked to school through fields full of baboons."

"Even so, nights when you work late, I'll drive you home." He didn't mention that it was he, not the big cat, that he feared she'd see slinking around the island after dark.

9

From the diner, Barlow headed north for ten miles, then once he figured the Breakfast Clubbers were home on Eden, he circled back. He didn't care to run into the wrong person in the wrong spot. The DJ on the car radio shrieked, "You're smack in the middle of a fourgasm. Four great hits in a row," and as Cal arrived at the zone of walk-in clinics, Lou Reed started crooning a golden oldie, "Coney Island Baby." Cal remembered the song from high school when he had, believe it or not, wanted to play football for the coach, "the straightest dude I ever knew." He and his teammates and their girlfriends spent hours discussing what the lyrics meant. The guys came down on the side of masculine initiation. "Because you know, someday, man, you gotta stand up straight, unless you're going to fall. Then you're going to die." But the girls pointed to the line "When you're all alone and lonely . . ." and made a case that Lou Reed was wailing about love.

Cal drove on. He didn't dare stop until the music did. The lyrics seemed aimed expressly at him and his time in the slam, when he couldn't quit obsessing, as Lou put it, about what you did and who you did and how your two-bit friends ripped you off. Then Lou slid into a refrain, "the glory of love," and ended by whispering that he'd give it all up for you, baby. Christ, what a crazy record, but no crazier than Barlow felt at the moment.

He pulled in at the most reputable-looking Doc-in-the-Box, a rare three-story structure. The handicapped parking places—there must have been a hundred of them—were all occupied. So Cal made do with a remote slot, shook out his chair, and zoomed over the zebra-striped speed bumps and heat blisters in the asphalt. Sun baked his hair down to its roots.

In the waiting room, a coffee table the size of a garbage scow slopped over with magazines—*Modern Maturity, Guns & Ammo, Spinal Column, Biker Babes.* And around it slumped patients whose posture didn't suggest much hope that any of them would get out of here alive. Several traveled with their own rolling IV trees from which fat drip bags swung. One woman had a tube up her nose and a canister of oxygen in her lap that she petted as fondly as a dog.

The spitting image of vitality and high spirits, Cal rolled over to the reception window, where the nurses appeared to be in worse health than any of the patients. Why was this always the case? he wondered. Why was the American medical profession a walking advertisement for obesity, diabetes, and coronary occlusion? Maybe nurses and paramedics overidentified with the sick.

Swaddled in a circus tent of a uniform, a woman of hippo dimensions handed him a clipboard and a ballpoint pen. "Fill this out, honey. Then have a seat till your number's called."

He didn't bother to point out that he had arrived preseated. Positioning himself beside a butt-polished chair, he scanned the questionnaire. Even innocuous inquiries had the potential to be tricky.

His instinct, as deeply ingrained as muscle memory, was to do as he did in the old days: lie about everything. Use an alias, a fake address, a stolen Social Security card, and a forged driver's license and pay the bill in cash. Why volunteer information that might fly back in his face during some future court date?

But now that his identity was false, he could answer every question truthfully. Or, that is, with a legally sanctioned lie. He did fudge the final one, though. Asked the reason for his visit, he scribbled "Consultation."

Then he riffled through the reading material on the table. Buried beneath *Modern Maturity* and *Spinal Column* lay a copy of the *Sports Illustrated* swimsuit issue. Only at a Doc-in-the-Box for the aged and dying would this hot-ticket item have remained unstolen.

Those *SI* babes, Barlow thought, you had to hand it to them for what they went through to sculpt themselves the way they were. Starvation diets, aerobic agony, cosmetic surgery, Brazilian crotch waxing. Then came the hard part—photo shoots in icy water or slithering half naked over scorching sand, always with a cheery smile. Never a worry in the world about their dental floss bikinis getting snagged in the wrong cracks or seaweed nesting in their G-strings. Cal, who struggled daily to keep his underwear out of his ass, admired their equanimity, among other attributes.

As he examined the snapshots, he monitored his pulse rate and heartbeat. He felt desire, he definitely did, but it was diffuse and extended weak tendrils below his waist. Still, it existed, the sexual urge, just as it did in the geezers at the Breakfast Club. Or was it, like his impulse to lie on the questionnaire, a muscle memory left over from a previous life?

A nurse called his number and dispatched him to a doctor on the second floor. Cal could have been an exhibitionist and climbed the staircase in his wheelchair. But he caught the elevator, where he confronted his face in the polished aluminum door. He had never liked his looks, the dark, long-lashed eyes, the swollen insolent mouth and mineral grain of his close-shaved jaw. Too ethnic. It still smarted that a girl in high school had dismissed him as "a hairy Italian."

The elevator jerked to a halt, and the door slid back in sections, collapsing into itself. Barlow appeared to do the same. His buff upper-body contours compressed into a sliver, then vanished along with his Velcro-tabbed tennis shoes, which looked clownishly large at the ends of his pipestem legs.

When Cal rolled into his office, the doctor stayed seated at a desk. He dealt with fifty patients a day. One more in a wheelchair didn't merit a special response.

He didn't look altogether well himself. His mustache drooped at the left corner of his mouth. A stroke or a harelip, Barlow thought. It was difficult to say whether the mustache hid the worst of the damage or exaggerated it.

"What can I do for you today, Mr. Barlow?"

Cal saw no percentage in inching up on the subject. "I'd like a prescription for Viagra."

"Hmmm," the doctor mused, crossing his legs, right ankle on left knee. He wore a pair of Hush Puppies. This troubled Cal. How much trust could you invest in a doctor who couldn't afford expensive shoes? "Any history of heart problems?"

"None."

"High blood pressure?"

"No. I'm in excellent general health."

"I see." Because the doctor slurred his words, this sounded like "I she." "How did you . . ." He searched for a euphemism, but not for long. "How'd you wind up in a wheelchair?"

"I got stabbed in the back."

"And your shecksual functioning? Any episodes of impudence?"

"Impudence?"

"You know." He let his wrist flop.

"I have sexual feelings. I'll say that much. I'm willing to try."

"Your genials are intact?"

Genials? This guy's speech impediment was about to turn an already embarrassing situation into burlesque. "Yes, my genitals are intact."

"Have you attempted intercourse?"

"No. I haven't had a chance. I've been in rehab, then resettling."

"On Eden," the doctor read off the clipboard. "Nice address. But for a man your age . . ."

"Not exactly a singles bar."

"How long since you last had shecks?"

This summoned up his boyhood, the scrotum-shriveling confessional box ritual. How long's it been? How many times? Alone or with others? Above or beneath the clothing? "It's been a while," Cal conceded. "But I figured, what the hell, I'd like to take a shot."

"I thought you said Viagra?"

"I did."

"It's a pill. Not an injection. The prognosis is better than with a vacuum pump and not as invasive as a surgical implant."

"That's what I'm here for. The pills."

The doctor nibbled at the lopsided caterpillar on his upper lip. "I'll let you have a complimentary six-pack. No sense paying till you've had a trial run. They're expensive. You know the drug companies— buy sheep, sell deer. Be sure to read the warning about side effects. You may have headaches or blue vision."

"Do I get a choice? I'll go with blue vision."

The doctor didn't laugh. He passed Cal a board of pills that were diamond-shaped and bore the inscription "VCR-50." "Take it an hour before shecks. Good luck."

Downstairs, after paying the bill, Barlow paused at the water cooler, drew a paper cone of tasteless liquid, and gulped his first blue beauty.

He hadn't driven five miles before he began to feel frisky. Maybe a placebo effect. But anything was an improvement. He motored up the road to Bare Assets. Advertising Lap Dancing and a Nude Interracial Love Revue, it was located in a low-slung building that might have been a storage barn before its reincarnation as a pleasure palace. With a megawatt midday sun burning down, a necklace of flashing lights superfluously framed the entrance. The parking lot was more packed than the one at the Doc-in-the-Box. The highway was empty and all the old devils were here. Bare Assets had no set-asides for the handicapped, no wheelchair ramp either, but it would have taken more than that to deter Cal.

He thundered up the steps and through the swinging doors to a perfumed antechamber. The bouncer collected a ten-dollar admission fee and advised customers of the ten-dollar minimum. When he spotted Barlow, he pulled a basset hound frown. "Sorry, pal. No way."

"What are you saying?"

"I'm saying I sympathize, but we don't allow panhandling. It creeps out the girls, not to mention the clientele."

"I'm not here to beg." Cal was indignant. "I came for the show."

"X-skoose me. That's the spirit." He palmed Cal's ten bucks and bowed him through the inner door.

The huddled gloom suggested an animal's lair, as did the dank warmth and the hormonal tang. Barlow bathed in it, let the sensory overload lave over him—the music, the ululating crowd, the chemical-altering medication, the gyrating girls and ambient testosterone. There must have been two hundred men here, but they registered as no more than pesky flies buzzing around a smorgasbord of bare flesh. The dancers dominated his attention.

Bumping and grinding, snaking up metal poles, executing splits, crawling around on all fours and arching their spines like cats in heat, they came in a jamboree of colors and sizes, races and chromosomal groupings. But Cal found their differences less entrancing than what they had in common. Enormous, spherically perfect breasts. Silicone, he supposed. All graduates of the school of hard knockers, and all method actresses. One finger in the mouth, another between the legs, they had grimacing, dreamy-eyed, fuck-me faces, like they were on the brink of the Big O and dared you to bring them off.

Each gal had creatively sheared her pubic hair. There were hearts, Mohawks, chevrons, Van Dykes, and Nike swooshes. Some had waxed themselves smooth as surfboards, the better to display their piercing. Not satisfied with tongue studs, nipple rings, and navel screws, they sported clit rings like zipper pulls. One tug and they'd peel apart.

You had to love it. At least Barlow did. Dancers onstage flashed their Mohawks and fletches. One lassoed a leg around the neck of a fellow at the bar. Another stretched out and played doctor. A few pranced from table to table, straddling laps and squirming.

Cal squirmed too. He didn't notice what the medication had accomplished until a slick-shaven blonde hooted, "Hey, get a load of Tripod Bob." Bestowing on him the benefit of a full frontal, she said, "Hi, I'm Nikki."

His eyes glazed over and threatened to roll back in his skull. But he held steady, marveling at the miracle. If science could create an elixir that allowed one appendage to be reborn, why not a pill to revitalize his legs? It didn't seem impossible. At the moment, nothing did. He might run, jump, fly.

Nikki, naked Nikki, lifted her arms over her head, elongating her rib cage like a Slinky, leaned back, and pressed her hands flat against the floor. Her body became a bridge. A swinging one. A swaying one. She shuffled in a syncopated rhythm. Barlow wouldn't have been surprised had she turned inside out.

"How about it, Tripod?" She fanned the bills in her garter belt. Cal slipped a five into the jackpot. The fleeting feel of her thigh sent a shiver through his system.

"You like a private dance?" she asked, her teeth clenched in preclimax tension. Or was it distaste? Though a world-class contortionist, Nikki possessed amateur theatrical skills and made a dog's breakfast of desire. But Barlow felt it keenly enough for both of them.

"How much?"

"Whatever you think it's worth."

"Lead me to it."

She stepped behind the chair to push him. He told her to go on ahead. The crowd cleared a path. The men and the performers applauded and shouted encouragement. Though grateful, he did no more than smile in acknowledgment. He couldn't risk losing his focus with grandstanding. Already distorted by a bluish tint, his eyes played tricks with distance and perspective. Nikki's jouncing buttocks appeared to be prehensile, grabbing and dragging him into a room as dark as a pocket.

She switched on a lamp that gave off a pink bubblegum glow, illuminating soundproofed walls. A chair and a single bed had been sheeted in clear plastic. Furniture condoms—what else could you call them? Cal had forgotten how punishingly squalid prostitution could be. Then Nikki made things worse.

"Are you a cop?" she demanded.

"Are you kidding?"

"Yes or no? You don't tell the truth, it's entrapment."

"I'm far from a fucking cop."

"Thata boy, Bob." She dropped the Tripod. Skimming her hands through his hair, caressing his chest and biceps, she said, "What a big guy you are. Big and hard." Careful not to bark her bare shins, she leaned over the back of his chair and whispered, "So what's on your mind?"

"I think you can guess."

"You gotta tell me, Bob. Otherwise I'm soliciting."

"I want a little loving."

"This isn't a country-western song, Bob. You have to be specific."

"I want sex."

"I bet you do." She slid a hand down into his loose pants. "Honest, now, Bob, am I liable to catch what you got?"

"Not unless you run into someone with a shiv."

"The syph?"

"A knife. I was stabbed."

"Poor guy. Wanna climb onto the bed?"

The plastic sheet didn't look inviting. A couple of crinkly thrusts and they'd both slither to the floor.

"What I'd like, I'd like you to move where I can see you," he said.

Holding the column of his heat, she spindled around in front of him. Defying gravity, her breasts didn't budge. When Cal cupped them in his hands, he might have been holding a pair of baseballs. There was the feel of stitching under his fingertips.

He sought out her clean-shaved cleft. The clit ring fit his finger like a wedding band. Nikki waggled her tail, moaning. "What now, Bob? Most guys, I sit on their laps and do a little dance."

He didn't feature Nikki squeezing in with him. Even if she managed to fit, the wheelchair was liable to collapse. "How about something different?" he said.

"Your call. First, let's release the beast." She lowered his baggy trousers and undershorts. "Whoa, Bob! You got a case of the Clintons."

"The what?"

"Looks like it's peeking around a corner, just like Slick Willie."

He curved at a pronounced angle to the left. Had all the Viagra gone to one side?

"Now what do we do about that?" Nikki asked.

"Kiss it," was the historical quote that came to Cal's lips.

"That'll cost a hundred bucks."

"So there *is* a price list."

"I don't do it for love, Bob."

"Then a hundred it is."

She rooted around under the mattress and produced a foil-wrapped package.

"Can't we do without that?"

"House rules." With one hand clutching Cal, she tore the package open with her teeth.

"I swear I won't come in your mouth."

"Hey, isn't that one of those famous lies—right up there with the check's in the mail?"

As she fitted on the condom, he feared the reduced sensitivity set him at an emotional remove. He might as well have been swaddled in the bed's plastic sheet. Was the pill wearing off? No, not possible.

Nikki picked up the tempo. Kneeling between his knees, she bobbed her head up and down. For added traction, she clung to the wheels and rocked the chair. When the cushion started to slide out from under him, she shoved a hand at it and struck something cold and solid.

Her lips loosened and she released a strangled scream. Sagging back on her haunches, she hollered, "What the fuck's this?" She flourished the steel-blue Beretta.

"Careful," he croaked.

"You claimed you weren't a cop."

"I'm not."

"This is entrapment. It'll never hold up in court."

"Forget court. The gun's for personal protection."

She crawled, then clambered to her feet. "I'm calling the bouncer."

"Don't! Please, don't." His happy reincarnation as Tripod Bob subsided in his lap. He pried off the latex and pulled up his pants. "I'll pay you."

"Damn right you will. All the work I done."

"Gimme the gun and I'll give you a hundred bucks for your trouble."

Tears dribbled from Nikki's eyes in sooty streaks of mascara. "How do I know, I give you the gun, you won't shoot me?"

"Take out the clip."

She blinked at the Beretta. She didn't know the trigger from the clip. "Why does my life suck?" This lament had more passion than any of her lubricious groans. As tears streamed down her cheeks, Nikki seemed to shed a final layer and stand before Barlow more naked than ever. A scared country girl with a clit ring. "I'm sick and tired," she said, "of men and their weirdness."

Ashamed of himself, Barlow dug the money from his pocket. "Lemme have the gun, honey, and we'll go our separate ways."

"Don't call me honey." She snatched the cash and handed him the Beretta. "You go first. Damned if I'm walking in front of you."

"Look, I apologize." He stuffed the Beretta back under the cushion. Heeling around in that tight space, he headed for the door. Behind him, Nikki flopped onto the bed. He heard her butt squeak on the plastic.

Out in the cacophony and testosterone crackle, the roistering crowd parted to let him pass. His exit prompted no applause, no response except averted eyes. The disconsolate slump of his shoulders, his thousand-yard stare, alerted them that all hadn't gone well in the cubicle. This happened at Bare Assets, just as it did elsewhere in the world, and there was nothing to do for it but go on with the show. Girls crooked their heels behind their heads, while men gazed on with the fixity of purpose of those beachfront property owners on Eden who searched the horizon at sundown for the green flash.

At the entrance, the bouncer chirped, "Have a nice day." Out on the parking lot, heat poured over the crown of Cal's head with the humid urgency of heavy rain. A blue cast tinted his eyes, as if he wore photosensitive glasses. He suffered a splitting headache. The transfer from the chair to the driver's seat was as draining as a desert trek. He left the door open, punched on the AC, and waited for the car to cool down. The radio swarmed over him, the DJ bellowing that this hour's fourgasm was about to begin.

Sometimes the ache that overcame Cal Barlow was a steady drizzle. Sometimes it damn near drowned him. Yet he tried to take something positive away from the experience. That's what the rehab doctors stressed. One inch at a time, they urged. Well, what the hell, today he raised the bar half a foot before he hit the wall.

10

As he dressed for his after-dark entertainment, Frank Pritchard considered the natural protection of black shoes, black slacks, a black turtleneck, and a black cap on his white hair. But what in other venues might be a perfect disguise would on Eden provoke suspicion and alarm. Nobody here wore black. Oh sure, the occasional woman in a cocktail dress. But never a man. To blend in, he'd do better to don full plumage—white shoes, plaid pants, a Hawaiian shirt as colorful as a calliope—and circulate unremarked among the male birds of paradise.

Amped up as he used to be as a boy before a ball game, he was raring to play and trusted he'd lose his jitters the instant the action started. Decked out as gaudily as an Easter egg, he paused in the garage and selected a can of blue spray paint. A quick shake, a test squirt on the newspapers in the recycle bin, and he was armed. Outside, on the hike-and-bike path, he joined the cancer-fearing crowd that exercised after sundown. Pritchard imitated the elbow-flapping, hip-waggling stride of a power walker. The aerosol can in his hand might be mistaken for a cell phone. Or he could claim it was insect repellent.

At the first cart track, he cut across the fairway. After nightfall, most people restricted themselves to lighted paths and steered clear of the golf course and its bosky dells, sand traps, and ankle-twisting divots. Alone under a rash of stars, Frank savored a gloating sense of forbidden fruit about to be gobbled, of unrepeatable pleasures. The first girl. The first million dollars. His appointment as corporate CEO. Flying on Air Force One.

But no, he thought, those were hollow milestones in a career that had ultimately made him miserable. Tonight was a contrary occasion, the bastard brother of the conventional success he had craved. He could only equate it with the delirium he experienced the few times he had allowed himself to cheat.

On the far side of the island, the McMansions of Acapulco Villas hogged up acres of prime real estate overlooking the ocean. The Atlantic pressed a shell to his ear; the shush of waves became louder, the scent of iodine deepened. His breathing, the thud of his blood, mimicked the rise and fall of the sea.

Bob Emery's baronial Spanish Provincial hulked behind a whitewashed wall whose pristine surface presented an inviting blank page. The dilemma, as for any aspiring author, was not just what topic to write about but how to express it. Vile obscenity struck Frank as too predictable and too tame compared with the violent threats he might have scribbled. And both lacked the keener pleasure of revealing Emery's secrets. The offshore accounts. His unreimbursed use of corporate jets for personal travel. The executive secretary who doubled as his mistress.

But Pritchard was afraid of betraying himself by insider knowledge. Wiser to work by implication, weaving menace in with mysterious remarks. In the end, the words gushed from the can, not his head, and the spray paint yanked his hand along in an untraceable script.

"Death to the fascist insect that preys on the blood of the people," he calligraphed in ornate cursive. Under it, in bold print, he added cryptic numbers, as if of Swiss accounts, cabalistic codes, or Satanic incantations.

From Bob Emery's place, he proceeded to the homes of other board members. On Arlen Graham's faux-Thai façade, he scrawled, "Florida demands complete penetration. Better death than dangling chads." On the garage door of the corporate comptroller's house he sprayed, "Check the books. Chuck the crooks." With paint fizzling from the atomizer in a faint mist, he squeezed out a final message to Ida Thurber, the token woman on the board. "Comes the revolution, the revels end."

Flinging the can aside, he hightailed it toward the fairway, a silver-haired citizen with a spring in his step and a song in his heart. He hadn't gone fifty yards when he recognized his mistake. The can might bear his fingerprints. Racing back, he wiped the tin cylinder on his shirt. Then no sooner had he dropped it again than he suspected it might contain a serial number or some other identifying mark. He stomped the can flat and tossed it into a water hazard, where it flickered and sank like a lure. He counted on a gator swallowing it. They ate anything.

Pritchard was surprisingly unfatigued, fuming with energy, yet plagued by a sense that something remained undone. Not that he had left incriminating evidence behind. More that something needed doing up ahead. Now that he had started, he didn't want to stop. What he wanted—the idea shaped itself out of a chaos of nonthought just as the microdots of jungle emerged from the sprawling grass of the golf course—he wanted to be with Ariel. The way he felt, he had it in him to sprint to Gumbo-Limbo Lane. Or maybe he'd meet her out jogging and they'd race to the trailer, where Nicholas would be sleeping and the two of them if they were quiet—

No, that was nuts. Worse than insane, it was sick. Ariel wasn't much older than Willow.

Still, he didn't head for home. He hurried toward Randi Dickson's townhouse via a route that swung past the mall and its grove of royal palms. At a boutique, closed for the night, a clutch of islanders stood transfixed in front of a blazing shop window. They were watching . . . they were watching watches. An opulent display of Patek Philippes, Blancpains, and Tag Heuers.

Bizarre as that was, Pritchard spotted an even eerier sight. Watching the watch watchers was a man in a dark suit. Lurking behind a palm trunk, he studied the crowd and never noticed Frank huff by. His hair was short, his shoulders bulky, his tie neatly knotted. A Mormon missionary out late canvassing for converts? Whatever, the man's conspicuous appearance reassured Frank that he had been smart not to wear black.

The light on Randi's porch dazzled as brightly as those at the boutique. Pritchard didn't bother to check on the anoles imprisoned behind the glass. What he had set in motion he was anxious to keep on track. He rang the bell, lost patience, and pounded the door.

"Who is it?" she called over the intercom.

"Me, Frank."

"It's late. I'm ready for bed."

"That's good."

"We'll talk in the morning."

"I need you now."

"Are you okay, Frank?"

"Never better. It's just something's changed."

A minute passed. Then another. Randi opened the door in a pair of green silk pajamas. Fresh lip gloss moistened her mouth. "Why, honey, you're soaking wet."

"I ran here," he said.

"That's not you. The boy who never exercises."

"It's the new me." He slammed the door and gathered her in his arms.

"Why, Frank . . ." she started. He didn't let her finish. He kissed her on the mouth, and after a moment's hesitation, she kissed him back. Her hands jumped from his neck to his shoulders, then to his hips, searching for a dry spot. Unable to find one, she pulled back and panted, "Let's get you out of these damp clothes."

"Good idea."

"And into a shower."

"No, I want you right now. Right here."

"What's happened to you? I thought you were depressed. I thought you couldn't be bothered."

"Oh, I'm bothered." He had his Hawaiian shirt off and was fussing with his zipper. Adaptable to evolving circumstances, Randi was quick to shed her pajamas. She feared his sweat would stain the silk. He took a long ardent look at her, tanned from sunbathing on the terrace, surgically tucked and trim. It was all she could do to hold him off until she folded the pajamas and laid them on the hall table.

"Did you take something?" she asked.

"A chance."

"You know what I mean."

"I took a chance. And now I'm going to take you."

The next morning they drove in Randi's Mercedes from the townhouse to Pritchard's more spacious home. He needed a shower and a change of clothes, and she needed a change in perspective and an opportunity to give her thoughts wider latitude. Usually she accepted events at face value—perhaps because she placed such a high value on her own face—but last night required close reassessment. It was so out of character for Frank. Pounding on her door, the tempestuous lovemaking . . . No, not lovemaking. It was straight sex—all elbows and knees, buttocks and head-banging there on the foyer rug. Despite his denials, she couldn't believe he hadn't been to a doctor for a prescription.

In the normal course of a romance, once she established what she regarded as intimacy with a man, she liked to let the relationship simmer while she assumed control. Most men's emotions had the longevity of a mayfly; they could exhaust the life cycle of an affair in a matter of days unless you steered them in a direction that you mapped out. But sometimes Randi improvised and released her deepest feelings from the cage where she habitually penned them. Today, the truth was, she wouldn't have minded if Frank had charged out of the shower and pinioned her to the floor again.

Of course, she could have chosen to go into the stall with him. But she stayed on the patio, sipping strong Italian coffee and munching the crusty wings, smeared with marmalade, off a croissant. As ruby-throated hummingbirds hovered in disappointment above the empty feeder, Randi's fleeting thoughts had the same random pattern as the quick-twitch flight of the birds.

She knew that she had to guard against impetuosity. The key to effective management, Frank had advised her back in the days when she could convince him to discuss business, was moderation. "Nothing's ever as good or bad as it seems," he had said. "Ups and downs are aspects of a continuum. It's like string theory, a complex mesh. In the standard deviation, it all evens out. Don't look at your stocks more than once a year."

That was before the bad overwhelmed the good and he sat strung out, staring at the tickertape crawl across the TV screen like an intestinal worm that was eating him up inside.

Her eyes flicked from the frustrated hummingbirds to CNN's business report. Wall Street hadn't opened, but there were the overnight numbers from Tokyo, Hong Kong, Zurich, and London. The names from the Far East—Nikkei and Hang Seng—were cute. But how could you take seriously an English market called the Footsie 500? It sounded like a Nascar race, a hobby for hillbillies. And as for the market in Helsinki, what sort of nitwit would invest in the Hex?

Not Randi. With her money as with her emotions, she bet on blue chips. Frank, for example, despite his recent slump, was a proven winner, sound in his fundamentals. You couldn't do better than his track record as a husband, father, and provider. Faithful to Dorothy, devoted to Willow, he was what any rational woman wanted. Now that she believed she had him, it came to her that it was shortsighted to suggest a cruise to Baja California. Why not something more ambitious—say a trip up the Amazon?

Frank joined her on the patio in his robe, the one emblazoned with astrological signs. Under it he wore swimming trunks. "Are you going in the pool?" she asked.

"I might. Look what Willow gave me."

He placed a three-dimensional tic-tac-toe board on the table between the butter dish and the marmalade jar. It was a gift that he had opened on Christmas morning and never touched again until now.

"Let's play," he said.

While it pleased Randi that he was back in the game, she had little talent or enthusiasm for cerebral recreation. She fumbled the marbles from hole to hole. With no chance of winning, her strategy was to delay losing. "You really should swim. You've got basically a good body. It just needs work."

"You've got a great body."

"What do you like best about it?" She coaxed his attention away from the board.

"Your smell and your taste."

Some women, she surmised, might view this as flattery. She'd rather be praised for what she had accomplished through hard work and surgery. Still, she had been tantalized by what he did to her with his tongue last night. As long as he didn't expect her to reciprocate. She made it clear to him she didn't do that. It just wasn't her.

"You know, Frank, you might be right about a cruise to Baja. I've had it up to here with sperm whales."

"Sperm what?"

"Whales. They're yesterday's news." Deftly as an origami artist fashioning a paper swan, she conjured for him a boat on a broad, slow river. Throbbing jungle. Jaguars skulking along the shore. Stilt villages, remote Indian tribes—

"I'll be damned," he exclaimed. "Look who's coming."

Two golf carts trundled off the fairway and through the rough. The lead E-Z-GO had a fringed roof, and Lonnie at the steering wheel. Seb slumped beside him in his Freedom from Cancer T-shirt, and Cal Barlow, braced by his blacksmith's arms, sat in back. The rest of the Breakfast Club—Tony, Adrian, and Steve—brought up the rear in a second cart. Everybody except Barlow was waving and hallooing.

Frank unlocked the patio's screen door and invited them in. But since Barlow couldn't leave the cart unless they carried him, they stayed where they were. Randi bustled over with the coffeepot. "Anyone like a cup?"

"Nah," Lonnie said. "We're in the middle of a round and I'm red hot."

"The bastard sank two birdies on the front nine," Seb groused.

"Even a blind squirrel finds an acorn every now and then."

"The reason we stopped," Cal said, "did you hear what happened last night over at Acapulco Villas?"

Randi felt drawn to him. Antimatter into a black hole, daylight into a dark star. Young, robust, his hair slick with perspiration or pomade, Barlow smiled at her, his teeth as white as a golf ball. "Somebody," he said, "tagged four houses with graffiti."

"Damn shame," Frank put in mildly. "They catch whoever did it?"

"Not yet. You know security on Eden," Steve said. "Apart from guarding the gates, they're clueless."

"They'll nab 'em in the end." Frank grinned at Barlow. "You taking up golf?"

"The boys woke me at daybreak and invited me to ride along with them."

"Best anybody can guess, it's someone from off island," Seb said. "Somebody that worked here and got fired."

"My first thought was teenagers," Tony said. "But there aren't any on Eden."

"Going by what the guy wrote," Lonnie said, "he has to be a weirdo."

Randi was starting to feel extraneous standing there holding the coffeepot. What was she? Betty Crocker waiting on the boys hand and foot? She had assumed Barlow was smiling at her. But he seemed to have eyes for Frank. Was the guy gay? Something about his mouth and smile made her think twice. What a waste if true.

"Remember Bob Emery's golf cart," she broke in. "That was suspicious, its rolling into the water. And his Hummer was vandalized."

"The theory is it's connected," Lonnie said. "Emery's house was one that got hit."

"Damn shame," Frank repeated. "Can't claim I always agree with Bob's business philosophy, but I empathize."

"He flew north this morning," Adrian said. "As a precaution, the company thought it better get him the hell out of Eden."

"An overreaction," Steve argued.

"No, it makes sense," Frank said, "to protect an important asset."

"But we can't let this change the way we live," Randi said. "Otherwise, they win."

"They?"

"Whoever's terrorizing the island."

"Let's not jump ahead of ourselves," Lonnie said. "Most likely Seb's right and it's a disgruntled ex-employee."

"How about getting back to the game?" Adrian asked.

"Before we go," Barlow said, "I'm thinking of joining some clubs. Frank said you might have suggestions."

"What are your interests?" Randi asked.

"How come you never ask me that?" Tony lamented.

"Because she can read your mind," Seb said.

"And an illiterate, dirty book it is," Adrian added.

"Are you interested in art?" Randi asked Cal. "There's a life drawing class."

"Hot dog! That means naked models," Tony said.

"No, our models wear bikinis. Sometimes we draw each other."

"That's atrocious," someone squealed from the far side of the patio.

Randi swiveled around. A towheaded little boy was dipping a foot into the pool. Then she noticed Ariel. She must have been turned sideways, Randi thought, and that's why she hadn't seen her straight off.

"I thought she quit," Randi whispered to Frank.

"I rehired her to organize my physical fitness program." Then to Barlow. "She's a trained masseuse. She'll take care of you too."

"What's this? Everybody's looking out for Cal," Seb complained.

Randi was tempted to pour hot coffee over Frank's head. Instead she told Cal, "Hope to see you in class."

The Breakfast Club waved goodbye, and the carts purred off like a pair of overweight cats. Coarse weeds in the rough scratched the undercarriages of the E-Z-GOs, the sound of fingernails on slate to Randi's ears.

book

two

1

Ariel in the A.M. possessed the frenetic metabolism of a jockey. Flitting through the confines of her trailer, anxious not to wake Nicholas, she dressed in jogging shorts and shoes, then ate a bowl of granola with yogurt and banana slices. While she did her stretches and crunches, the boy woke on his own. Sometimes he joined her down on the floor, imitating her exertions, complete with groans, as she twisted into pretzel-like poses. Other days, when he was cranky, she spoke to him in Xhosa, a click language whose tongue trills and glottal stops got him laughing.

Once he was dressed and fed, they went outside, where the air smelled of dying flowers. A tree had shed its blossoms on the garden— or the lawn, as Americans referred to their fenced-in rectangles of grass. Nicholas crawled up into the three-wheeled stroller, and Ariel strapped him in as if for liftoff. The carriage bore a Land Rover label, the same as the all-terrain vehicles that she had bounced around in as a girl, fording dry washes in the veldt and wild torrents during the rainy season. Though she had denied to Mr. Pritchard that she missed home, she treasured memories of South Africa.

Her morning run to Eden recalled Cape Town. True, the road to the island didn't offer much topographical variation—no mountains, no massive rock falls into the sea—but the gum trees and palms and bougainvillea were familiar, and so were the tumbledown neighborhoods and the tinfoil chime of wind through barbed wire. From breezeblock and wooden hovels such as you saw in every black township, there wafted plumes of smoke from cooking fires and the smell of roasting mealie—or corn, as they called it here. Fenced by chainlink and thornbushes, the yards full of yapping dogs resembled stock kraals in some rural dorp.

She liked Americans. Even the ones on the island were mostly amiable and generous. But the strange thing about them was how strenuously they refused to acknowledge their strangeness. We're all middle-class, they maintained, all in the same boat together. Not a dime's worth of difference between us. Yet despite their insistence on sameness, they struck Ariel as dissimilar as chalk and cheese, gazelles and giraffes. What possible comparison was there between the chosen people on Eden and the blacks, coloreds, and Asians who, at this hour, trudged along the weedy verges of the highway toward jobs in rich men's houses?

As she sprinted past her neighbors, Ariel questioned her place in this scheme of things. With no family ties and only the most tenuous connection to the community, she was no better and no wealthier than the people she lived among, but even they regarded her as an outsider. That she was white just added to the irony that whatever she might say about the oddness of Americans, their innocence or ignorance, she was the one who had traveled such a great distance to the country of limitless opportunity and wound up a single mother at

the end of the road, clinging by her fingernails to the last teardrop of
another continent.

At least she had Nicholas and, luckily, she had Frank Pritchard.
Nicholas was lucky to have him too, and every time she saw the two
of them sitting together in that shaded corner of the patio watching
TV, she suffered a heart pang. Was Mr. Pritchard the father Nicholas
needed now that her husband—no, ex-husband—was gone? And
where did Ariel fit in?

She already had a father and didn't need another. What she
needed, she thought, would have embarrassed her to put into words.
Even thinking about it seemed a sin to a South African, whinging self-
pity being a mortal offense. But she wanted someone in her life the
way Mr. Pritchard was with Willow and had been with Dorothy—
tender and attentive, never bullying and obtrusive. Over the Christmas holidays, she had watched him dote on his daughter, and for
months during Dorothy's sickness she had seen him trying to cheer
his wife. Diminished and heartsick as he often was these days, he remained the kind of man you could admire and count on for . . . for
what exactly?

The strands of her thoughts became so tangled, it was impossible
to unbraid them and distinguish what she hoped for Nicholas from
what she hoped for herself. As if racing toward clarity, Ariel forced
herself to run faster. Nicholas liked that and giggled in giddiness
at the speed. It made her feel like singing. She fetched about for
one of the Zulu lullabies she had grown up with, but they were all
mixed in her mind with that Paul Simon album that featured South
African backup singers. So she sang to her son, "I'm going to Graceland, Graceland, Tennessee. My companion is the child of my first
marriage."

Then she struggled with the lyrics to "Diamonds on the Soles of
Her Shoes." A girl making the sign of a teaspoon, a boy making the

sign of a wave? What did that mean? Still, Ariel liked to picture her own shoes gleaming with jewels, barely skimming the ground. A rich girl, not in money. In fleetness of foot.

On the causeway, her clunky K-Swiss trainers thumped the concrete. Around the pylons, in the placid ocean, high-priced debris from Eden—famous-label boxes, designer-brand mineral water bottles, empty magnums of champagne—collected in floating islets. Fishermen who cast their lines between these islets shouted "Good morning" as they did each day when she swept by. But serene at the wheel of an Infiniti sedan, Frank's friend Lonnie sailed along without seeing her. Like a lot of residents of Eden, his future lay far in the past and he watched it recede in his rearview mirror.

Sight of the backward-looking old man called Dorothy to mind again. "My only worry is Frank," she had confided to Ariel. "It's hard on him. When my hair fell out after chemotherapy, I didn't care. I never liked it anyway. As a little girl, as a teenager and a young woman, then when I was middle-aged and it turned gray, I never once liked my hair. So why should I cry about it now? I'll buy a wig and look like I always wanted to. But Frank, he's not adaptable. You're going to have to help him."

Because of her affection for Dorothy and Mr. Pritchard's kindness to her, Ariel had always felt warmly disposed toward him. After the funeral, when he railed against fate and the perfidy of the board, she was of course on his side, and even though it seemed a girly sort of self-indulgence to form an emotional bond with her boss, she knew one existed between them, unexpressed and unacknowledged but still there. That's what made it doubly painful to watch him go downhill and recognize that she couldn't—and he wouldn't let her—help him. And that's why she had been so susceptible when he begged her to come back. At last he was willing to put himself in her hands and let her cure him.

At the gate, the guards greeted Ariel. The man with the hose misted them with spray, and Nicholas squealed in delight. Onto the island they rolled. As usual it looked as if it had been licked clean. While property owners valued a natural environment, they didn't care for the leaf rot and seaweedy rankness of the subtropics. Whenever high tide tossed up something unpleasant from the ocean, maintenance crews with rakes and shovels swooped down on it.

Out on the golf course, alligators loafed on the shores of water hazards, sunning themselves, their tails curled in a scrim of jagged letter J's. Everybody on Eden thought they were marvelous, the more monstrous and murderous the better. Scaly little horrors in the shallows, armor-plated behemoths on the muddy banks, these upset nobody.

But insects were a different matter. Each week a nuclear winter of pesticides rained down on the island as tank trucks spray-bombed mosquitoes, midges, and no-see-ums into oblivion. In theory, this scorched-earth campaign had eradicated roaches. In reality, whenever a three-inch scuttler zipped across a kitchen floor, antennae waving like buggy whips, islanders assured one another that it was a palmetto bug, a harmless outdoor creature that had blundered indoors. Nothing to get riled about.

Edenites, Ariel thought, treated the recent vandalism much as they did roaches—as if it weren't really there or had already been (or soon would be) eliminated. They wouldn't admit what was obvious to her. This man—she couldn't conceive that it might be a woman—was having everybody on, winding people up for his own pleasure. A clown, not a criminal, he recalled the annual fundraiser at her country high school. Sectioning the soccer pitch into squares, the school auctioned off each patch of sod to the highest bidder. Then a cow was led onto the field, and wherever it shat, that was the prize-winning patch. South Africans got a good laugh out of such antics, but islanders blanked out any joke at their expense.

At the tennis courts Ariel spotted a parked VW and heard the rhythmic *thwock!* of ground strokes. She paused next to a manatee sculpted of stone. When you pressed the manatee's flippers, water gushed out of its mouth. Concealed behind the fountain, a man in a dark suit watched Randi's son, Freddy, rally with Cal Barlow. They were hitting on one of the hard courts, Freddy in his spotless whites, Barlow bare-chested in his wheelchair.

As Cal rifled each shot back and Freddy walloped him another, the man in the suit didn't follow the flight of the ball. He kept his eyes on Cal, his gaze so intense it was difficult to say whether he was admiring him or drawing a bead on him.

Ariel, too, had a hard time taking her eyes off Barlow. Racquet in one hand, his free hand powering the chair, he stayed in constant motion, swiveling and spinning. Just as Freddy danced on the balls of his feet, poised to change direction in a split second, Cal danced on wheels. In the lone concession to his handicap, he was permitted two bounces, but often he rushed the net and volleyed before the ball touched the court.

"What are you doing here?" the man in the dark suit demanded when he noticed Ariel. His peremptory tone raised her hackles.

"What's it look like I'm doing? I'm bloody well watching them knock up."

As he lifted his hand toward his inside breast pocket, he might have been a policeman about to write her a ticket. "You like knocking up, huh? You've done that before, I see."

"Mommy, let's go," Nicholas said. "Push me fast."

"There's a good idea, Mommy. Go fast." The man spoke with the arrogance of someone accustomed to issuing orders and being obeyed. This only increased Ariel's obstinacy.

"We'll go in a minute," she told Nicholas. "I want to watch Mr. Barlow."

"You know him, do you? Where's he live?"

Ariel ignored the question. Because of his dark suit and beaked features, the man reminded her of a crow.

"Isn't he remarkable?" said a woman's voice. It was Randi, who had slipped up behind them.

The man removed his hand from his pocket, and after a moment hurried off to the hike-and-bike trail.

"Who's that?" Randi asked.

"I have no idea. He was here when I came."

"He draws a crowd, doesn't he?" She was watching Cal. "A beautiful human being."

Ariel had never known what to make of her. She suspected Randi had her eyes—at least one eye—on Mr. Pritchard. Did she have the other on Barlow? Or was she steering Ariel in that direction, clearing a path for herself with Frank? This wouldn't have annoyed her half as much if she hadn't had an intuition that Mr. Pritchard was also pushing her toward his neighbor, acting as matchmaker or a mischief-maker.

After gulping a drink from the manatee's mouth, Ariel sang out, "Cheerio," and ran off. At the pace she was going, she expected to overtake the man in the dark suit, but he had vanished.

2

The surface of Frank's pool shimmered like a mosaic of blue tiles on the dome of a mosque, every irregular facet dazzled by its own sun. At a signal from Ariel, he plunged into the glitter. Underwater, he felt he existed at the eye of a diamond, integral to a harmonious design. A curious sense of well-being coursed through his oxygenated blood. Everything, it seemed, was about to get better.

At the shallow end of the pool, Ariel poised birdlike on one foot. Paddling toward her, Frank longed to embrace her thighs and bury his face at the prominent juncture of the wishbone. Bathed in the same chlorine-scented molecules, he was persuaded that they shared a powerful connection. But Ariel didn't appear to be aware of it. All business in her red Speedo swimsuit, she instructed him to latch onto the side of the pool and demonstrate his kick.

Frank scissored his ankles in a desultory fashion and stared over at Nicholas, who, in turn, stared at the TV. With the preternatural technical proficiency that kids develop these days, the mop-topped boy had no trouble wielding the remote control, switching from the Business Channel to a *Simpsons* rerun.

"Faster," Ariel ordered. "Throw yourself into it from the hips down to your toes. It's like dancing."

She kicked up a foamy storm beside him, setting a pace he couldn't match. As he flagged and sank, she stood up and propped one hand under his knees, the other under his solar plexus. "Keep it up. This is good for your cardiovascular, and it'll increase your flexibility and stamina."

At her touch, his heart seized, and for an instant water flooded his mouth. Then he torqued into a higher gear. He might have been skating the surface tension of the pool like a pond skimmer.

"Slow down," she said, "before you hyperventilate."

He surrendered to her hands.

"Don't stop," she said. "Space out your strokes. Good. You've got it. Okay, relax now."

He planted his feet on the bottom, fighting for equilibrium. His head belled back and forth, his chest heaved, and his belly quaked. Ashamed to have her see him like this, he quipped, "I'm not at my fighting weight."

"We'll have you in good nick in no time." She pressed two fingers to his throat, checking his pulse.

"Spot on," she said. "Rapid, but strong and steady." Even in his depleted state, he wanted to move her hand to his mouth and nuzzle the hollow of her palm. But as soon as he caught his breath, she suggested that they swim a few laps to cool down. "Don't thrash about," she said. "Let the water do its work. It'll help you if you let it."

While Pritchard did an awkward crawl, Ariel advanced in an effortless sidestroke, her head out of the water to watch his form. "When I was a girl," she said, "this is what we called social swimming. Just pottering along with a pal and having a nice chat."

Too busy gasping for air to reply, Frank nevertheless liked the illusion that they were in this together. They might have been sprawled in bed on a rumpled blue sheet, the world around them all the same lovely shade of blue. If his lungs hadn't been bursting, he would gladly have gone on this way forever.

But when the blue world started to blacken, Frank had to stop. He knelt in the shallows so that only his face was above the waterline. He didn't want her to see his sad-sack condition.

"Well done," she said. "That's a good day's work. You have the makings of a world-beater."

Ariel hoisted herself out of the pool and readjusted the leg bands of her Speedo. While her back was to him, he clawed up the aluminum ladder and flopped onto a chaise longue. Sunlight beat down, burning his shoulders, but he couldn't quit shivering. Nicholas cut his eyes from the Simpsons and shot him a sympathetic look. It spoke volumes when children considered you an object of pity.

As Ariel went into the house, her damp footprints described a sine curve of graceful scallops across the patio. A childhood of shoeless running hadn't flattened her feet. Almost at once, she was back with a towel that she draped over Frank.

"We'll do more and better tomorrow." She dug her thumbs into his throbbing shoulders.

"Assuming I'm ambulatory."

"You'll be fine. You're a man." She pronounced it *mun*. "Not a little gull."

Her hands and voice and nearness warmed him, and he found himself flirting with the notion of returning the favor and rubbing Ariel down. What kind of *mun* was he becoming?

"It's time I went and tended to Mr. Barlow," she said. "Lie here in the sun and you'll soon be dry as a nun's underpants."

Pritchard wanted to ask where she got these expressions, but he was more concerned, as he had been from the beginning, about her going to Barlow's place. "I'll come along."

"No point in that," she told him.

He lurched to his feet and was staggered by a violent head rush. "Always a pleasure to see Cal. What about Nicholas? Shall we bring him?"

"He's fine here."

"But if he falls into the pool?"

"He swims like a fish."

From the rear screen door, they padded over an expanse of cropped grass, springy as a carpet under their bare feet. Cal was in his wheelchair next to the pool, sunbathing in his skimpy *cache-sex*. Frank was glad he had wrapped himself in the wet towel.

Barlow sang out a musical greeting, dealt Frank a playful jab in the gut, and shook hands with Ariel. Pritchard had trouble following what was said. Everything except an acute awareness of his own slack, pasty physique was crowded out of his head by the younger man's aura of potency and total untrustworthiness. How had it ever seemed a smart idea to introduce this guy to Ariel?

Reluctant to leave, equally reluctant to stay, he couldn't bear to watch Ariel touch him. Cal's legs might be useless, but what about the rest of him? Frank clasped a paternal—no, a possessive—hand to her arm. She shrugged him off and said, "Let me get orientated here."

"Sure. I'd better go back to Nicholas."

He trekked across the hi-shag lawn, lifted the little boy out of his chair, and sat with him on his lap.

"Are you okay?" Nicholas asked.

"Yeah, I wanted to watch TV with you."

He had a clear view of the patio where Ariel and Barlow were engaged in an animated conversation. But of course he couldn't hear them. Crouched in front of the wheelchair, she examined his legs at close quarters, flexing and chafing them. Though eager to eavesdrop, Pritchard refused to pick up the binoculars and read their lips. He wouldn't lower himself to that.

On TV a Japanese cartoon had replaced *The Simpsons*. Woodenly dubbed into something closer to Esperanto than English, it showed a pterodactyl tearing Tokyo to pieces and pecking the population to death.

"I don't like this," Frank said. "Let's watch *Animal Planet*."

"Do we have to?"

"Don't you like animals?"

"I guess."

There was a program about a family of raccoons every bit as rambunctious and incorrigible as the Simpsons or those foulmouthed knuckleheads on *South Park*. Frank was desperate to smoke, but didn't because of his promise to Ariel. He also didn't glance next door.

A full-grown male raccoon could weigh as much as forty pounds, the commentator claimed. Ring-tailed critters with prehensile paws, they could climb, jump, squeeze through the tightest cracks, and prise open doors and windows. Ingenious as well as agile, they gathered clams and dropped them on rocks to break the shells and devour the innards.

"If there's any doubt how determined they are, and how destructive," the announcer said as the camera panned a raiding party in a Dempsey Dumpster, "last summer raccoons shut down a nuclear power plant in Port Gibson, Mississippi. Burrowing under security barriers, they short-circuited the plant and knocked it out of business for days. Just imagine what they could do to your home."

"I want one," Nicholas exclaimed.

"How about a dog instead?"

"Borrring."

Unable to hold out another second, Pritchard let his eyes roam toward Ariel and Cal. But they had gone into the house. Maybe she needed to stretch him out flat for a massage. Frank pictured her painfully unkinking Barlow's legs. Or perhaps Cal was letting her inspect the prescriptions in his medicine chest. But why guess? He was paying Ariel. Was it too much to expect a report?

Presently a maintenance crew arrived to clean Cal's pool. He wouldn't pull anything inappropriate with them around. And surely Ariel wouldn't permit liberties. Still, Frank stewed and fretted and suffered pangs of jealousy such as he hadn't experienced in fifty years.

That evening after Ariel and Nicholas left, Pritchard microwaved a Lean Cuisine—under torture he couldn't have identified the meat—and ate it off its aluminum tray, washed down by half a bottle of Châteauneuf-du-Pape 1973. Then he put on his game face and his disguise as a Honolulu lounge singer, and crossed the golf course to the clubhouse, his pockets full of toothpicks. Slightly tipsy from wine and sore from swimming, he didn't rush. He savored the moment, the whole linked chain of minutes.

As always at this hour, the club parking lot was crowded and the valets were busy. Edenites congregated here every night for drinks and dinner, cards and billiards, and what passed for conversation. As he circulated among the cars, he heard a husband and wife discuss the shortcomings of the state's antipoverty program. "Do you know the poorest people you'll ever meet?" the man asked. His wife said that she didn't. "Young golf pros," her hubby explained. "And nobody gives them a damn thing."

With Bob Emery's Hummer safely garaged, Frank searched for another board member's or corporate fellow traveler's automobile. There was an Audi TT coupe that belonged to Arnold Pease, the in-house counsel, and a Porsche Boxster owned by a male-menopausal regional sales manager. Pritchard jammed a toothpick into the Audi's door lock and snapped it off. To ensure that the splinter couldn't be extracted—that the entire locking mechanism would have to be replaced—he punched in a second toothpick, pushing the first one in deeper. He did the same to the door on the passenger side and for good measure, inserted toothpicks into the trunk lock and the gas cap as well.

As he moved on to the Porsche, his heart hammered as it had that afternoon when Ariel laid her hands on him, lifting him in the water so that he felt lighter than air. Barlow had been right about the rewards of low-tech retaliation. Why bother with sophisticated chicanery when a sliver of wood could lay his enemies low and raise his own spirits? And to do this in the name of justice, punishing deserving parties, heightened the endorphin glow.

Pressing his fingers to his throat as Ariel did when she monitored his heartbeat, he set off at a fast trot to Tahiti Townhouses. He liked to top off one triumph with another. The rampages and Randi, an appetizer and an entrée, both courses crucial to the full meal, the banquet, his life had become.

He no longer knocked at her door. Randi had given him a key. Letting himself in, he crept from room to room in the dark, leaving his clothes behind like a cat burglar marking an escape route. She was in bed, eyes shut, pretending to sleep. Maybe she actually was in a dreamy half-doze. Frank couldn't tell. But he knew she liked it this way, with him playing the stealthy intruder and her the hapless prey, he fantasizing that he had coaxed a marble statue to life, she reveling in the belief that even while unconscious she had the power to arouse him.

Lifting the hem of her nightgown, he heard a slight alteration in

the timbre of her breathing. As his finger caressed in dwindling circles, her hips shifted, her spine arched. Still she kept her eyes screwed
tight. It amazed him how long she mimicked sleep—right up to the
instant she cried out and locked her ankles around his waist. "Oh,
Frank! It's you. I was afraid it was the night stalker."

"You're safe with me," he said.

"But I don't want to be safe. Don't stop."

"I don't plan to."

3

He didn't stop with Ariel either. Every day he did his stretches and warm-up exercises, then dived into the pool at her command. Though he groused that she was crippling him, he gloried in her hands-on closeness and in the intoxicating attention she showered upon him. When she insisted on giving him a massage for his aches and pains, it turned out that his reluctance to let her touch him had been well placed. As she ground her elbows and knuckles into his back, Frank groaned in what might sound like rapture but was purest agony. She drilled into an especially gnarled clump of ganglia, and he screamed, "What the hell was that?"

"Toxins," Ariel told him.

"Are you implying I'm an ugly sack of poison? Bile, I'll admit to. But toxins?"

"I'm loosening pressure points where muscles are starting to calcify."

He held back from asking whether this was what she did to Barlow. If Cal's treatment hurt half as much, Pritchard had nothing to worry about. Which didn't, however, prevent him from worrying. Not just about Cal, but about what he was doing with Randi when Ariel, although Frank wouldn't admit it, was the one he wanted to be with.

He also held back from asking Ariel about her ex-husband and what she did alone at night in the trailer. Instead he said, "Tell me about Africa."

"That's a lot of territory."

"Tell me about the parts you know best."

"That's South Africa."

"Say you were there, what would you be doing today?"

"Probably the same thing—treating a patient."

"Where would you live?"

"Cape Town, if I had a choice. Working at Groote Schuur Hospital. Relax," she said. "You're tensing up."

"What would you do when you weren't working?"

"Train for the Comrade's Run. I've always wanted to do that."

"Sounds like a Communist event," he said.

"It's a hundred-K endurance race from Pietermaritzburg down to Durban."

"But what would you do for fun?"

"For me the Comrade's would be fun. It's not a pressurized event. The challenge is simply to finish. I enjoy training when I have a goal and when I have a beautiful place to run."

"Are you saying Eden doesn't qualify?"

"It's fine. But it can't compare to the coast from Cape Town to Landudno. I used to train along the ocean there. The waves were so big I'd feel them shaking the ground under my feet. Then on the return trip, I'd take Chapman's Peak Drive and jog beside Table Mountain."

As she talked and manipulated his spine, he pictured her there. He would have liked to imagine himself running beside her, but even in fantasy he didn't envision himself as a marathoner. And this led by a roundabout route to a fear that Ariel might reemigrate to South Africa. For all he knew, she was an illegal alien, at risk of deportation. Would she let him hire the meanest, most expensive lawyer to fight the INS? He couldn't bear to lose her.

Not that he felt he had her by anything except the slenderest thread. Hell, he had a hard time convincing her to accept a ride home. That night, after ten minutes of protest, she finally agreed to fold the stroller into the Jag's minuscule trunk, buckle Nicholas into the jump seat, and strap herself into the passenger seat. From the causeway, they watched the tin roofs of the huddled town, which had glowed brassy gold all day, turn molten silver in moonlight. As they approached Gumbo-Limbo Lane, Frank wished she would invite him in. She didn't, but he acted as if she had and said, "Sorry I can't have dinner with you. I've got things to do."

"Thanks for the ride. Remember to drink lots of liquids," she said. "Keep yourself hydrated. That's the key."

"See you tomorrow." Nicholas scrambled out.

At loose ends and eager for a pick-me-up, Frank stopped at the Bait Boutique and bought a bucket of chopped fish heads, chicken skin, and coagulated blood. The whiskery gent who sold him the chum swore it would attract sharks. "If that's what you're after."

"That's exactly what I'm after."

He proceeded to Eden's marina, the berth of a hundred magnificent yachts yawing at anchor. Halyards pinged quiet music from aluminum masts. Broad and stately as Cleopatra's barges, cabin cruisers wallowed in water clearer than Pritchard's swimming pool. Hirelings with long-handled nets had sieved every speck of debris out of the harbor.

Lugging a two-gallon bucket, to all appearances a proud boat owner intent on polishing his deck, he walked onto a pier that was rubberized and crosshatched for better traction. No gull, sandpiper, or pelican shit defiled it. There were no birds at all at the dock except for carved wooden owls attached to pilings to frighten off feathered marauders.

One motorsailer had a preening nameplate, MRY-BORD. Registered in Nassau. Nobody was topside, no lights below. Although lamps were lit on several vessels in distant slips, Frank saw nobody and heard no voices. The fleet was moored for the night, sleeping in its antiseptic port.

The joke hereabouts—maybe at every high-end marina—was that a yacht was a hole in the ocean that you shoveled money into. Pritchard intended to change the punch line and reduce Bob Emery's motorsailer to a slop jar of chicken slime and fish scales. Careful to keep his shoes and pant cuffs clean, he sloshed the putrid soup over the teak decks and brass fittings, then baptized the captain's chair with blood.

The stains and stench were enough to enrage any self-respecting seaman. But these were only previews of catastrophic coming attractions. Toppling the wooden owls from their pilings, Frank transformed the MRY-BORD into a landing strip for live birds. By daybreak it would bob like a carcass under shrouds of scavengers that would scar the deck, score the brass with their sharp beaks, and stucco the boat from bow to stern with guano so deep it would take power tools to chip it off.

Exultant, Pritchard was leaving the pier when a small runabout, its motor off, glided ashore. A man in a dark suit dropped anchor and vaulted onto dry land. Lithe as a cat, but not nearly as sharp of vision, he bumped into Frank, recoiled, and reached for something under his armpit. The bucket tumbled from Frank's hand, clownishly hobbling his feet. He couldn't run, could barely keep from falling.

"What are you doing here?" the man demanded.

Pritchard thought it must be someone he knew. There were no strangers in paradise. But nobody he knew would have spoken to him like that. "I might ask you the same question."

"Let me see your ID."

"I live here. You're the trespasser." Frank brazened it out, figuring that if the fellow hadn't noticed him until they collided, then he hadn't seen what he'd done to Emery's motorsailer. Still, there was a blood-spattered bucket between them.

The man flashed what might have been a badge. Then again, in the moonlight, it could have been any metal object. "I'm investigating suspicious behavior."

"Are you with security?"

"I'm working undercover."

Frank wanted a closer look at him, but didn't dare lean in and bring his own face into sharper focus. At this distance, he had the impression of looking at another carved wooden owl—beaked features, beady eyes, predatory intensity.

"Things on Eden aren't what they should be," the man said. "Some people aren't who they seem."

"If you're talking about the vandal—"

"It's a lot worse than that."

"I wouldn't know," Frank said. "I'm out looking for night crawlers."

"Night what?"

"Crawlers. Worms. For bait." He picked up the bucket. "If you don't mind, I'll carry these home."

"You got a car?"

"Yes."

"Get in it and go. From now on, be careful. Stay on lighted paths. You notice anything, call us."

"Well, good luck," Frank said.

"You too. And hey, don't mention this. It'll be tough to catch the guy unless we have the element of surprise."

The Jag stuttered and snorted as if the plugs were shot or the fuel line clogged. But it was Pritchard's trembling foot on the accelerator that caused the backfiring. For the rest of the night he was deeply shaken and couldn't sleep. Then at seven A.M. the phone rang.

Lonnie, who docked his cabin cruiser at the marina, sounded apoplectic. "You wouldn't believe the birds," he said. "It's like that Hitchcock movie. Talk about a shit storm. You can barely see Bob Emery's boat for all the feathers and crap."

"They have any idea who did it?"

"Seb still believes it's an outsider. But I'm starting to think it has to be somebody on the island."

"I suppose I qualify as a suspect. Bob and I weren't always on the best terms."

"Nah, nobody buys that. I'd almost rather you were doing it. What people are afraid of is worse. It's why we can't call in the state troopers. What if it's someone from Assisted Living? You know, all the Alzheimer's and dementia patients and pill poppers. If one of them is running wild, we could have a sad situation."

"I see what you mean."

"No sense humiliating somebody's family. So what I understand, security's keeping things quiet. Investigating at their own speed."

"I see," Frank repeated, and what he saw was no reason to mention his run-in with the undercover agent.

. . .

Ariel arrived an hour later and suggested—it sounded more like a dropped gauntlet—that he race Barlow.

"Me on foot and him in the wheelchair?" Frank asked.

"Don't be silly. The two of you swimming."

"Is this his idea?"

"No. Mine."

"I'm giving away, what? Thirty years to him?"

"He's giving away two legs. I'd call that even."

It wasn't. Not by a long shot. Cal beat him every day for ten days in a row. Pritchard had never liked losing and had hoped that senior mellowness would dull the disappointment. But it didn't. Especially not with Ariel watching from the sidelines, cheering them on.

Frank bore down. He poured into these freestyle sprints the same reckless spirit he brought to his nightly escapades, and the gap between them narrowed. In another week they were swimming neck and neck. But afterward, Frank had to haul himself out of the water like a creature emerging from primordial muck. Panting, he crawled, and Cal crab-walked, onto dry land, and the two of them collapsed belly down on the patio.

"You're getting faster," Barlow told him. "Better."

"I could hardly have gotten worse."

This was a lie. The way he was headed a couple of weeks ago, sinking into a bog of gloom, he still hadn't bottomed out. There were fathoms more he could have fallen. Randi and Ariel deserved some credit for pulling him out of his tailspin, and so did Cal. But when Barlow went on to say, "Don't you think you've made your point? Don't you think you oughta cool the pranks?" Frank pretended not to understand.

"Don't bullshit me," Cal said. "I'm the guy, in case you forgot, who encouraged you to play dirty. But you accomplished what you wanted. You shot a rocket—several of them—up Bob Emery's ass. You ran him off the island."

"This was never just about Emery. There are other issues, other people."

"Yeah, and you stuck it to them too. How long's this shit list of yours? Why not quit while you're ahead?"

Frank smoothed suntan oil over his belly. It was firmer and flatter than it had been since college. He considered admitting his fear that if he quit, he'd lose a miraculously refound side of his life. He considered mentioning the Beretta, their implied pact. Instead he said, "I'll think it over."

"Yeah, do that. You know"—Barlow motioned for the tube of Bain de Soleil—"the whole time I was in rehab I had a mad-on far worse than yours. I hung onto it like it was cash, something precious I couldn't afford to lose if I wanted to survive. But then it dawned on me that I better let go or the rest of me would die."

"Look, I'm just trying to live and enjoy my golden years."

Barlow streaked lotion over his cheekbones and down the bridge of his nose. A chief applying war paint. "One thing I'm curious—this living and enjoyment of yours, does it include Ariel?"

"What kind of question is that?"

"Don't act all Frank Lloyd Righteous on me. I see how you look at her. Are you telling me you're never tempted to cop a feel of that ass?"

"Sounds like you've given it plenty of thought yourself—like you're the one tempted to grab."

"Not me." Eyes shut against the glare, he tilted his face to the sun. His tan had the texture of shellac. "She's not my type. I prefer more meat on the bones."

"So what do you do for sex?" Frank asked, thinking blunt cruelty was no better than he deserved.

Barlow rolled with it. No defensive reaction. "There's some hot stuff over on the highway."

"I'd be careful if I were you."

"Always wear a raincoat. That your motto, Frank?"

His motto was Mind Your Own Business. But he said nothing.

"Of course," Cal went on, "Bare Assets doesn't have anything half as nice as Ariel. You two are the cute couple on campus."

"Don't start that again. If I were sleeping with her, do you think I'd let her bring Nicholas along? You think I'd trust her with you?"

Barlow grinned. "I assumed you were a generous friend, a sharing person."

"I don't care for this line of discussion. My daughter's almost Ariel's age."

"No kidding." He cracked an eye open. "You never let on you had children. Where is she?"

"In Europe."

"You never mentioned her to me."

"Don't act hurt. You're not exactly a fountain of personal information yourself. Ever married? Any kids?"

Barlow let a minute pass. "You don't feel like talking about your daughter, I respect that. I got my own reasons for not discussing my boy."

"It's not that I don't want to talk about Willow. It's just—"

"Just what?"

"I miss her. I wish she lived where I saw more of her."

"Fly where she is. You got the time. You got the dough."

"Maybe I will," Frank said. "Maybe I will. But you know how it is. Sometimes it's better for a kid to have some space."

Both of Barlow's eyes were open now. The sun cream on his face slanted at sad angles. He sighed. "Here I start razzing you and I end up bumming myself out."

"You miss your son?"

He nodded. "Sometimes in my weaker moments I even miss his mother."

"No chance of a reconciliation? No chance of them joining you on Eden?"

"You don't mind," he said, "I'd rather not talk about it." He dragged himself over to the wheelchair, his feet trailing behind like something that didn't belong to him. Or, Frank thought, they belonged to him, but like wheel-less toys that he tugged along.

4

In his living room that night, Barlow grabbed the remote control and gunned on the TV. How many hours had he wasted in the slam sitting slack-jawed in front of the tube, trying, as he did now, not to think about his son? Not to wonder about his wife?

Well, you do the crime, you have to do the time. That was the best that most cons had to offer in the way of wisdom and consolation. How and why they wound up on the wrong side of the law was as unfathomable to them as the next day's weather. But early in life, Barlow knew he had made a choice, a career decision. Convinced of his street smarts, he believed he'd never get caught. Then once caught, he believed he'd never be betrayed—which proved, he guessed, how dirt-road dumb he had been.

He spun through the channels with the boredom of somebody playing Russian roulette with every chamber empty. Another reminder of the joint. The incessant arguments, the stupid, nonstop wrangles about what to watch. Tits and ass or basketball? A documentary about serial killers? The glamorized blood and guts of *ER?* All that bickering left him eager for the blissful freedom to choose his own program. But once you were out, you realized there was nothing on television. The Weather Channel. The Garden Channel. The Shopping Channel. The Real Estate Channel. Three Spanish-language channels. Talking heads on cable networks nattering about weapons of mass destruction and the number of Michael Jackson's face peels. Nothing.

Discovery and National Geographic were broadcasting downers. One show about land mines littering the Third World, the other about mad-cow disease. Problems, problems and no solution in sight. Barlow bet he could fix things. Ship the fucking sick cows to Cambodia and let them loose in the minefields. Bingo! Both problems solved!

He flipped to ESPN and resigned himself to watching ski races from Austria. Interchangeable zombies in helmets and frictionless shell suits zoomed down alleys of snow, past the flickering shadows of pine trees. They reminded him of the Levolor blinds in his bedroom, how they never quite shut out the sun. There were always thin orange blades stabbing between the slats, piercing as memories.

They had some hot stuff over on the highway, he had bragged to Pritchard. Not that he was getting any of it. The board of Viagra tablets lay like a reproach on the top shelf of his medicine chest. Five rounds remained. After his debacle with Nikki in the condomized cubicle, he hadn't had the balls to revisit Bare Assets. He could have eaten a pill and polished his knob in the comfort of his home. But that was too much like being back in the heaving, hard-breathing, crotch-grabbing Big House.

Strange how much life on Eden resembled prison. Lompoc, let's say. Minimum security. Those Club Feds could be depressing places, undermined by the very things—dorm living and open doors all day—that were supposed to make them desirable. You couldn't even take a crap in privacy. Couldn't share a secret without someone blabbing it in group therapy. And with so many brownnosing white-collar offenders slammed up together, it was risky to bribe the guards to smuggle in booze and drugs. Numb-nuts businessmen, angling for time off for good behavior, would rat you out.

Bored by the skiers—not enough of them tumbled ass over tea-kettle to hold his attention—Barlow admired the background Alps and steepled villages painted the color of Italian ices. As he started doing curls and reverse curls with a fifty-pound dumbbell, he mused what it might be like to live in cuckoo-clock Austria. Not that the Witness Protection Program would finance such a lark. But if he decided to bug out of the golf glee of Eden, who'd know? Who'd care? The mob might chase him, but he doubted the cops would bother. Unless he caused trouble, they'd just as soon be shut of him.

Yet tempting as it was to split and take his chances, he knew he'd have to travel with a piss-poor companion—himself. And wherever he went, he'd have to down his daily ration of meds, monitor his sad ass for bedsores, and hire somebody to keep his legs from kinking.

Maybe he could talk Frank into tagging along. Not just for practical help and purposes of camouflage. He enjoyed the old guy's company, their conversations, even the disagreements. Which made him regret that thus far he had revealed almost nothing about himself except lies.

He hadn't even been honest with Pritchard about Ariel. Although he generally subscribed to the principle that a heavy-legged woman promised a light and lively ride, he was drawn to her whippet thinness. Once as she massaged him, he had cupped a palm to her butt. Round and firm as a couple of apples. He could hold both her cheeks in one hand.

She gave him a down-her-delicate-nose glance of disdain, like that would rattle him. Rather than let go, he squeezed her ass, and she shifted her hand to his belly, fingering the muscles of his abdomen as if searching the lower segments of his six-pack for a pop-top. Just when he thought she might grab his cock, she seized a fistful of sinew and twisted.

"I spent a season rehabbing the Springboks," she said. "Do you seriously think that after that randy bunch of rugger-buggers I can't deal with the likes of you?"

He dropped his hand from her rump.

"Point taken?" She twisted harder.

"Okay, I get it. You're spoken for. You're Frank's girl."

"Wot?" She released his skin, and it snapped back like elastic.

"I know he's sweet on you. Till now I didn't know where you stood."

"You're talking bollocks."

"Not me. It's you. Look how you're blushing."

"Sure, I like him. But it's not what you think. He's a good person and he's had a hard time. If you could have seen him with his wife."

"I've seen him with you. That's all I need."

"Just shut up," she said, "and let me get on with it. I wouldn't even be doing this for you if it weren't for Mr. Pritchard."

When the phone rang, Cal jabbed the mute button on the remote control. An involuntary reflex. His next reflex was that it had to be a wrong number.

"What about Art?" a woman asked.

"Nobody here by that name, lady."

"It's me, Randi. Remember? You said you wanted to sign up for art class."

The voice, then the face, registered. Frank's friend. The blonde with the coffeepot and the smile. Somewhere in age between Pritchard and him. But quite tasty.

"Look, I gotta confess," Cal said, "my whole life I never held a paintbrush."

"This is a course in drawing. No paint. We use pencils and charcoal."

"Pencils I have experience with. Charcoal I'm familiar with from barbecuing."

She let out a throaty laugh, like he was the funniest man alive.

"When do we start?" he asked.

"Tonight."

"Lemme see. You caught me at a busy time. I got a calendar someplace. Yeah, luckily I'm clear."

"I could pick you up," she said, "if that'd help."

"Not much space in that Mercedes of yours. Might be tough getting in and out with my chair."

"Shall we meet at the community center, at the mall?"

"Sure. Is there someplace I can buy pencils and paper?"

"I have plenty of supplies. We'll share."

Cal hung up feeling like he had better chill a moment and catch his breath. He swallowed an antispasticity pill and ate a banana for the potassium. In the bathroom, he had trouble peeing as he did sometimes when he was nervous and in a hurry. He poked his stomach, the way he had been taught to do. This pump priming occasionally caused bruises, but it got him going.

Then he showered and changed clothes, performing each movement with the exactitude of a gymnast. Doctors had drummed it into him that everything was an opportunity to practice. But practice for what? He pondered the question in front of the medicine chest and decided it was self-deluded to fire a blue beauty. He was headed to art class, not a lap-dancing club. Why have sex on the brain while he had a pencil, not his cock, in his hand?

As for the Beretta, he debated whether to bring it along. Bad enough that Pritchard knew about it. But he didn't like to go out unarmed. Then too the feds had the right to enter the house whenever they pleased. If they shook down the premises and found the pistol, he was finished. Safer all around to keep it under the wheelchair cushion.

Randi was waiting for him on the mall parking lot, peering over the low roofline of her 230 SLK. She appeared to have dressed for a cocktail party in a pair of smart white slacks and a fitted burgundy top, the type, if he remembered right, that snapped between the thighs. Maybe he should have worn something classier than a T-shirt and loose cotton trousers. In compensation, he injected extra swagger, a show-offy athleticism, into his exit from the VW.

She toted a black leather case, a big one like models lugged around the streets of Manhattan. "Art supplies," she explained as she led him into the mall's atrium, where the splash of a fountain competed with the drizzle of Muzak. An auditory fog enveloped them as they progressed through this cathedral of commerce whose intersecting passageways each promised a fascinating destination but ended at another parking lot.

"Some people when they move to Eden complain about culture shock," Randi said. "Like they're shocked because there's no culture. But honestly the island has plenty to offer. There's a repertory theater, a choral group, a foreign-film society, a couple of book clubs."

"Yeah, it's a happening spot," Cal agreed.

"I don't even think of it as an island. To me it's a microcosm."

Of what? he wanted to ask. Like most women when they walked beside his wheelchair, Randi didn't know where to aim her eyes. Up? Down? Straight ahead? What was the correct protocol with cripples?

While her gaze wavered, he checked her out. She looked to be in splendid shape. Cinched waist, taut butt, perky breasts. Didn't show much mileage anywhere except her neck. Those faint circles in soft flesh. Rings of Venus he had heard them called.

In an alcove surrounded by elephant-ear plants, a clutch of old-sters huddled over lap boards. Cal dreaded that this might be the art class, this pathetic, palsied group fiddling with sheaves of paper. But the papers weren't sketchpads. They were spreadsheets, and everyone was chattering into a cell phone.

"The investment club," Randi whispered.

"Who are they talking to at this hour? Brokers in Asia?"

"I think they're just, you know, practicing."

For what? Barlow wondered as he had earlier about himself. They might claim they didn't care about the current down cycle; they were in the market for the long haul. But most of them didn't look like they'd make it to the next annual report.

"Here we are," Randi said.

The community center was a multipurpose space lit like an inter-rogation chamber. Cal imagined detectives behind the mirror wall studying his every eye twitch and tremble. At the far end of the room, a gooseneck microphone drooped over a lonely podium. At the near end, blue foam mats had been stacked after a yoga class. In the center of the floor, men and women at easels stared with peculiar fixity at a padded box several feet square. It might have been a pedestal for a statue or a potted palm. Nothing was on it now—not that you'd know this from the fierce attention these people paid it.

Randi unpacked her case and handed him a sketchpad. Then like a fisherman tweezing up a hand-tied fly, she passed him a single stick of charcoal. "Careful," she warned. "It makes a mess."

When she introduced him to the club, he caught no names, only noted that this was a younger crowd of creative types. He counted three men with mustaches, a few middle-aged women with long frizzy hair. Members of both sexes wore those rope-soled canvas shoes that tourists brought home from France. A black guy, a big mother with the heft of a middle linebacker, had a shaved head as slick as a bowling ball and deep-set eyes like finger holes. If it wasn't surprising enough to have a soul brother in the class, the guy spoke with a plummy British accent.

"We're privileged tonight to have a professional model," he said. "I trust it won't cause controversy"—he pronounced it con-*trawv*-esy—"but she'll be posing topless."

The mirrored wall parted and out pranced a woman in a terry-cloth bathrobe. She might have been fresh from a shower and an hour of hard labor at the makeup table. She had really caked it on—foundation and glitter, eyeliner and purple lipstick. When she shed the robe, revealing the surgical perfection of her breasts, Barlow recognized Nikki from Bare Assets.

She gave no sign that she recalled him. Her memory bank must have been a blur of male faces and members. Hopping up onto the pedestal, she struck a cat-in-heat pose, down on all fours, spine arched, teeth clenched in that grimace of counterfeit desire or genuine disgust that Barlow had noticed on all the girls at Bare Assets. Despite the bikini bottom, she looked naked without her garter belt and wad of bills.

"I believe," the black dude said, "a less theatrical pose would be preferable."

"Your dollar, your call," Nikki said. "Tell me what makes you happy."

"Please lie down on your side. Extend one leg and crook the other. Now let your arm fall back behind your head."

"You got it."

Cal angled the sketchpad in front of his face like a sun reflector.

He still feared Nikki might sing out that she never forgot a customer who packed heat. But when she rolled over, canting her rump in his direction, he felt safe lowering the pad to his lap.

"Isn't the human body amazing?" Randi murmured. "I mean, for an artist, what could be more intriguing than those contours, the subtle chiaroscuro of light and dark? It makes me wish I had more talent. I see it, but I can't get it down on paper."

It made Cal wish he had more testosterone and functioning neuroreceptors. He saw Nikki and wanted to get her up on her hands and knees again, with him jamming from behind. He felt something. It wasn't his imagination or memory. It was genuine desire, but desire so detached from arousal that chemicals would have to bridge the gap.

He thanked God he hadn't downed a pill before class. Otherwise he would have had a built-in easel in his lap. The rebirth of Tripod Bob. As it was, he could regard Nikki with something approaching artistic objectivity. He could, as Randi recommended, reduce her to geometrical shapes and shadings. He could hold the stick of charcoal at arm's length and study her as if against a grid. He could analyze the conical solidity of one upthrust breast and the stippled shadow beneath the other.

What he demonstrably could *not* do was draw her. Scratching at the pad, he milled gray powder onto his hands and down the legs of his pants. He was transforming himself, not the paper, into a pointillist doodle.

After an hour, the model requested a ten-minute break and climbed down off her pedestal. Roaming around, she criticized their efforts, pointing out errors of perspective. What was she? A roving instructor? Barlow's sketch resembled something on a lavatory wall— a hasty ideogram of hard-core porn and wretched technique. Not wanting her to see it or him, he vamoosed to the atrium and looked in on the investment club. They were still phoning in practice puts and calls.

By the time he returned, Nikki had disappeared. The black guy, with the calm authority of a British Airways pilot apologizing for a brief bout of turbulence, announced, "There's been a scheduling mix-up. Our model had a man-date-ry appointment elsewhere. We need a replacement. Any volunteers?"

In the whelming silence, Cal figured Nikki had pocketed a few bucks from this gig, then hustled over to the highway for the more lucrative Beaverama.

"What about you?" Randi asked him. "We're bored with drawing each other. You'd be a marvelous change after the model's soft lines."

Although grateful for any excuse to stop grinding the charcoal, Cal hesitated. Not normally shy, he felt self-conscious in front of a roomful of strangers. But then Randi said, "Please. You have such terrific definition," and he thought, What the hell. Clambering from the wheelchair onto the pedestal, he stripped off his T-shirt. It was no bad thing to see the look in their eyes. For the last few years he hadn't savored much that might pass for admiration, so he seized the moment. He fanned out his lats, flexed his delts, and deepened the divide of his pecs.

When Randi suggested that he pull down his pants and pose in boxer shorts, he hesitated again. He didn't relish baring his legs and the scar on his spine. His attenuated thighs, the licorice-stick calves, the feet that folded in on themselves like dying flowers—sight of his lower body suddenly provoked in Cal something close to panic. It was almost as bad as the first days of rehab—that fear that he was in quicksand up to his chest and might keep on sinking until he didn't have a mouth to scream. But Randi said, "Perfect. You're perfect," and that broke the spell.

"Do Christina," someone shouted.

Cal drew the line at female impersonation and drag queen crap. They could find another sucker.

"The Wyeth painting," the same person said.

"Are you talking to me?" Barlow demanded.

Randi stepped to the pedestal and gently realigned his legs. She had him prop his weight on one hand and swivel his face in the opposite direction. "That's it," she said. "*Christina's World.*"

Afterward, Cal didn't do the rounds as Nikki had done to see what the artists had made of him. He was satisfied with Randi's approval. Still, it was an extra boost to his morale when the black guy invited him back next week, saying, "We can't get enough of you."

Out in the atrium, the Muzak had died, the fountain was dry. The investment club had packed up its spreadsheets and abandoned the alcove. Cal's wheels whirred down the corridor, a lullaby of the mall's long day.

"Let a lady buy you a drink?" Randi asked.

Among the few establishments still open, there was a bar with a fifties motif. Pink and black upholstery. Wrought-iron tables. Wall hangings of poodles and hot rods and hepcats in pegged pants. A jukebox belted out numbers from the pre-rock era—"Tennessee Waltz," "Lisbon Antigua," "Old Cape Cod."

"I was a kid when my parents listened to this schmaltz," Randi said, settling into a booth. "That was before you were born."

Cal took a big icy bite of his Scotch on the rocks. "We're about the same age," he lied. "Which raises the question why you live here."

"Why do you?" She wiped the charcoal from her fingers with a pink napkin, then sipped a Cosmopolitan.

"Short story," he said. "I need somewhere that's flat, not too many stairs, not too much traffic, and nobody's liable to mug me in the street."

"You're in heaven. Or you were before the night stalker."

"What I gather, he doesn't bother people, just property."

"So far. Let's hope it stays that way."

"I think you can count on it. Now it's your turn," he prompted her.

"Frank tells me you had a work-related accident."

"Hey, we don't want to talk about that."

"Do we really want to discuss how I ended up on the island?"

"That was the deal. Play fair."

"Well, I was married. Moved here with my husband. When that didn't pan out, it made sense to stick around. After all, Freddy's on Eden."

"He lives with you?"

"No, he has his own apartment. But I like to be close by."

"Yeah, and there's Frank." Cal swirled the cubes in his glass, locking all instruments on maxi-cool, not wanting her to think it mattered to him one way or the other.

"Frank's an old friend," she said. "Actually his wife was my friend. After Dorothy died, I, you know, I've been there for him."

"And that's how you two got to be more than friends?" He didn't put a lot into it, just laid it out, not so much a softball question as a simple statement of fact.

"We care about each other. From time to time, we cry on one another's shoulder. But 'good friends' pretty much describes our status."

Barlow didn't feature Pritchard crying on anybody's shoulder or doing the caring-sharing, deeply meaningful bit. "Sorry to pry," he said.

She finished the Cosmopolitan. "You know, there are Assisted Living units that have a fifties décor. They pipe in music like this. Apparently it soothes the Alzheimer's patients. Reminds them of happy days. But frankly," she said, smiling, "it leaves me cold. Shall we go back to my place for a nightcap and something slightly more up-to-date?"

"I'd like that, Randi, I really would. But it's late and that art took it out of me."

She held the smile, clenching her teeth like Nikki. "I was hoping to persuade you to pose for me. A private session."

What could he say? Gimme half an hour to rush home and drop a blue beauty? He reached across the table and squeezed her hand. "How about a rain check? Tomorrow night, let's say."

"What's wrong with the day?" she asked. "The light's better for sketching."

"I'd be up for that."

5

What nobody appreciated, Randi thought, was her vulnerability. She had never been a naturally cheerful or optimistic person, but she had developed a sunny disposition the same way she had flattened her stomach and trimmed inches off her hips—through hard work. And just as a personal trainer had helped her lose weight, she had hired specialists to tidy up her moods with couch sessions, hormone replacement therapy, and other pharmaceuticals.

True, she still had her foibles. She tended to forget things. Frank joked that like a primitive tribeswoman, she always left on at least one electrical appliance, as if it were a fire that she feared she'd never be able to start again. And he chided her for obsessing too much about money. But she had taken some wicked hits in her time. She had survived several major market corrections and full-blown recessions, including that killer during the second Reagan administration. She had written off a million in losses during the NASDAQ nosedive and retreated to bonds to lick her wounds. Now she had gone into Ginny Maes, Reits and Grits, and half a dozen other acronymic investments.

Having weathered so many crises, she felt a power affinity for Cal Barlow. Like her, he was positive and upbeat, and last night as he swung out of his car and into the wheelchair with such élan, she realized he had the qualities she admired in a man—physical grace, sensitivity, and spirituality, all combined in one hard, muscular package.

Granted, Frank had his points too, but they had gotten jumbled in her mind with Cal's. For Randi, men were seldom an either/or proposition. Her brain didn't function in a binary fashion. Without being entirely conscious of it, she intuited patterns, tantalizing correspondences. Liking one man didn't preclude others. If she could contrive to have them both, where was the harm?

The fact was, Frank alone no longer satisfied her. She had started to lie awake in bed at night, wondering whether he would come. Wondering whether she would. For the first time since her teens, during those tornado-tormented summers in Kentucky, she turned out the lights early and touched herself. Her excuse—and she felt she needed one—was that she was warming up for Pritchard. But now she had her doubts about the source of her heat.

She blamed Frank for barging in on her and she blamed him when he didn't show up. She blamed him for the fire he had ignited and blamed him for leaving her on her own to extinguish it. But above all, she blamed him for Cal Barlow. She would never have met the man had she not sat on Frank's patio, spying through his binoculars.

Cal wasn't even her type. Muscle boys and lifeguards had never held any appeal for her, and she wasn't usually a woman who viewed her role in life as a helpmate or healer. The first time she saw his withered legs, the first time she heard him talk—he sounded like a New York cabdriver—that should have ended things right there. But somehow it hadn't.

In the past, she had conceived of the dynamics of sexual desire as operating on the same principle as a self-cleaning oven. To her, love-making was a sort of cyclical sanitary process that only trashy, ill-educated people allowed to become central to their lives. Those with more sophistication kept it in perspective. When oil splatters and gumminess built up, they simply rejiggered the control button. But all this fooling around with Frank had thrown a permanent switch in Randi and now she required constant maintenance.

The next day while she waited for Barlow, Frank called to ask why she hadn't stopped by that morning. She said she was expecting a repairman to come fix her stove. "I hear him at the door," she said, then rang off.

But it was a false alarm. No sign of Barlow. In the living room, she pushed the peacock chair into a corner, widening the space between the rattan couch and the coffee table, opening a path for him to roll out to the privacy of the terrace. They would sit there, she decided, on a pair of chaise longues that overlooked the lake, a protected bird sanctuary, off-limits to boaters and swimmers. As ibises and spoonbills took flight from the shrubbery along the shoreline, there was often a hushed clapping of wings. When Randi sunbathed nude on the terrace, she liked to make believe the soft beating sound was applause for her.

Another hour passed, and when Barlow still hadn't arrived, she started to worry. It was demeaning to phone him, but she had the excuse that he was differently abled and might have had an accident. "Have you changed your mind?" she asked, unable to keep a certain frostiness out of her voice.

"Not at all," he said. "I just wasn't sure when you wanted to get together." Since daybreak, Cal had been sitting with a glass of water and a tab of Viagra, ready to fire up. "I'll be right over."

"How do you intend to get here?"

"Drive."

"I'd rather you didn't."

"Hey, I'm sorry I'm late."

"I'd rather you leave your car at the mall. Parking's tight at Tahiti Townhouses." She couldn't risk having Frank or Freddy see his VW in her driveway. "Do you mind?"

"Not a bit."

The instant she hung up, this all seemed like a very bad idea. She debated calling him back, telling him to forget it. This isn't me, she thought. It's not in my nature. This isn't happening.

While that mantra shuttled back and forth in her mind, she brushed her hair. She sprayed cologne on her wrists and the crooks of her knees. A fresh lemony scent. Then she raised the garage door with the electric gizmo and lingered in the shadows watching for Cal. As he rolled around the corner and up the street, through a dazzle of mica chips in the asphalt, he was smiling. At what she couldn't guess. He couldn't see her. Yet the smile had a radiant effect on Randi. How could she resist a man with such a sunny disposition?

"I hope it wasn't too far." After he glided into the garage, she scrolled down the door.

"You kidding? I didn't break a sweat."

Three steps led from the garage to the house. Randi hadn't considered how he would get up them. Was there a board to improvise a ramp? But before she had time to react, he tilted back in the wheelchair and mounted the stairs with the equipoise of a gyroscope spinning up an incline.

"Why don't we sketch outside?" she suggested.

"Let's get to it." His voice rang with irrepressible cheer. "Where's my pad and pencil?"

"You don't need them. You're here to pose."

"I thought—my presumption—you'd do me while I did you."

"No, a model has to stay still. And how am I supposed to draw you if you have a sketchpad in front of you?"

"It's your party. Next time's my turn." He thumped over the aluminum track of the sliding door and onto the terrace.

"Why don't you relax on the chaise longue?"

"Mind if I take off my T-shirt?"

"Oh, I insist. Here, let me help you skin the rabbit."

Her tone was facetious, mock maternal. But that wasn't how she felt as he stripped to his shorts. Bracing on the armrests of his chair, he performed a flawless dismount onto the chaise longue. When Randi touched the patch of scar tissue at the base of his spine, Cal shivered.

"Let's get that ugliness outta sight." He rolled onto his side, facing her.

"Is it from your accident or an operation?" she asked, perching on the other chaise longue.

"A bit of both. I got cut in the accident, and the doctors, what they did, they had to open me wider and fuse the vertebrae before they sewed me back up."

"That's awful, Cal. Tell me how it happened." She picked up a pad and made random strokes in charcoal.

"It's a long story. The short version, some people I worked with were undependable. I should have expected trouble. The type of enterprise I was in, things constantly go wrong."

"What kind of business was it?" she asked.

"A bunch of different things. The one in question, I suppose you'd call it electrical supply. There was a blowup and I caught a chunk of steel in my spine."

She winced. She respected his desire to be brief, but had to tamp down the urge to pry for details. While she thought a woman was wise to retain a last veil of mystery, she liked to tear it off a man and learn what lay beneath.

"What do you make of this outbreak of crime on the island?" she asked.

"Haven't given it much thought," he said. "I'm a homebody these days."

"Home is where these things have been happening. When you think of the thousands we spend on security, it makes you wonder."

"Wonder what?"

"Whether we're safe."

"You're safe with me. I guarantee that."

His confidence moved her. He resembled a brawny gladiator. Russell Crowe in that movie. Only more ethnic. He might have been a praetorian guard protecting the corrupt aristocracy—Joaquin Phoenix and those Roman perverts.

"I can't help being frightened," she said, "when I'm alone at night."

"It's just some fool letting off steam, having a little fun."

She arched an eyebrow. "Is that your idea of fun? Scaring people half to death?"

"No. Mine's laying out here with you, looking at the lagoon and the birds. You wouldn't know anybody else lived on Eden."

She dashed a hand at her forehead. The charcoal left a sooty smudge, like ashes on a penitent. "Could I ask a favor?"

"Of course."

"Would you mind slipping off your boxers?"

He looked at her. She looked back at him. "It's a tradition as old as art," she explained. "Think of the statue of David. Think of Adam on the ceiling of the Sistine Chapel."

"Well, if it was good enough for them." Boyishly shy, he eased the elastic band of his boxers down over his hips and tugged them off his ankles. After a moment, he said, "It's not fair that you're dressed and I'm not."

"The artist's prerogative."

"Don't models have any privileges? 'Specially unpaid volunteers?"

"What would you like?"

"I'd feel more comfortable if you moved over here and kept me company."

She crossed the space between them as if to draw him at close range. But he removed the pad from her hands, and she skated the flat of her palm over the segmented muscles of his stomach and chest. The slight granulation of charcoal served as a lubricant. When he clasped a hand to the back of her neck and pulled her down for a kiss, she liked his smell, the taste of his tongue, the enfolding power of his arms. All so different from the men she had known.

She undressed looking down at him, and what she saw surprised her. Thickly swollen, sturdily erect, he had a distinct curve. He clasped the back of her neck again and urged her head lower. "I need a little encouragement," he whispered.

She didn't do this. I'm not the type. It's not in my nature. Yet while the mantra occupied her mind, her lips did what Barlow asked, and as long as she kept telling herself that this wasn't her, she found that she could abide it.

Barlow lay back, and Randi straddled him, posting at her own speed. The corner he rounded inside her led where nothing and nobody had ever touched her before. He hit bone. He hit it again and gasped. She gasped too and thought he was howling. But the howl throbbed up from her own throat, and she collapsed onto the brown beach of his chest and listened to birds oar away against the sky in rousing applause.

6

The Breakfast Club's annual deep-sea fishing trip was an event that usually Pritchard preferred to skip. He didn't care for catching fish, ripping the hook from their ravaged mouths, appalled by their dying eyes. He cared even less for not catching fish, pissing away a day in a deck chair swilling beer. In a millisecond he could process the whole slow arc of an angler's experience. Up early in the morning, intoxicated by life's manifold glories. Two hours later, paralyzed by its inherent meaninglessness. The urge to live in the moment swiftly overtaken by the imperative to escape it. But Cal was eager to go, and Frank regarded it as his duty to encourage his neighbor's enthusiasms.

As for his own enthusiasms, he was loath to admit that he had any. Bad enough that Barlow was aware of his rowdy misdemeanors. He didn't want him to find out about Randi. What they did was nobody's business. The last few nights, as a matter of fact, she herself hadn't seemed entirely aware of what they did in bed. Her pretense of sleep had become unnervingly convincing.

But his feelings for Ariel were the most difficult to deal with. He hadn't just hidden them from Barlow. He had largely concealed them from himself and transferred them to Nicholas. Leading the little boy by the hand around the patio, he explained the operating principles of the air-conditioning unit, the pool filtration system, and the gas-powered grill that he hadn't barbecued on in over a year. He attempted to teach him the solution to Rubik's Cube and had carried him to the deep end of the pool to demonstrate Archimedes' Law. He let him have free rein of the house, unlimited access to the Jacuzzi, and almost complete control of the TV.

While Ariel tended to Cal, Pritchard rattled on to Nicholas about the advent of high-definition television and the future of interactive electronics. Meanwhile on Animal Planet, that hyperthyroid Australian, the Crocodile Hunter, lifted a poisonous snake six inches from his lips and crooned, "Isn't she a bee-ooty?" Nicholas said, "Ugh," and channel-surfed to a program about the Florida panther.

A genetic bottleneck threatened the big cat with extinction. It wasn't just pollution and a shrinking habitat that had reduced its population. Inbreeding had resulted in crooked tails and cowlicks, heart defects and heightened susceptibility to parasites and disease. Worse yet—Frank cringed—most male panthers were cryptorchid, with one or both testicles undescended, and scrotal sacks teeming with malformed sperm.

The news didn't bother Nicholas. He dozed off on Frank's lap, a dreamy reminder of Willow sleeping in his arms as a little girl. He must have held Dorothy like this as well. He knew he had, but he couldn't summon up specific instances. Oh, he remembered the sex, especially the first few years of marriage, when they made love in as many different settings and circumstances and positions as possible. He had wanted her never to forget, had hoped she would always associate him with her life's most profound experiences. But as for simply holding her in his arms, no, there was nothing solid.

Swept through with sorrow, Pritchard had the vertiginous sense of leaning over a precipice, struggling to retrieve what had disappeared. He hugged Nicholas. How foolish not to hold on to what you loved as long as you could. Everything fell away soon enough. Why let it go without a fight?

That evening, as Ariel was about to set off for the mainland, he wanted to plead with her to stay. Instead, he asked Nicholas to spend the night with him watching cartoons. This joshing bit of nonsense allowed him to say he'd be lonely until the little boy returned tomorrow—when what he meant was he'd miss Nicholas's mother.

The day of the fishing trip, he scribbled Ariel a note. "Be back this afternoon. Cal and I'll be full of aches and pains from reeling in whales. We'll need a massage."

The Breakfast Club convened at the marina as dawn spilled its mango brilliance over the flotilla of yachts. The pier had been scrubbed down, and a new batch of wooden owls commanded the pilings. Bob Emery's motorsailer languished in dry dock, where its ruined deck was being refurbished. Frank noted the absence of the dark-suited investigator's runabout. The incident still troubled him. Having come within a hair's breadth of getting caught, Pritchard had taken a hiatus from his high jinks for the past week.

Lonnie owned a forty-foot Bertram cruiser, and he manned the helm in a captain's hat, alternately toying with the boat's gauges and his own chest. Freddy had hired on as first mate, and the lanky blond tennis pro helped the Breakfast Clubbers aboard one by one. Tony had a gimpy knee, Steve a herniated disk. Adrian, in Bermuda shorts, had varicose veins like pickled octopuses plastered to his calves. "If you can't cure it, you gotta endure it," he said.

"Don't start with the cornball slogans," Lonnie told him.

"Don't scorn corn," Adrian shot back.

Freddy arranged a soft landing for Seb, who was bare-chested for a change. His skin had a razor-burned look from defibrillator paddles. Hair that had been yanked out by the roots resprouted in grizzled tufts. "Who do we have here?" Seb said to Freddy. "Handsome young fella, a poor man's Brad Pitt. A homeless person's Brad Pitt."

Freddy laughed, but didn't join in the badinage. Few had ever heard him say anything except, "Bend your knees and watch the ball." The consensus was he suffered inner ear trouble, as in nothing between them. The alternative theory was that Randi had spoiled him and he needed treatment for affluenza.

As Barlow negotiated the ramp, Freddy worried whether the wheelchair would leave skid marks on the deck. Lonnie said he didn't give a damn, and Freddy hoisted Cal and it over the gunnels and wedged him into a corner.

Lonnie motored slowly out of the marina, then accelerated into ocean swells. He watched where he was headed, not, as in a car, where he had been. Steve cracked open the first round of beers, and Freddy began baiting hooks.

"Catch a whiff." Tony dredged in a breath. "Only two things smell like that. One's fish."

"You know, after Dubya Dubya Two, I served in Japan," Seb said.

"So you told us a thousand times."

"The women there claimed Americans smelled like corpses, like rotten meat."

"Yeah, well, what did Jap women smell like?" Lonnie asked.

"Nothing. Even down there they had no smell."

"Was that good or bad?"

"A question of your point of view. Sometimes white bread's all you want. Sometimes a man likes tang to his poon."

Tony laughed and spouted beer from his nose. "Tastee Freeze," Adrian shouted.

Frank moved next to Cal, who stared into the stiff breeze, his hair blown back and brilliantined to his scalp. His prominent chin and cheekbones looked aerodynamically designed; his upper torso as sharp-edged as metal that had been milled on a lathe. While the garrulous wisecracking guys razzed one another, Pritchard told Barlow that several miles offshore one of the last coral reefs in the continental United States swagged from Eden down to Key West. At low tide, it broke the ocean's surface in isolated spots. At high tide it lay no deeper than a few feet beneath the Atlantic. It was dying, the reef was. Pollution had killed it, and so had divers who snapped off souvenir sea fans and antlers of coral.

"Chrissake, Frank, give the poor guy a break," Tony complained.

"Give us all a break," Steve said. "We came to fish. Not to listen to a lecture."

"You know, Frank, you may be suffering from a major senior malady," said Adrian, a former adman who had a cruel tongue. "Irony-deficiency anemia."

"I'd like to see the reef," Barlow protested.

"Fine, go see it," Lonnie said. "Take the dinghy. My blessings. But let's not talk it to death before it dies of natural causes."

"I'll go with him. Are there masks and snorkels on board?" Frank asked.

"Don't let a little teasing chase you away," Tony said.

"I'm not sure this is such a terrific idea," Freddy said. "How're we going to get the wheelchair into the dinghy?"

"I don't need it," Cal said.

"What if the boat capsizes?"

"Hey, Freddy, you think his wheelchair floats?" Adrian asked.

"I can swim," Cal said.

"In a race I bet he'd beat the Bertram back to the marina," Frank said.

To everyone's astonishment except Pritchard's, Cal scuttled out of the chair, chinned on a davit, and deposited himself in the dinghy. Once they lowered the inflated rubber Zodiac into the sea, Frank climbed aboard too, and Barlow rowed them toward the reef.

"I'll drop anchor," Lonnie called. "We'll fish here till you get back."

The Atlantic was calm, the sun hot, the rocking of the dinghy soporific. Yet Frank felt wired as he did at night ramping around Eden. He was sure Cal could swim ashore from this distance. He doubted he could. Still, he wouldn't have missed this. Despite all the arcana he had accumulated about coral reefs, he had never seen one firsthand and never dived in a mask and snorkel anyplace except his pool. Now was his chance—as in many cases, maybe his last.

He assumed it was the same for Cal—a first. But then Barlow took charge and instructed him to spit into his mask and polish the Plexiglas. "I don't wear fins," he said. "They're useless to me. But you'd better put them on."

"You've done this before?"

"Yeah. Not that I know anything about the history of coral like you do. My boss treated me to a couple of trips to the Caribbean. Year-end bonuses. Mostly I shot fish. Too bad we don't have a speargun."

"Watching fish is good enough for me," Frank said.

"We run into anything scary," Cal said, "a shark or a barracuda, don't panic. Swim back real slow to the dinghy."

Barlow hiked his rump up onto the side of the boat and pressed a hand to his mask. Frank followed his lead. On the count of three they flipped over backward and sank into a seething eruption of bubbles.

As the water buoyed them to the surface, Pritchard had the sense that he was scudding like a cloud above high sierras of coral. Schools of fish as flashily plumed as tropical birds flew by. Stunned by the beauty and his own apparent ability to fly, he forgot to breathe. Then a squid pumped past him like a disembodied lung and reminded him to suck in air through the plastic tube.

Cal lay spread-eagled on the ocean, his legs to all appearances alive, his body whole again. He pointed to a sea turtle, to three tarpon hurtling by like a freight train, to a lazy leopard ray trolling its barbed tail along the bottom. Though it was true that pollution was skeletonizing the reef, and he and Barlow were swimming over the bones of a moribund ecosystem, the sea fans and weeds waved in a welcoming fashion, and beds of brain coral looked inviting enough to sleep on. Pritchard wouldn't have minded spending the night here, his flesh glowing with phosphorescence. Why had he wasted so many months moping on the patio? Why had he and Dorothy never done this? Christened by these beneficent waters, she might have lived. Was it too late for him?

By the time Cal said they should swim back to the dinghy, Frank was waterlogged and his fingers had the consistency of corduroy. But the snorkeling had exhilarated him, and he did the rowing on the return trip to the Bertram. "I haven't been honest with you," he confided.

"Hope you're telling me you took my advice and stopped your trick-or-treating."

"I'm lying low for a while. But I'm not ready to quit."

"Too bad."

Frank feathered the oars, then dug in and pulled hard. "It's Ariel. My feelings for her, I suppose they're not paternal after all."

"Well, whatta you know." Where the mask had clamped onto Cal's face, a red oval framed his smile. "What was it the man in the movie said? 'Welcome back to the wonderful world of pussy.'"

"That's not what I'm saying," Frank objected.

"Fine. Say it how you'd say it."

"I feel silly talking about this. At my age, to admit you're falling for your physiotherapist sounds one step removed from senility. You know the progression—cheerleader, homecoming queen, trophy wife, mistress. What's next? Falling in love with my proctologist?"

"You think too much. They warn a man not to let the little head tell the big head how to live. But it's just as bad when the big head's too bossy."

"Thanks, professor, for your explication of the mind/body problem."

"No, seriously, what's the big mystery? Ariel's attractive. Not my type, but a doll. Plus she gives a great massage. What's not to love?"

"The question is where does it lead?"

"Same place everything does. Relax and you might have some fun as you find out where you're going. Don't let her get away."

"Quiet," someone shouted from the Bertram. "You're scaring the fish."

"We thought you rowed to Havana," a different voice hollered.

"We hoped you had. More beer for the rest of us."

Freddy hauled up a string of pompanos and yellowtail snappers that writhed like an ornamental Japanese kite. After he put them on ice, he came astern to help Pritchard and Barlow aboard. The dinghy was reattached to its davits, and Lonnie set a course for the marina. At Seb's instigation, they sang choruses of "Roll Me Over in the Clover" until nobody could remember any more obscene couplets.

Toasted by the sun and salted by the sea, reeking of beer, fish, and live bait, Frank looked forward to a cold shower and a massage. While Ariel worked him over, he'd describe the reef and invite her out to the

coral beds. He pictured the two of them floating on the ocean, holding hands as you saw couples do as they skydived out of airplanes.
People sometimes got married like that, airborne or underwater.

"Jesus, will you get a load of this," Lonnie exclaimed.

As he maneuvered the Bertram into its slip, the Breakfast Club
gaped at an extraordinary scene—a traffic jam of golf carts on the marina parking lot. Cranky from the day's heat, sailors, skin divers and
water skiers were snarled like dodge-'em car drivers at a carnival. The
air over Eden crackled with shouts and curses, the tinny beep of
horns, and the dull thud of rubber bumpers against fiberglass fenders.
For an instant the platoons of hired help paused at their chores and
watched with poorly disguised glee the insane antics of their em-
ployers. Then just as abruptly as it had clotted, the traffic dissolved
into the peaceful arteries of the island.

At Frank's house, Ariel stretched under the porte cochere while
Nicholas snoozed in the stroller beside her. Unlimbering the piano-
wire tightness of her hamstrings, she bent at the hips and flattened
her palms against the ground. Ritual preparation for the jog to
Gumbo-Limbo Lane.

"Do you have to go already?" he asked.

"You've got company." She did a set of toe raises. "I had them wait
in the living room."

A gunmetal-gray golf cart, the kind favored by island security of-
ficers, was parked behind a pigeon plum bush. An extension cord
linked it to an electrical outlet. "I let them plug in," Ariel said. "Their
batteries needed charging. Hope you don't mind."

"Not at all." He spoke quietly to keep from waking Nicholas. "Stay
awhile. I'll get rid of them."

"Can't do it," she said. "They've been here for hours. They're not leaving until they talk to you."

"What do they want?"

"The tossers wouldn't tell me. They treated me like a bloody servant. Told me to fix coffee. I told them to bugger off to Starbucks." She jogged in place. "They came back with cappuccino. Nothing for me."

Through his nostrils, Pritchard sounded a trumpet of annoyance. "I've been snorkeling out at the reef. I wanted to talk to you about it."

"Been there," she said, pumping her knees higher. "It's not bad, but it doesn't compare to the coral in the Indian Ocean. Catch you to-morrow," she shouted over her shoulder, shoving the buggy past the slowpokes on the hike-and-bike trail.

Frank felt left in the dust. How had he fallen so far behind? Every-body, it seemed, had done what he was only now getting around to. He'd have to hurry if he hoped to catch up.

He entered the living room as if sweeping into corporate head-quarters, an executive in a chalk-striped suit, not a sun-flushed guy in damp bathing trunks. He gave no indication that he noticed—and he definitely offered no apology for—the distressed state of the place. Many of the knickknacks he had savaged had been discarded, but he had glued back together a few photographs, bowls, and vases, and he had held on to the Eames chair with its split upholstery and the Knoll couch with its dented chrome frame. The only item in showroom condition was the ceremonial sword on the chipped mantelpiece.

"Gentlemen," he greeted them. "Don't get up."

But they did, juggling trashcan-sized containers of chocolate-sprinkled cappuccino. One wore the lettuce-green uniform of Eden's gerontocratic security force. The other, younger and burlier, was dressed in blue jeans and a faded work shirt. Either he had been sum-moned to duty unexpectedly or he, too, was working under cover.

The older man—Ned, his name tag identified him—had the deferential, forelock-tugging manner of most of the retirees who guarded the causeway. "I reckon you know—" He reseated himself, with the cappuccino propped between his knees. "We've had a series . . . a series of incidents. We don't like to alarm residents, but we've been investigating."

"I'm sure you have." Frank folded a towel on an Eames chair and parked his butt on it. He might have showered and changed first. But this way if the questioning took an ugly turn he'd interrupt and claim he had to dry off and put on clean clothes.

"We'd like to keep this a community affair," Ned said. "No use causing a ruckus and creating the wrong impression. We hired Andre Mingle here on a hush-hush temporary basis."

"And you're what?" Frank inquired of the beefy fellow.

"A security consultant. Troubleshooter. That type thing." Seated on the Knoll sofa, elbows on knees, Mingle gazed at the mangled décor. What's wrong with this picture? was etched on his face. But the words never reached his mouth.

Pritchard craved a cigarette. He would have suggested they move out to the patio so he could smoke, but the men appeared to be ill at ease in this souvenir cemetery and he didn't want them to become comfortable.

"We thought you might help us," Mingle said.

"Whatever I can do." Frank crossed his legs, then promptly uncrossed them. His thighs were salt-chafed.

"Going back a month or more, do you recall seeing a stranger on Eden?"

He refused to mention the man in the dark suit unless or until they did. That would only lead them to ask why Frank had been at the marina that night. He smiled. "You're the first, Mr. Mingle."

"Call me Andy. Glad you've got a sense of humor. Some folks on the island are pretty hot under the collar. So like I say, if you'd cast your mind back, maybe you remember your whereabouts when the perpetrator struck."

"Didn't he or she strike several different times?"

"We've recorded a dozen incidents," Ned said.

"And you're asking me what I was doing all those nights?"

"If you could," Mingle said.

"Are you asking everybody on Eden to account for his or her whereabouts?"

"Not everybody. Only certain individuals."

"There's a pattern," Ned added.

"Is there?" Frank's teeth, his tongue, his larynx and lungs screamed for smoke.

"All these incidents," Mingle said, "involved attacks on property belonging to persons directly or indirectly linked to the same company."

"Your old company," Ned said.

Pritchard chuckled ruefully. "My old company doesn't exist. Look at the big board. The logo's gone. It's not listed on the Dow, the S&P, or the NASDAQ. The only place you see the label these days is in a junkyard."

"But the company as it was reorganized has virtually the same executives and board members," Ned said.

"Except for me. I'm not involved anymore."

"Still, you get the drift," Mingle said.

"Afraid I don't."

"Glad to fill you in," Mingle said. "But first, to the best of your recollection, where were you those nights?"

Frank gazed at the ceiling, not as if racking his brain to remember, but steely-eyed, as though perturbed by an impertinent middle manager who was in his office on sufferance. "I'm a widower, Andy. I live alone. I stay home most nights."

"What about the girl?"

"What girl?"

"The one that answered the door."

"She's a board-certified physiotherapist. She comes during the day to treat me and my neighbor."

"The crippled fellow?" Ned asked.

"Differently abled," Frank corrected him.

"Has she noticed anything out of the ordinary? Somebody that doesn't belong?"

"Not that she's mentioned to me."

"Those nights you were home alone," Mingle said, "ever see or hear anything unusual?"

He shook his head. "Since my wife died, I've had trouble sleeping. Generally I take a pill and go to bed early."

"Insomnia," Ned said. "I'm a fellow sufferer."

"This pattern, getting back to it," Mingle said. "We're worried about you, Mr. Pritchard. Because of your previous association with the company, we're afraid you might be on the hit list."

"Really?" He performed a credible charade of shock. "Is that what you think?"

"It's a hypothetical we have to consider."

"Don't mean to scare you," Ned said, "but we suggest you stay alert."

"I will. But I'm not going to change the way I live. Because then they win."

"I admire your spirit. But it stands to reason," Mingle said, "if we know you were the CEO, then this guy that has a wild hair against the company knows too."

"Is it really as serious as you make it sound?" Frank asked. "Whoever it is has been guilty of some horseplay and petty damage. I don't see the danger."

"The potential's there. Next thing you know, he'll target people. That's the profile."

"The profile?"

"Of this psychopath we're dealing with."

"So that's how you have him pegged?"

"Absolutely." Mingle pushed off the sofa. Ned pried himself up too. "He's gotta be a sicko. Who else would attack a paradise like Eden?"

"Somebody with your background, Mr. Pritchard, has no experience of how the criminal mind operates," Ned said.

"Thanks for the warning. I'll keep my eyes peeled."

"You do that," Mingle said. "And, hey, change out of those wet trunks before you catch cold."

Frank wanted to tell him that in his own house he'd wear wet trunks as long as he damn well pleased. And as for the cockamamie profile they had concocted, they could take and shove it. Instead, he thanked them for their concern, praised their vigilance, and showed them to the door.

7

The two men lolled next to the pool, recovering after their daily race. When Pritchard described his encounter with Ned and Andy Mingle, Barlow wasn't surprised. "They're on to something. But it's simple," Cal said. "What you do is fuck up your own house. End of story. You flip from suspect to victim."

"I'm not sure they see me as a suspect," Frank said.

"Trust me, the nature of cops, they wouldn't question you if they didn't."

"Isn't it possible they just wanted to warn me to be careful?"

"What's the difference? They've twigged that you worked for the company and have never been a target—unlike every other executive on the island. Don't let them jump to conclusions. Heave a brick through your window and put this bullshit behind you."

"I'm not finished. Not by a long shot."

"Who's left to punish?"

Frank made a lazy circular motion of his hand. There were too many candidates to count.

"You're pushing your luck, Frank. Declare victory and retire."

He despaired of explaining to Barlow that retaliation had become secondary. He feared sliding back into the deep hole he had dug himself out of. "Trashing my place has its appeal," Frank confessed, remembering the delirium of ransacking his house, then rising phoenix-like from the shattered belongings. "But that would bring Ned and Andy back, and I'm not in the mood for more of their questions."

"That's what worries me—your mood."

"Look, I'm happy."

"Happy's one thing." A vertical frown line bisected Cal's forehead. "But this euphoria of yours, don't let it carry you away and lose contact with reality."

"I guess what I need is to get off the island and clear my head."

"Good idea."

"I'll drive into the 'Glades. Check out how the other half lives."

"It's not the other half. Ninety-nine point nine percent of the world doesn't live like this. Want company?" Cal asked.

"No, thanks. I'll think better on my own."

Since Randi often dropped by to watch Lou Dobbs with him in the evening, Pritchard called and left a message that he'd be out and wouldn't be home till late. He had an appointment, he said, with an estate planner to discuss issues pertaining to a generation-skipping trust. This was the sort of high-serious conference that she wouldn't question.

In the garage, he revved the XKE. A sixty-six-year-old man at the wheel of a '66 roadster might strike some as andropausal nonsense, but he believed in a synergy of man and machine, and was heartened that the Jag had served him so well this winter. It, like him, had required only a little exercise and a change of pace to shake off the rust.

Exuberant as a schoolboy playing hooky, he sped off to the mainland, plowing into the desolate interior. In this part of the state, to travel in that direction was to enter the bush, the outback. Away from the candy floss of the coast and its ant heaps of domesticity, ten minutes from the interstate and a mile from the poured concrete pylons of a failed condominium development, a road with a number, no name, plunged him into Third World poverty. Towns no better than *bidonvilles* housed migrant fruit pickers in cinderblock shacks. Signs on liquor stores, police stations, and missions had subtitles in Spanish, Creole, Arabic, and what might have been Mandarin.

There were dense green fields where Haitians hacked at sugarcane, flooded rice patties where Asians waded knee-deep in mud, and tomato patches—or were they strawberry beds?—where Hispanics cultivated plants in Potemkin villages constructed of plastic sheeting. Lush, arable land alternated with thirsty earth that was ash-gray and unsettled by wind. Farther on, mangrove jungles ribbed both sides of the road, and Pritchard had the impression of being trapped in an enormous raffia basket woven in a wickerwork factory by madmen. Vine-draped trees wallowed in tobacco-colored water, the bark mossy, the branches weighted down by air plants. The Jaguar's tires shredded amphibians that had oozed up from the swamp and tried, unsuccessfully, to cross the road.

Eventually he arrived at a Miccosukee Indian reservation. Or so it was identified. What he saw were picnic tables under thatched roofs as shabby as bad toupees; Stygian canals streaked with yellow algae, like stomach purges of pure bile; airboats propelled by industrial-strength fans; Quonset huts that housed casinos. Judging by the chock-a-block parking lots, there was no shortage of gamblers. A tout in an orange Day-Glo vest pinwheeled his arms, urging Pritchard to stop.

But he drove on to an establishment called Jungle Fever. See 'em Here, the billboard declared. Critters! Crocs! Gators! Snakes! Frank parked in the shade of a palm tree whose trunk was swaddled in burlap, like a leg in blood-brown bandages.

Outside the car, the air dripped heat and smell. A compound of animal odors—the rotten breath of carnivores, the taint of old meat, the fetidness of burrows and stagnant ponds, and what could only have been beasts that had died in captivity—flooded his nostrils. Behind a tall fence, amid a miniature Alcatraz of cages, a heavyset man stepped out of the admission booth as if to confront rather than welcome him. His scowling mug suggested that Jungle Fever didn't take kindly to unannounced visitors. Maybe, Frank thought, he should have phoned ahead for a reservation.

"Looking for something?" Holstered on the man's hip, a pistol made a ready perch for his hand.

"Good day. How are you?" Pritchard sounded as though he might be selling something. He also sounded as though he was holding his nose. He decided the hell with it and inhaled the awful stench. "I've always meant to stop here. I love animals."

"Me, I can take 'em or leave 'em. It's a living." His hand hopped from the pistol to his hair. He had a ponytail, shaggy as a feather duster.

"I'm in the market for a pet," Frank said.

"I show 'em. Don't generally sell 'em. What are you after?"

"Haven't made up my mind. I've got a little boy at home and I'd love to surprise him."

"Grandson?"

"Son," Frank said. "Second marriage."

"It's a great life if you don't weaken. I'm on my fifth."

"About your animals . . ."

"Plenty to choose from."

"I'd like to look them over."

"It'll cost you five bucks. That's to get in. You buy something, we'll apply the admission fee to the purchase price."

He and the man wandered between the close-set cages.

"Your gun," Pritchard said, "is it for protection against the animals?"

"On my own property, it's for protection against whatever."

"You wouldn't happen to have a Florida panther, would you?"

"Hell no. Anybody tells you different is a damn liar."

"No offense," Frank said.

"They catch you with an endangered species, the state doesn't just confiscate it without a red cent of compensation. It fines your ass off and shuts down your business. So don't mention panthers to me."

They stopped at what appeared to be a great green bowl of pesto. On closer inspection, several alligators floated in the sauce, only their unflinching eyes and dark nostrils visible. A neighboring cage was empty except for straw, vegetable matter, and a discarded rattle from a diamondback. For the first time in days Frank was conscious of his eye spider competing for attention, yoyoing up and down.

"Now, Florida panthers," the guy ran on, unable to quit yammering, "they hardly exist as such. About a hundred left, total. Sixty percent of them are half-breeds crossed with western cougars the government shipped in. Western cougars are no more endangered than you and me. There's over eighty thousand of them."

"In Florida?" he asked, incredulous.

"Hell no. All over the US of A, they're pushing east, swimming the Mississippi. You got 'em in the suburbs of Kansas City, gobbling up deer that the goddamn antihunting lobby let overrun the country."

Unlike the hopped-up owner, the reptiles at Jungle Fever seemed terminally sunk in torpor. Hadn't they been fed? Or had they gorged themselves comatose?

"This panther crap"—the man was seething—"is just another excuse for the state to grab private land for public parks. Habitats for endangered species, they claim. I don't even want to talk about it."

"I won't mention another word."

"It's like these so-called Indians. Native Americans, you're supposed to say. You ask me, they ain't any more native than the panther. They're mongrels. Interbred for generations." He snorted. "Say Miccosukee to me, and I say Microwave. That's what I call them. The Microwave tribe, fat off welfare, rich on gambling, building houses you and me couldn't afford in a lifetime."

At last they arrived at an animal that was manifestly alive and hell-bent on escape. Skittering up chicken-wire walls, swinging upside down from the ceiling, a well-nourished raccoon rattled its cage.

"What do coons cost?" Frank asked.

"Whoa, man, you said a pet for your kid. This ain't what you're after. Look at them claws, them teeth. That baby's faster than a fart with a red ring around it and it's flat-out ferocious. It'll rip your boy a brand-new asshole."

"I don't plan to let him play with it. We'll keep it in a cage."

"You better. It breaks loose in your house, you might as well burn the mother down. You hear what happened to that nuclear power plant in Mississippi?"

"Saw it on TV," Frank said. "But somebody caught this one. How hard can it be?"

"I trapped it in the woods. I didn't dig it out of the attic insulation or an air-conditioning duct. You might could catch it in a house if you stayed at it long enough, but by then you wouldn't have any electricity or plumbing left."

"I'll take it. How much?"

"Fifty bucks. Forty-five minus your admission. But get this straight. I ain't buying it back and I sure as hell ain't traveling to your home to trap the son of a bitch."

"You've got a deal. Now if you'll sell me a cage, something that'll fit in the trunk of my car, I'll be on my way. You've made a little boy very happy."

Retracing his route, Pritchard ignored the posted speed limit and hurtled through the rural backwaters, the alien enclaves and agrarian squalor. For miles he drove beside a levy, looking out on a wind-stenciled lake that surged at eye level. He might have been hydroplaning at the crest of a wave. In all this beckoning space, it struck him as nonsensical not to do everything to excess. Small may be beautiful, as the ecofreaks maintained, but out in flat, sodden Florida, he felt huge, he felt electric. While tree-huggers preached uplifting homilies about sustainable growth and limited resources, there was nothing to compare with the rush of busting loose big-time. After a long period of indifference to earthly delights, he was now nothing but raw appetite, and in his wake, along with exhaust, he wanted to strew chaos as profligate as charity.

In the thronged slurbs along the shore, high-rises formed ladders, each terrace another rung to the foil glint of heaven. Frank stopped at a bakery and asked the bewildered owner to hold the sweets and sell him an empty cake box. The biggest one in stock. That proved to be a pink contraption that could have accommodated a four-tier wedding cake, with a doll-size couple on top. Its folding sides curved together into a cupola that doubled as a carry handle.

At a picnic area near the causeway to Eden, couples lounged on the beach, admiring the slow churn of ocean and the lovely, off-limits island. In an iron hibachi, provided by the municipality and embedded in concrete to prevent theft, charcoal cooked someone's dinner. A man of impressive girth had dragged an aluminum lawn chair into the shallow murmuring surf and stretched out on it. From one angle, the scene appeared to Frank to be of sea-sorrow—a dead Viking warrior waiting to be set alight and launched toward the watery embrace of eternity. But from a different perspective, the man on the lawn chair looked like the happy vacationer that he was, resting up for the evening fish fry.

With everybody else absorbed in contemplation of the Atlantic, Pritchard went to the rear of the Jag and raised the trunk lid. The caged raccoon exploded like a hairball from hell. Its furious antics were almost funny. It might have been a gremlin from one of those cartoons he and Nicholas watched, a creature capable of chewing steel bars and spitting out bullets.

Letting the four sides of the cake box fall outward, he positioned the cage on it and folded the flaps back into a cupola. The box rumbled until darkness deceived the raccoon into thinking it was time to sleep. Then he put it on the passenger seat beside him, secured by the seat belt. At the gates of Eden, guards saw nothing peculiar about an islander bringing home a pastry treat.

Rather than pillage his own house, Frank intended to broaden the original bull's-eye and strike a target that had nothing to do with his old company. He accepted that there would be collateral damage. But it wasn't as if anybody on the island was completely innocent.

Normally he would have hiked across the fairway, steeped in anticipatory pleasure. But the caged raccoon was too heavy to carry that far. So he drove to the club, sweeping up to the Monticello replica, where a parking valet said, "Take that package for you, sir?"

"No thanks. A surprise birthday party. I'll deliver it myself."

He held the cake box as gingerly as a baby's bassinet. The coon coughed and chattered. The valet didn't hear this as he slid behind the wheel and burned rubber toward the parking lot. The clubhouse bar was thick with predinner drinkers. Frank could do nothing there without being seen. A few early birds made the dining room another unwise choice. Ditto the library and the snooker parlor. By now the box quaked like a defective bomb about to blow up in his face.

Frank ducked into the men's room, which was deserted. The unflattering mirror over the sink showed a white-haired wraith carrying a pink cardboard palace. He passed quickly down the row of stalls until he located one with an air vent in the rear wall. He locked the door, lowered the toilet lid, and balanced the noisy box on the commode. Then with the wafer-thin tab of his Tiffany key ring, he unscrewed the louvered screen from the air vent and verified that it didn't lead outdoors. No, it tunneled into the bowels of the clubhouse, connecting a warren of crawl spaces, drying closets, and laundry chutes. What a playground for a rambunctious raccoon—a funfair of wires and insulation, food cupboards, and the climbing frames of curtain rods and chandeliers. Pritchard's greatest regret was that he wouldn't be around to witness the carnage.

As he lifted the cage from the box, the coon snarled like a chainsaw. To put a finger wrong was to invite dismemberment. Fur flew as he positioned the cage over the air vent and slid the door open. The raccoon, in its frenzy, failed to spot that escape route. Frank raked the bars with his key ring to drive it into the duct. But the coon took a swipe with its prehensile claw, jarred his hand, and knocked the keys loose.

Pritchard lunged for them and missed. Bouncing off the box, they jangled to the floor so that he had to squat down and scrabble blindly, all the while struggling to keep the open door of the cage pressed to the wall. The coon jibbered and screeched and tried to eat his fingers. As Frank stood up, the raccoon sprang at his face, bounced off the bars, and ricocheted into the duct. With a dexterity born of desperation, Pritchard dropped the cage, slapped the louvered screen into place, and screwed it tight.

Afterward, he paused for a second glance at the mirror. Better now. His skin glowed with rude good health, his eyes gleamed. He beat his flyaway hair into shape, tucked in his shirttail, and sauntered out of the men's room with the empty cage concealed in the pink box. The raccoon was already kettle-drumming behind the baseboards. Frank saw friends, greeted them by name, and explained away the box as a take-out dinner. When the valet fetched the Jag, Frank said, "I got the date wrong." He plopped the box onto the passenger seat. "Guess I'll have to eat it myself."

Ravenous as he was, he could have consumed an entire wedding cake, including the spun sugar couple on top. Instead, he nuked a Lean Cuisine and killed three-quarters of a bottle of vintage Bordeaux. Still fizzing with adrenaline, he watched a Tom Hanks movie about a man marooned on a desert island, desperate to rejoin his fiancée and his high-flying colleagues at FedEx. Pritchard granted the premise, envied the protagonist's resourcefulness, and admired his guts for knocking out his rotten tooth. But as Hanks started crossing months and years off a stone calendar, then talking to a volleyball, a needling disquiet commenced in Frank's stomach. This was all too reminiscent of his former life, back when he had been cast aside.

He liked to believe he'd never sink that low again. Still, it had happened once and not that long ago. What was to prevent him from plummeting a second time? True, he had Barlow, the equivalent of the wise and compassionate ball, Wilson. And he had Ariel for massages and to feed his fantasy life, and Nicholas to sit on his lap. But for nights like this when the pressure to leap out of his skin, if not off a cliff, became intolerable, there was only Randi.

Extinguishing the front porch lights so that he wouldn't have to face the frying anoles, Frank sampled the outside air. It smelled of the ocean, with an added spice of jasmine. He wondered how long he would have to live in Florida before it acquired the specific gravity of the gray town in Ohio where he had grown up, delivered newspapers, made Eagle Scout at the age of sixteen, and played coronet in the pep band before leaving for college. There he had met Dorothy, and on nights not unlike this he had walked a mile across campus through fallen leaves and wood smoke on the chance, the mere chance, that she might kiss him.

There were many paths to Randi's. He chose one that meandered past a par-five hole whose green appeared to be upholstered with billiard table felt. He didn't run. He wanted to take his time and reflect. Not about where he was headed, but where he had been. Like Tom Hanks, he sensed something hanging over him. A place and a person he'd like to get back to. But after all the tribulations of constructing a raft and improvising a sail out of a sheet of plastic from an airplane toilet, Hanks had returned to his girl only to discover that she was married. Pritchard would have been heartbroken. But phlegmatic Tom simply went on to deliver a long overdue FedEx. Frank hated that ending. Maybe he hated any ending, happy or otherwise.

Round and dimpled as a brand-new Acushnet golf ball, the moon lighted the fairway a luminous silver. As he crested a knoll, he spied an elongated shape next to a water hazard. It might have been a fallen branch. But that was the sort of debris seldom seen on Eden. It had to be an alligator, a mature male basking after a meal.

He edged nearer, his shoes soundless in the damp grass. Compared with the gators in the reeking bouillabaisse that afternoon, this one looked odd. The tail it flicked back and forth had a distinct bend near the tip.

Frank did a double take. That was no reptile tail. It was a cat's.

He flattened himself to the fairway in the same tense posture as the panther. Long as him and almost as thick-set, the cat lowered its head, lapping at the water. Pritchard thanked God, actually uttered a prayer of gratitude, that he had lived to see such an impressive beast on the loose.

Abruptly the cat pitched upright and whirled on him. Too late, Frank realized he had done everything wrong. With a panther, you didn't crouch down and make yourself into a compact morsel. You stood tall and waved your arms, bold and menacing.

When he did this now, the panther growled and turned tail. Neither swift nor stealthy, it retreated like a sore-footed, swag-bellied retiree.

It's dying. The panther was on its last legs. The idea descended on Pritchard with the weight of a mallet, nailing him to the ground. That's why the big cat wasn't back in the canebrakes or in the jigsaw puzzle of the Everglades. Its time was short, and like many a citizen of Eden, it had gravitated to the golf course to await the inevitable.

Frank broke and ran toward Tahiti Townhouses.

8

Randi savored the sort of contentment she associated with finishing her federal income tax return or her Christmas shopping. She and Cal had just rounded off a marathon session in bed that melted her heart and set her legs chiming like a tuning fork. With a staying power unparalleled in her experience, curved inside her like a question mark— he referred to his member as pleasure-bent—he asked things of her that she had never known were in her power to give.

Not that the giving was a one-way street. She got. She took. On top, she was in a position to ask probing questions of her own and to touch a few unexplored bases. Gazing down at the brawn beneath her, the dark eyes, black hair, and rapacious white teeth, she pictured herself riding a panther, a sleek animal you didn't dare dismount until it was spent. Although utterly involved, she treasured the slight distance, the different perspective. It allowed her to reflect while the rest of her cantered along in an instinctual groove.

Now that she knew Cal almost as well as Frank, she considered the contrasting talents they brought to sex. There was the younger man's attentiveness, the older one's impetuosity; the muscle boy's tenderness, the white-haired gent's pile-driving ardor; Barlow's afterglow of gratitude, Pritchard's spell-stopped resumption of an agenda that excluded her.

Would it sound too silly, she wondered, to say she loved them both? She certainly depended on them and reckoned that with their respective debits and credits they added up to a full man. Not a perfect one, but a complete one. Which was why she didn't feel any guilt. She couldn't very well be accused of infidelity if they were parts of the same person.

The trick was to arrange things so that they didn't learn about each other and she didn't lose either of them. She believed she could handle Cal. But Frank posed a challenge of an altogether different order of magnitude. Foothills versus Himalayas. She still hoped to marry him and she knew this meant negotiating a Maginot Line of difficulties. The idea of going through that grinder made her appreciate Barlow's sweetness all the more.

From the bedroom, the two of them adjourned to the living room for an interval of postcoital intimacy, bathed by the television's generous glow. Though it was bliss to linger beside his wheelchair as they watched *Cast Away*, she kept glancing at the clock. Randi knew that Frank was at a meeting with his estate planner, but she feared he might return before Barlow left. Or almost as bad, he might show up before she had a chance to shower and change the damp, body-warmed sheets.

"Honestly, now," Cal said. "Helen Hunt, what's your opinion? Is she beautiful or not?"

Randi had often pondered the enigma of the TV sitcom star who had graduated to movie roles. Something about her upper lip didn't look right. But in a benevolent mood, she said, "I think she makes the best of what she's got. What do you think?"

"Not bad."

"Come on, she's lovely. Look at that hair, those eyes."

"I've seen better. I've had better." He squeezed her inner thigh. "What it proves is how tastes have changed. A Hollywood star used to be somebody you never believed in your wildest dreams you could fuck."

"Oooh, I don't like that word."

Pausing, Barlow appeared to debate whether to take it back. "Okay, make love to. With old-time stars, much as you might fantasize, you never thought you'd get them in the sack. Character actors were the ones you believed you'd have a shot at."

"I see what you're saying. Today's stars are actually character actors."

In Randi's estimation, this was no bad thing. To have sexually plausible characters in leading roles involved the viewer more deeply in their plight, even when it was a stupid one. Like plunking Tom Hanks down alone on an island. Why not put Helen Hunt there with him? Why let him become so lonely and loony he babbles at a volleyball? To watch people talk to themselves you didn't need to tune in to the cable channel. Just visit the chatterboxes in Assisted Living. Randi prayed that she'd never end up like that, counting the peas in her potpie.

Yet after Tom Hanks lost weight from his low-carb diet of roots and berries and fish, he did look damned attractive, looked, in fact, like a leaner, paler version of Cal. Randi toyed with the idea of enticing him into a quickie after *Cast Away*. But she couldn't succumb to every desire. She had to get him out to the garage, on the road home, not into bed again.

"You know, honey, I wish we lived on a desert island," she said. "But the reality is—"

"It's rougher than it looks. I've sort of been marooned before, and believe me, I'd rather be with you. Someday I have to tell you about that part of my life."

"I'd love to hear it. But not now. I'm not a night person. I'm a day person. And there's Frank. I never know when he'll drop by for one of his pity parties."

"It's tough for me to feature him that way."

"Men are less guarded around women. More sharing. It's not so hard for him to discuss stuff he hides from everybody else."

"If you say so."

She half-wished Cal would protest or show some jealousy. Maybe demand that she tell Frank that they were in love and stop seeing him. Not that she would do it, but at least then she'd have a better notion of his feelings. As it was, he displayed so little curiosity—forget about jealousy—she wondered whether it would bother him to find out she was a two-timer. For a degrading moment, she entertained the nightmare possibility that the two men were in this together, trading her back and forth like a cheap party favor.

No, that was pathetic. Like fretting about whether she had switched off the stove.

"Hate to rush you," she said, "but I have to get my beauty rest."

"Lemme hit the bathroom before I go."

"There's one in the hall, across from the door to the garage."

She was glad to have him headed in that direction. But once they reached the cloakroom, she realized it wouldn't accommodate his wheelchair.

"No sweat." Cal stretched, grabbed the porcelain rim of the sink, and swung himself over to the toilet seat. But the transfer wasn't a smooth one. The cushion tumbled from his chair and the 9-mm Beretta Parabellum clattered to the floor.

In a heart clot of fear and confusion, Randi felt some hideous secret, some device that paraplegics depended on, had been revealed to her. The gun, with its glinting steel barrel and intricate cross-hatchings on the handle, was mesmerizing. She had never seen anything uglier and, at the same time, so beautiful. Her legs shivered as they did during sex.

"It's for protection." Cal broke the silence.

"I don't understand."

"Case you haven't noticed"—he bent down to retrieve the pistol—"I'm crippled. Defenseless."

"Against what? Nobody's going to hurt you."

"You positive of that? There's this nut prowling around the island. I wouldn't shoot anybody. But I like carrying something to back him off."

"Oh, baby, I'm sorry." She stroked his corded shoulders. "The gun scared me, that's all."

"I get scared too. Parking at the mall, chugging over here in the dark, what if I bumped into a panther?"

"It'd run the other way. They're very skittish. It's the night stalker that concerns me."

"Me too," he said. "They start off with petty crime, but sooner or later they're out for blood."

"*They?* Do you think there's more than one?"

"A figure of speech. The thing is—be candid now—if you can't stand me bringing a weapon, we'll have to meet at my house."

"No, no. I'll get over it." She plumped the cushion back onto his chair. "Why don't I let you have some privacy?"

As he slid the Beretta back into its hiding place, Randi heard a noise. It could have been the click of the safety. The click of a chambered round. The click of the trigger. But to her horror it was Pritchard's key at the front door.

She clamped a hand over Cal's mouth and gestured wildly toward the garage. There was no mistaking her meaning. Go! "Is that you, Frank?" she called. "Wait a sec. I'm in the bathroom."

Barlow catapulted off the toilet seat and into the chair. Canted on two wheels, he crossed the hall and jounced down the short flight of garage steps. Randi shut that door behind him and hurried to the front door, where Frank was jabbing his key.

"I was just thinking about you," she exclaimed.

He didn't swoop in to embrace her. He hung back, shaken, his skin matte-gray with mottled highlights. He exuded a musk that reminded her of a penned-up animal. How did men work themselves to such a fever pitch just thinking about sex?

"Come in," she said, regretting that she hadn't showered. Cal's spunk leaked between her legs.

"I saw it," he said.

She feared he meant Cal. "Saw what?"

"I swear to God, it was terrible. We have to talk."

"Not out here. Inside."

"There's no time." Urgency etched his voice. The key in his hand was leveled at her chest like a gun barrel.

"What are you telling me, Frank?"

"The panther."

"The what?"

"The panther. I saw it."

She released a startled yelp, yanked him into the townhouse, and slammed the door. Was the musky smell from the big cat? She made herself small in his arms and pressed her face to his shirtfront. At close range, the scent reminded her of a raccoon that had once raided her garbage can. "Thank God you're not hurt. It must have been awful."

"It was very sad."

This was more like the Frank Pritchard she knew, the man who processed most emotions as melancholy. She led him into the living room, anxious to get him out of earshot of the garage. "Tell me about it."

The peacock chair creaked under his weight. "I shouldn't be sitting here," he said. "I should be doing something."

"Shall we call security?"

"No, they'll kill it."

"Don't be silly. They don't even kill alligators that eat pet dogs. They'll tranquilize it and take it where it belongs."

"Where's that?"

"The Everglades. Or a zoo."

He shook his head. "I can't stand to think of it in a cage. And it won't survive in the Everglades. It's dying."

"How do you know?"

"It's fat and slow. It ran like an old man."

She sat beside him, as she had with Cal, and held his hand. How different they were, right down to the texture of their palms. She listened for the electronic whir of the rising garage door. Would Frank recognize it? "Why don't we go into the bedroom? Wash up and lie down until you're feeling better."

"I feel fine. It's the panther that needs help."

Randi burst into tears. The shock, the late hour, his close shave with the panther—she had every good reason to cry, and one bad one. She heard the garage door and wanted to distract Pritchard.

"It's okay, it's okay," he said, trying to console her. "If it's dying, I guess it's better off on the golf course. I just pray the maintenance men don't—"

She pushed his hand away. "I don't give a damn about the panther. It's you. You're awful. You don't love me. We never even have a conversation."

"That's not fair. We're having one now."

"Yeah, about a panther. I bet you talk about other things with Ariel."

"Is that what's bugging you? That I have a personal trainer?"

"Personal trainer my foot."

"Don't you understand? The reason I hired her is for Cal. He has to be stretched. His legs shrivel up."

This interested Randi. She knew next to nothing about Barlow's physical specifics, apart from his sexual performance. But now that she had Frank on the defensive, she couldn't get sidetracked by medical lore.

"All you care about is sex," she said. "Soon as we started that, it's like you're embarrassed to be seen with me." Haggard as she looked at the moment—no makeup, eyes puffy and red-rimmed, mouth raw from servicing Cal—it might have been a mistake, she thought, to suggest that he was ashamed of her appearance. "And you never want to travel. I bring home brochures about cruises and safaris and you don't even read them."

"I'm happy on Eden."

"Happy! Who are you kidding? You've been miserable for more than a year."

"I'm better now."

"Are you, Frank?"

"Yes," he said with the wariness of a businessman who senses he's being backed into a corner. "I'm beginning to recover."

"That's good. I'm glad for you." She plucked a Kleenex from a dispenser on an end table and dabbed at her eyes. "But I worry about the future. About where we go from here."

"In April or May, I'll decide what to do this summer and—"

"This isn't about summer. This is about us."

"Look, if you're dead set on a cruise—"

"For Chrissake, Frank, you can't be this opaque. You're playing dumb and stringing me along."

His slow reply—or rather no reply—revealed volumes, and it occurred to her how much hard work lay ahead. The question wasn't *whether* to stomp her foot on the shovel and dig in. It was *when*. What could she accomplish at this hour? The wisest course might be to coax him into bed and send him home with a sample of what he'd miss if he lost her. Then again, a gritty assertion of independence might set the tone for future negotiations.

Randi balled up the Kleenex. "We're adults, Frank. Why play games like a couple of kids? I don't have to spell this out for you."

In the ensuing silence, it dawned on her that she was wrong. She did have to spell it out for him.

"We've known each other a long time," she said, "and been through a lot. I respect your memories of Dorothy and your relationship with Willow. But we have to honor what we have. Life is for the living." She wondered whether to mention love and decided that it didn't suit the conversation. "The point is how we handle the next step."

"You're asking me to take a huge amount on board at one time. At . . ." He consulted his wristwatch. ". . . At midnight. After I've had a run-in with a dying panther." He spoke slowly, with the gravity of a man who wants a woman to think she's being frivolous. "If we're going to have this conversation, I'd rather do it the right way."

"Do what? Are you afraid to say the word?"

"If we're going to discuss marriage, I'd rather do it during the day."

"And what would you rather do at night?" She anticipated that he would suggest they have sex. She hoped he'd suggest that so she could say no.

Instead, he said, "I should go home. I've got some serious thinking to do."

"Fine, Frank," she said coolly. "Let me hear from you once you know what you want."

After he left, Randi unfolded her thighs and they released an almost audible adhesive rip. At last, she could shower. First, however, she opened the door to the garage to be sure that Barlow had gone.

She half-hoped that he hadn't. She half-hoped that the other half of the whole man she had cobbled together from mismatched parts would spend the night. But he wasn't there, and as she headed for the bathroom, she speculated how much money Cal had. If he was rich, maybe she should marry him. Then an extraordinary thought presented itself: Since she was already rich, why did it matter if he had money?

9

Occasionally Barlow came to on Eden with the same sense of befuddlement as when he had swum up out of the ether in the prison hospital. Back then he believed he was in hell. Now, though not quite in heaven, he thought he had graduated to limbo, a well-appointed antechamber where he was blessed by damned good luck. Not only had he escaped from Tahiti Townhouses without Frank catching him, he had gotten away with his lie about the gun. As long as Randi didn't blab to anybody about the Beretta, he was safe.

And why should she? She was a chick who dug secrets. After the initial shock, she seemed to get a buzz out of the gun. An extraordinary woman, he thought as he breezed along the street toward the mall. Okay, she had a few years on him, but what did that matter compared to what she was willing to do to please him?

It had been obvious at the start she had no taste for going down on him, but she got better at it every time, gradually cutting back on the tooth play. That nipping and noshing that some women equated with passion. Why was it so hard to persuade them to be kind to the equipment? He had been with women who complained that men treated their clits like they meant to erase them. Then they turned around and grabbed your balls like a bag of shot.

Randi, by contrast, was a quick study and, in her way, a sweetheart. He hated to sound like a sap or one of those girls that has a soft spot for the guy that busted her cherry. But after the long dry spell he'd been through, Cal couldn't help seeing her as bountiful and loving.

Still, despite his gratitude, he didn't buy that malarkey about Frank dropping by at night to cry on her shoulder. What sort of simpleton did she take him for? Pritchard, it wouldn't surprise him, was dipping his wick too. He didn't like it. In fact, it was painful to think about. But how could Cal complain when he hadn't been aboveboard with Frank? Balance of power. That was the best he could hope for. As long as everyone got some of what he wanted and had something on everybody else, they were all easy-breezy.

Of course, the old hot-blooded Cal would never have swallowed such shit. Share a woman? Not on your life. Back then you crossed the line, you got chopped. But here on Eden, under the sway of Viagra, his life had acquired a soothing blue sheen and a milder tempo. Sometimes he listened to himself reasoning with Frank and was stunned how mellow and law-abiding he sounded. Love, sex, grieving, business ethics—he was like an agony aunt full of advice about any subject, a ready dispenser of fortune-cookie wisdom.

Trucking along, Barlow admired the neatly trimmed oleanders, all color-coded so that pink, red, and white bushes alternated at regular intervals. Symmetrical flower beds lay like tatted antimacassars across barbered lawns. In the colonnade of royal palms on the mall parking lot, any tree that was slightly out of true had been buttressed with two-by-fours to force it into line. He understood Frank's compulsion to mess with this meticulous design, but Cal knew the island was as good as life was likely to get for him. Grappling from his chair into the VW, he wondered how to convince Pritchard of this. To be honest, though, Barlow had to admit that before a shiv severed his spine, no one could have argued him into being the person he was now. In his experience, people changed only when they had no choice.

He nudged the steering wheel and nursed the VW along at a 17 mph dawdle. Pale moths dispersed in his high beams like particles in a physics experiment. Then a mad scientist, lanky and silver-haired, blundered into the scope. Frank looked rumpled and flustered, as if he had gone through a trash compactor. Had Randi given him the bum's rush? Or had she, in a fit of madness, spilled the beans about her other lover?

"Hey, sailor," Barlow called. "Looking for a ride home?"

"You'll never guess what I saw." Frank circled to the passenger side and piled in. "I saw the panther."

"No shit."

"It was on the golf course, drinking from a water hazard."

"Jesus, I'm jealous. I'd love to see it."

"That's what I thought until I did."

"It scared you?" He caught a whiff of Pritchard. "It smelled bad?"

"It's dying."

"How could you tell?"

"It was fat and ran like every joint in its body ached. Like it was a hundred years old."

Cal laughed. "Maybe it ate a meal it couldn't digest. One of your enemies."

"This is no laughing matter. Don't tell anyone. I don't want security harassing it when it's on its last legs." Then Pritchard asked, "Where've you been at this hour?"

"Getting my oil changed."

"Over on the highway?"

"That's where the service stations are." He coasted into Frank's driveway. "You oughta try it sometime."

"That's all I need. A dose of some incurable disease."

What could Cal say? He already had one. Everybody did. "Let's go to the reef again soon."

"Yeah, I'd like that." Shouldering open the door, Frank climbed out. His lower back crackled like dry kindling.

"Everything okay there?" An E-Z-GO approached them, a plump specimen in a lettuce-green uniform at the controls. "Oh, it's you, Mr. Pritchard," the security guard said. "Just making the rounds. Can't be too careful on a night like this." Ned climbed from the cart. "You gentlemen hear the news?"

"We've been out for the evening," Cal said.

Ned shined a pencil-size flashlight into the car. "Evening, Mr. Barlow. There was a ruckus at the clubhouse. Someone set a raccoon loose. It ripped through the place like shot through a goose. You know how coons are."

"No, how are they?"

"They're as bad as roaches. It ain't so much what they carry off and eat. It's what they fall into and ruin for everybody else."

"How can you be sure it didn't wander into the club on its own?" Frank asked.

"They found where somebody unscrewed a vent and let the coon into the duck."

"The duck?"

"The AC duck. It chewed up the insulation, crashed through the snooker room ceiling, and scared the bejabbers out of the pool players. Then it broke damn near every glass and bottle in the bar. Attacked its reflection in the mirror and cracked that too."

"Did they catch it?" Frank asked.

"Nope. It scurried back into the duck and over to the dining room. Scattered hair and food all over the tables and got away."

"What sort of lowlife would do such a thing?" Cal said.

"Had to be the same one did the other stuff."

"Thought there was a pattern," Frank said. "Thought this lunatic had zeroed in on my old company. I've been on the alert ever since you warned me."

"Stay on it, Mr. Pritchard. He's breaking out into the general population. There's no predicting where he'll strike next. G'night, gentlemen."

As Ned reversed down the driveway, Cal muttered, "You're begging for it, Frank. You won't be satisfied until you're behind bars, will you? What if one of these assholes shoots you?"

"You're the one who suggested dirty tricks. You said—I believe I'm quoting accurately—a stink bomb can be as effective as a car bomb."

"Don't blame it on me. I was trying to keep you from gunning people down. Which is what you said you had in mind."

"I don't blame anybody. I'm having a ball, just like you advised."

"Quit with this I 'advised' bullshit. Like I'm your consigliere or your accomplice. My advice is knock it off."

"Yeah, maybe the raccoon should be my swan song. Maybe things should subside as suddenly as they started. Grant Eden a respite to examine its conscience."

"I got a better idea. Examine your own."

Cal woke early the next morning and went out by the pool. For a change it was cool enough to wear a sweatsuit. The fairways and greens sparkled with dew, and the first golf carts left silvery tracks in the grass. He hadn't slept well. Worrying about Frank had kept him awake. It seemed to him his neighbor wanted to get caught. A paradoxical impulse as old as crime. When it wasn't a desire to be punished, it was a wish to explain, to have your day in court and a chance to expound your grievances.

But what worried Barlow wasn't just the shit Pritchard might bring down on his own head. When a guy got collared, he sometimes copped a plea. And what was more logical than for his neighbor to roll over on him? Just mentioning Cal would be enough to incriminate him. If the police poked into his past, he'd be a perfect fall guy.

He hated thinking like this. That ex-con paranoia, the constant toting up of pluses and minuses, the temptation to squeal on a friend before he ratted on you. He wasn't that guy anymore. Or was he?

When the glass door to the house rasped open on its aluminum runner, Cal flung his head around and groped under the seat cushion. A man in a dark suit and tie stepped out onto the patio, and Barlow was relieved he hadn't pulled the gun. He didn't recognize this guy, but he knew the type. The polished shoes and buzz-cut hair, the swagger, the hawk face. Cal assumed it was a federal agent. They walked right in. Didn't bother to knock or ring the bell. They unlocked the front door with their own key, the feds did, to remind you who was boss and that Uncle Sam paid the bills.

"Yo, Cal!" he yodeled. "Enjoying the good life?"

"Let's do this inside."

The man brushed past him to the pool, hands on hips, the lapels of his jacket spread wide. He drank in a lungful of chlorine fumes. "What did you do to deserve Utopia? A place like this could make even a toad like you a better person."

"I don't wanna talk here." Cal feared that Frank might come out onto his patio and see them.

"Gimme a break. You spend every day in the sun while I'm in an office without windows."

Cal didn't wait. He wheeled into the house. The buzz-cut boyo circled the patio, snooping around. Then he came in too. Hands still on hips, jacket open to show off his flat, hard belly and shoulder holster, he nosed around the kitchen, the pantry, examining the oven and the refrigerator, paying particular attention to the freezer compartment.

"Make yourself at home," Barlow drawled. "Pour yourself a glass of orange juice."

"Don't mind if I do. Hey, Tropicana! The high-priced brand. Love those chewy pieces of pulp. You can taste it's the real thing, not some cheap concentrate."

The juice mustached his upper lip with a yellow streak. Cal thought it improved his close-shaved kisser. The man tossed the living room, not a heavy-handed shakedown like in maximum security, but sufficient to serve notice that nothing got by him. Barlow hoped there wouldn't be a body search. Most of them skipped that. Squeamish about frisking him. Afraid they'd catch something. He didn't see this fastidious guy rooting around under his ass and busting his knuckles on the Beretta.

While the man checked out the bedrooms and bathroom, Cal waited in front of the TV, feigning interest in a National Geographic rerun about a mastodon preserved in Siberian permafrost. When he returned to the living room, Cal said, "I'd like to see some identification. Just to know who I'm dealing with."

"A tip, my friend. You should ask first. How do you know I'm not a hit man?" He flashed an ID. Name of Joseph Delk. On a perp that would sound like an alias. On this dildo, it was a perfect fit.

He plopped down in the La-Z-Boy and put up his feet. Even the soles of his shoes appeared to have been polished. "Suppose you're asking yourself why I'm here."

"Tell you the truth," Cal said pleasantly, "I don't give a shit."

Delk plowed on as if Barlow hadn't spoken. "Figured you might be suffering from ADD. As in we haven't been paying you enough attention. But you're always in our thoughts."

"You make a fella feel loved." He turned off the TV.

"You keeping your pecker clean?"

"Doing my best."

"You should be great at it, given the incentive. The alternative."

"What can I tell you?" He turned his hands palms up. "I mean, that you'll believe."

Delk ran the tip of his tongue over his upper lip, licking off the orange juice residue. "Tell me what you do day to day?"

"I swim, I work out, I've joined a few clubs."

"Must be plenty of people in wheelchairs for you to hang with."

"I eat breakfast once a week with a bunch of guys. Sometimes I ride in the cart with them when they play golf. They take me fishing."

"Tell me more." Delk's eyes were far away, not on Barlow.

"I'm in an art class."

"Next thing you'll be peddling me portraits of Elvis on velvet."

Cal had had about enough of this. "Nah. My medium's wood. I could offer you a cut-rate price on an asshole for a hobbyhorse."

Delk made a temple of his fingertips. His head bobbed like a doll's in the rear window of a car. "Looking back at your life as a whole—"

"Hey, even crippled, I wouldn't say my life's a hole."

"—what would you say is the most valuable lesson you ever learned?"

Barlow scratched his chin, deep in thought. His fingernails grated as if against sandpaper. "When I was ten or eleven, somewhere in there, my father owned an Oldsmobile with metallic green enamel and a white convertible top. My father loved that car and he taught me that with just a bucket of water, a bar of soap, and a chamois, you can keep an automobile looking cherry."

Delk collapsed the temple. "Hearing you talk like that, I have to question how much you've been rehabilitated, how much the taxpayer's investment is paying off." He unholstered a .38 Special from under his armpit and aimed it at Cal. "It's time you learned a real lesson."

"What the fuck's this? Capital punishment for telling a joke?" Barlow went rigid in the wheelchair. "What kind of cowboy are you, Delk? Isn't the rule you don't pull a firearm unless your life's in danger and you mean to use it?"

"Maybe I mean to use it."

The fine tremor of Cal's feet became serious shakes. In his day, he had dealt with some true freaks in law enforcement. But this one took the cake. The fruitcake. "What'd I do?" he asked.

"For starters, you didn't tell the truth. I ask what you've been doing and you don't mention your new girlfriend."

"Excuse me, my mistake, I thought your job was keeping me safe. Not poking your nose into my sex life."

Delk leered. "That's the only thing interesting about you. How you have sex in a wheelchair."

"There's no law against what I do in the bedroom."

"But there is one against vandalizing cars and boats and houses. You didn't mention the crime spree on Eden."

"There's no crime spree. It's some senile dementia patient playing Halloween trick-or-treat."

"You still think this is a joke, don't you?" But it was Delk, not Barlow, who was grinning. "These incidents, when you add them up, have the earmarks of a protection racket. You raise hell till people agree the security guards can't cut the mustard. Then you say for a price you'll make the problem stop."

"Chrissake, how am I supposed to run that scam from a wheelchair? What do I threaten them with? That I'll bump into their shins at high speed?"

"I'm tired of your talk." Delk cocked the hammer on the .38.

"Are you nuts? You'd kill me in my own house for suspicion I trashed a golf cart?"

"I'm taking you off the island and dealing with you there."

"You got no right. No probable cause. I want to speak to a lawyer."

"Call him once we get where we're going."

"I'm not going anywhere. I have ties to the community. Neighbors who'll vouch for me."

The phone rang. Cal let it ring. He was too upset to answer. But it gave him an idea. "You guys already know everything I do. You have the phone tapped. You've probably got the whole house bugged."

Delk didn't deny it. He didn't confirm it either. But a bewildered look crossed his bird-beaked face. Clearly it had slipped his mind that everything he said, all his over-the-top macho posturing, might be recorded. He motioned for Cal to pick up the phone.

"Did I wake you?" It was Frank. "Catch you in the shower?"

"Yeah."

"You sound funny, like you're out of breath."

"Doing my exercises."

"Look, Ariel's early. She wants to work with you first today."

"Send her over." Barlow set the receiver back on its cradle. "My physiotherapist," he told Delk. "She'll be here in a second."

Delk let the hammer down on the .38 and reholstered it. Shaken, he stood up, unsure which way to go.

"Use the front door," Cal said.

"We're not finished. I'll be back."

"Wait and you'll see this prowler'll turn out to be somebody with Alzheimer's."

"It'll take more than that to get you off the hook."

"Then you better bring papers next time. Because I'm not going anywhere unless there's a court order."

They heard Ariel calling from the patio.

"That's the thing about life," Delk said. "You never know where you're going."

Cal waited until Delk was gone, then rolled outside, delighted as never before to see Ariel. Smiling, he strangled the urge to rush next door and strangle Frank Pritchard.

10

"I didn't sleep ten minutes last night," Frank lamented. "I can't get the panther out of my mind."

"Believe me," Barlow said, "there's bigger things to worry about."

"I'm afraid it's in pain. I'm afraid the guards'll hunt it down."

"The guards couldn't catch a cold."

"It deserves to die with dignity. Somebody may have to put it out of its misery."

"Look, if you're hinting around for me to shoot it, get that thought right the hell out of your head. We gotta talk."

"I'm listening."

"Not now. Not here."

At the wheel of the VW, Cal's arms were extended in a state of dynamic tension, quivering from the effort of maintaining the island's absurd speed limit. The mood he was in, he didn't trust himself to talk and drive at the same time. And after the way Delk had reacted to the suggestion that his house was bugged, Barlow didn't dare discuss things there. Frank's place was also out of the question. Ariel and her kid might overhear, and Randi could drop by at any moment. So Cal headed for the mangrove forest, the last stand of aboriginal vegetation, a leafy maze of cavelike canals on the west coast of Eden.

"It isn't just the panther keeping me awake," Frank said. "My bedroom faces east. Soon as the sun rises, it's right in my eyes."

"Wear one of those sleep masks they hand out on airplanes."

"And it's noisy. Frogs and crickets croak all night, then first thing in the morning birds and golfers start in."

"So wear earplugs." He passed an ancient couple pedaling tricycles. They looked like a couple of overweight kids on the brink of heat prostration.

"Sometimes I can't catch my breath," Frank said. "I wake up gasping for air."

Familiar with that feeling—Cal's chest had been constricted since Delk's visit—he had no sympathy to spare. "Wear one of those thingamajigs that spreads your nose. Like football players do. Breathe Rights."

"But the worst thing is, the real reason I can't sleep, Randi's bugging me to marry her."

Forks of autonomic dysreflexia pronged Barlow's arms. The VW accelerated to 30 mph. An unexpected pang of jealousy accompanied the muscle spasm. He was losing her just when he realized he might love her. "Congratulations," he managed to say. "When's the happy day?"

"Not in my lifetime." Frank rubbed his palms on the knees of his tan pants. Didn't he ever wear a different color?

"She's an attractive woman." Cal throttled back on the speed. "And she strikes me as a warm, loving person."

"What we both love is my money."

"You're being too hard on her." Much as he didn't care to convince Frank to marry Randi, he felt compelled to defend her. "I've gotten to know her in art class, and I like her. Everybody does."

"She has her good points. But there's Willow to consider."

"Consider how? You never see her."

"Still, she's my daughter, and I have to think of her feelings. Then there's Freddy. Where does he fit in?"

"Yeah, and there's Ariel."

When Pritchard groaned, Cal's spirits soared. Maybe the Rube Goldberg machinery of their enmeshed lives would continue to clunk along.

"The way I feel about Ariel," Frank conceded, "I guess you're right. It wouldn't be fair to marry Randi."

"Of course it wouldn't. You sleep with her yet?"

"Which one?" Pritchard turned Jesuitical.

"I already assumed you're banging Randi. I'm talking about Ariel."

"You have a marvelous knack for expression that reminds me of our former in-house counsel. His typical opening salvo was a telegram, 'Fuck you. Harsh letter follows.'"

Frank's answer, Cal noticed, never quite connected with his question. But this wasn't the time to press the issue. He needed to save his energy for more urgent matters.

Where the smooth-paved macadam ended and a gravel path commenced, the foliage became more the way it was on the mainland, back on those country roads that corkscrewed into the Everglades. Wind-tortured West Indian mahogany and green buttonwood trees. Crooked limbs and knobby knees. Crippled vegetation that might have been a memorial garden for Cal.

His eyes jumped around, searching for a straight line, a level surface. They landed on a boardwalk that bisected the mangroves. Bird-watchers humped along it, stooped under the weight of binoculars and cameras. Shuffling from one observation platform to the next, they congregated at wildlife markers like choirs consulting musical scores.

"How far do we have to go," Frank asked, "before we talk?"

If he had a choice, Cal never would have talked. Or he'd have done it in a rowboat, in the middle of the Atlantic, right before he pushed Pritchard overboard in a lead-lined barrel. Furiously retracing the chain of wrongheaded decisions that had led him to this predicament, he wanted to blame everything on Frank. But without Cal's early encouragement, would his neighbor have done anything worse than shoving Bob Emery's golf cart into a water hazard?

Beneath a sapodilla tree bowed by fruit, there was a shack no bigger than a privy where an island employee rented out kayaks for excursions into the swamp. Suddenly excited, Frank exclaimed that he had rowed here many times. Forgetting his sleepiness and his breathlessness and his worry about the panther, he acted like a tour guide, as if he had arranged this day's outing for Barlow. He and the booth attendant lowered Cal into the rear seat of a fiberglass kayak. Then Frank folded his spare frame into the front seat and shoved them out onto the sluggish current.

A mistake. Barlow feared he was forging another link in his error chain. They should have held this powwow someplace else. The kayak seat was hard enough to cause pressure sores. And it wobbled under his ass. He didn't relish the idea of tipping over into the scummy water.

"Those webs you see"—Frank was in full lecture mode, leaving Cal to do all the paddling—"they were spun by golden orb weavers. Their filaments have the tensile strength of steel."

Cal could believe it. The spiders looked big enough to build bridges. Big enough to destroy bridges. He ducked under the low-hanging webs.

On the back of Frank's head, the white hair had a yellow tinge from the sun, just as Barlow's father had had a tarnished halo from his hatband. That was the only similarity between the two men. He didn't regard Pritchard as a paternal surrogate. If anything, he felt fatherly and protective toward the old guy. Which didn't, however, preclude being fed up with his refusal to listen to reason.

"Mangroves come in three types," Frank gibbered on. "Red, white, and black."

"Black and white and read all over." Cal tried to dam the Niagara of information.

"Black mangroves have white specks on their leaves from sweating out saltwater. They reproduce by means of beanlike pods. When the pods fall from the trees, some of them sink into the mud and root there. Others float for miles before they sprout and form islands."

"Hey, give it a rest, okay?"

Pritchard's head drooped, straining the frail tendons at the back of his neck. Cal softened his voice. "Let's enjoy the scenery and have a quiet moment."

He hated to hurt Frank's feelings. He knew he meant to make things educational and interesting. But Cal needed silence to get his thoughts straight.

The canal widened into a pond where fish flashed through swales of green weeds. They were big, these fish, but they torpedoed into the air as if weightless, and when they knifed back into the water, pelicans crash-dived after them. Ungainly as canvas bags stuffed with coat hangers, the birds belly-flopped with the artlessness of cannonballers. How did those klutzes ever catch fish? If only the fittest survived, it was obvious bloody-fanged nature gave no points for style. Desire and dimwitted persistence carried the day.

Cal steered to shore, and as he moored the kayak to a black mangrove, dozens of crabs skittered off its arthritic roots.

"Indians built this mound ages ago." Frank started up again, pointing to a hummock littered with oyster shells. "They ate a diet of crustaceans and—"

"They claim oysters are great for sex," Barlow broke in. "I don't know whether to believe it. I once ate three dozen and only thirty worked."

That got a chuckle from Pritchard. He turned around to face Cal. Midges and mosquitoes hung like a beaded curtain between them. "What's so important that you dragged me out to one of my favorite spots?"

"Glad you like it, Frank. Hope it puts you in a receptive frame of mind. Because I've got a favor to ask."

"Name it and I'll do it."

Cal skinned off his T-shirt. The paisley shade of the mangroves cooled his chest. On the mound of shells a long-legged, harpoon-beaked bird strutted about, lifting and planting its talons as noiselessly as a burglar. It reminded him of Delk. "I want you to hit my house," he said.

A frown—close to a scowl—gouged Pritchard's forehead. "I don't get it."

"The security people told you they noticed a pattern. All the victims were connected to your old company. Well, since you won't hit your own house and throw them off the scent, why not hit mine? That'll help us both."

"I broke the pattern with the raccoon."

"Break it again so they don't miss the message."

A flock of pelicans kamikazied into the pond, creating a ripple that rocked the kayak. "Is this some sort of insurance deal?" Frank asked. "You want me to trash your property so you can collect damages? I have to say that's pretty low."

"Look who's talking. The king of low blows."

Under his crown of silver hair, the king glowered. "I never did anything to enrich myself. I never bothered anybody who didn't deserve it. I may have been legally wrong, but it was for moral reasons."

"Yeah, well, I got my reasons too."

"What are they? Last night you were begging me to stop."

"It's a simple favor I'm asking. I've done one for you," Cal said. "I never let on to anybody that you're the prowler."

"And I never told anyone about your pistol."

Barlow hadn't expected this grudging, niggling attitude. "All right, then, we're even. It's pure kindness, a good turn, I'm asking."

"How's vandalizing your house an act of kindness?"

"Chrissakes, do you want me to claim it's a matter of life and death?"

"Is it?"

"You could make that case."

"Then make it."

"You must have been hell at collective bargaining."

"Not bad."

"Not bad my ass. You'd have left the teamsters peeing in their pants."

Frank's eyes presented fathoms of inscrutability. It was impossible to guess what he was thinking. Or whether he was thinking. Whatever he took in, he projected nothing Cal could read. "The law paid me a visit yesterday," Barlow said.

"Was it Ned and a fellow named Mingle, all puffed up with beefy self-importance?"

"No, this guy was alone. From off the island."

Pritchard's eyebrows jackknifed. "I was under the impression that Eden intended to keep things in-house, so to speak."

"It may be too late for that. You see, there's this rumor circulating—
it's spread to some strange places—that I'm responsible for your grab-
assing around."

"That's ludicrous. What's the proof?"

"Look, the law, whether you know it or not, can cause plenty of
trouble without proof."

"Nonsense! This isn't a banana republic. Some sinkhole without
due process."

"That may be your experience. My experience, the police decide
to bust your chops, they do it."

"Do what? Are they threatening to arrest you? And what's this experience of yours?"

"They don't need to arrest you to ruin you. They take pleasure
fucking people over." Cal hesitated, swinging between stark alterna-
tives. Zip his lip and run that risk. Or confide and accept the other
risk. Finally he released the trapeze. "I don't like to disappoint you,
Frank, but I got a record. That's why I'm under suspicion."

Poker-faced, Pritchard assimilated this with no evidence of shock.
"A record for what?"

"Call it white-collar crime."

"No, let's call it what the court called it."

"They called it tax fraud."

In the shadow of the mangroves, Frank was leaf-patterned. He
laughed, and the light and dark spots shifted over his white shirt.
"Hell, half the island has had scrapes with the IRS."

"I had more than a scrape. I did time."

This got Pritchard's attention. "So you're what? On parole?"

"Let's leave it that I'm in a position where they can yank my chain."

"Why would they keep you on a short leash? And how do they tie
tax fraud in with somebody keying cars and setting loose a raccoon?"

Cal squirmed on the fiberglass seat. He felt nothing below the waist, but he feared that his bones were bruising his skin, lacerating it from the inside out. What kind of life was it where just sitting peacefully on your ass caused abscesses?

"You're not leveling with me," Frank pushed him.

"It's not easy to explain."

"Neither is wrecking your house. If you want me to do that, I need to know why you were in jail."

"Have it your way. You ever hear of a bust-out scheme?"

"Not by name. Maybe if you described it."

"That was my specialty," Cal said. "Bust-out schemes. They're not all that different from leveraged buyouts or hostile takeovers. Bet you know a thing or two about them."

Pritchard didn't answer. Didn't budge. The net of light and dark splotches held steady on him.

"What we did," Cal said, "my partners and me, we'd invest in a company whose sales spike in a particular season. As a for instance, consumer electronics—computers, TVs, sound systems, car radios, etcetera—which the public tends to buy in bunches right before Christmas. The way the cash flows it's not a steady twenty-five percent per quarter. These outlets'll do thirty-five percent of their annual business in November and more than that in December. So what you do in a bust-out, you establish a line of credit with your vendors and for six months you pay the bills religiously. Then when the big Christmas rush rolls around, you increase your inventory five or ten times and run up a huge debt."

"Which you have no intention of paying," Frank interrupted.

"That's the magic question. Did you have criminal intent? No way, you plead in bankruptcy court. You sold the whole inventory and owe your suppliers millions of bucks. Your creditors clamor for the money, but you can't pay because—"

"Because you skimmed everything into an offshore account."

"That's the allegation. But your defense is inept management. You overspent. You kept poor records. Your accountants were crap. You suffered high shrinkage. It takes months, years, to dig down to what everybody believes is the bottom of things. By then your creditors have wasted a fortune on lawyers and they face another fortune in court costs if the case goes to trial. In the end, they settle for twenty cents on the dollar. So you bust out with a pretty penny."

"You're a crook," Frank said.

"Hey, I'm no Ken Lay. I may not even be as bad as Bob Emery."

"You're a crook," he repeated with such vehemence that the bird lifted off the shell mound in a clatter of wings.

This hurt more than Cal would have expected. "Let's get the time scheme straight. I *was* a crook. I paid my debt to society."

"And now you're out of jail where you belong and are living in luxury on millions of dollars of stolen money."

"Not even close. I'm on a fixed income. I barely limp along day to day. And because of your monkeyshines, which they pin on me, I'm about to lose the little I have left."

"Ain't that a pity," Pritchard gloated. "I'd call that a salutary secondary gain."

"And I'd call you a self-righteous prick. What kind of scumbag lets his crippled neighbor take the rap for him?"

"Who are you calling a scumbag?" Frank lurched forward. But the rocking kayak threatened to dump them both into the water. He sat back.

Cal raised his hands, not in surrender, but to signal that they should calm down. Normally he adhered to the Israeli strategy. Don't negotiate with terrorists. Just bomb. But although he knew in a pissing contest that he could hurt Pritchard with embarrassing accusations, he had no cushion under his own ass. He'd wind up on the street, a smudge on the asphalt.

"You know, Frank," he said, "this makes me sad. I thought we were kindred spirits."

"Bullshit, you just didn't want me telling anybody about your gun. Now I know why."

"You only think you do."

"Now I understand a lot of things about you."

"Me too. I understand why you're alone in that house. Why your daughter lives in Europe. Why your company kicked you off the board."

The distress this brought to Frank's face was dreadful to see. "I don't have to listen to this from the likes of you." He thrashed his paddle, as if to separate his half of the kayak from Barlow's. His end swung out into the down-pouring sun.

"You complain about corporate-greed pigs. But how are you different?" Cal taunted him. "I don't notice you've missed many meals. This hard-on you have for justice, it's just resentment that they shit-canned you. In your day, I bet you had both feet in the trough."

Frank continued beating his paddle, frantic to row away from the awful words. "Let me go," he demanded.

"You think you're always the guy calling the shots, don't you? Always the guy in charge. Like you're the last man on earth that has the angels on his side."

Breathing hard, Pritchard floated back into the shade. "I want to leave," he said between pants. "Unless you have that gun on you and mean to use it, I intend to untie the line."

"Listen to you. I assumed—excuse my mistake—we were pals. Now you make me out to be a murderer."

"Don't switch this around. You lied to me from the start."

"I didn't lie. I just didn't tell you every detail. Can you blame me? Look how you react when I come clean."

"You still haven't told me the truth. Not all of it." He looked around, like he might jump ship and wade ashore.

"You want to hear the rest of it? You might as well so you'll know what'll happen to me if you don't help."

"I'm not interested."

"I'm going to tell you anyway." By now Cal was every bit as furious as Frank. "All the bust-outs I pulled, the cops never made a charge stick. But raking through my financial records, they found one measly tax dodge and blew it up into a federal case. I landed in Allenwood Prison serving three to five."

"You have my sincerest sympathy."

"I'm not finished. The feds, they squeezed me to turn state's evidence. I refused. Still, my partners were worried that I'd rat them out, so they had me shanked. I survived. But I couldn't go back to jail. That was a death sentence. So I testified, and the feds put me in the Witness Protection Program."

Along with leafy polka dots, incredulity flittered over Pritchard's face. "And the morons sent you to Eden?" he roared. "Next door to me?"

"Yeah. Go figure."

"What's your real name?"

"You don't want to know. All you need to know is the feds see your dumb-ass pranks and think it's me starting a protection racket. They're threatening to kick me off Eden and out of the program."

"It's the end of the gravy train. Not the end of the world."

"For me it's the end, period! Without protection, the mob'll pick me off in a week."

Frank's shoulders sagged. He laid the paddle across his knees. "I don't see how it helps to have me hit your house."

"It's a no-brainer. You do my place and the feds'll realize I'm not behind all the shit you pulled."

"Not necessarily. They might decide you did it yourself to throw them off track."

"No, we'll fix it so they won't. I'll be way the hell and gone, sur-rounded by witnesses, when it happens. If you make this your last job, I'm sure they'll let me stay."

Frank rubbed his palms over his pants, erasing the crease. "What if I get caught?"

"That's never worried you before."

"But your house is right next door."

"Look, nobody'll catch you. Wear gloves and don't leave finger-prints. We'll plan it out step by step."

Pritchard looked glum, disconsolate. He brushed at his shirt, as if to whisk away the leaf shade. "This agent that paid you a visit, was he wearing a dark suit, short hair, a face like an owl?"

"A lot of cops fit that description. Why do you ask?"

"I might have run into him at the marina. I was afraid he saw me splattering Bob Emery's boat with chicken guts."

"Must not have. It's me he's after. This is the only way to get him off my back," Cal swore. "And it'll put you in the clear too."

"The hardest thing," Frank said, "is going to be living without it."

It? Barlow thought he meant their friendship, their talks, the swim-ming races. But Frank said, "I depend on what I do at night to get me through the day."

"We'll find better things."

"Okay, I'll do it."

Unknotting the rope, Cal came away with salt on his hands. These mangrove roots were like pretzels, their shape and white crust.

Pritchard swung around, facing forward, baring the stringy vul-nerability of his neck. In measured strokes, they sculled to the middle of the pond. Fish flew out of the water and pelicans piled in on top of them. Ecologically minded Edenites might regard this as a heartening example of the life cycle, but for Barlow it was a reminder of his low perch in the food chain. All Frank had to do was repeat what he had been told and Cal might as well stick the barrel of the Beretta into his own mouth.

"I still don't understand," Frank said, "how you ended up a criminal."

"I didn't. I ended up in a wheelchair."

"I mean before that, how did you become one?"

"Ever been to Italy, Frank?"

"If you're going to say all Italians are in the Mafia and you had no choice, that's BS."

"No, I'm saying I took my son to Rome when he was little and we climbed that hill behind the wedding cake monument where there's a view of the Forum. Sammy looked at those domes and columns with no buildings attached, and the holes full of rubble, and he thought somebody had nuked the place. 'What happened?' he asked me. But how could I tell him?"

Pritchard shook his head, perplexed.

"It's history, Frank. A long, sad tale. There's not enough time to explain it and you wouldn't believe me if I did."

book

three

1

The boundaries of Frank's life reshrank to the dimensions of his mesh-screened patio. Sometimes they seemed to have shrunk to the circumference of his skull. He skipped that week's Breakfast Club meeting. He spotted friends on the golf course and didn't call out to them. When the wind kicked up, it carried the ocean's scent and memories of that afternoon of snorkeling, but he didn't go back to the reef. After the kayak trip, he no longer even crossed to Barlow's pool for their races. He swam in his own pool with Ariel, then sat with Nicholas on his lap while she went next door to treat Cal.

Although she offered to massage him, Frank said no thanks. Now that he had acknowledged that he loved her, he didn't trust himself to let her touch him.

He resented Cal for the cruelty of his accusations, not to mention their possible accuracy. Though tempted to launch a counteroffensive, what could he do? Call Barlow mean names? Bend the spokes of his wheelchair? Pee in his pool? The guy had already invited him to blitz his house.

Then there was Randi. He was supposed to be weighing her marriage ultimatum. But he couldn't do it. Oh, he could think about it. He just couldn't marry her. To wed a woman like Randi, it struck him, was to enter a kind of Witness Protection Program—one where she got a new name, he got a bogus identity, and they remained a mystery to each other.

Still, he didn't want to hurt her, and when after days of silence she called him, he didn't spoil the pretense that she had phoned on civic business. There was a proposal to plow up the asphalt hike-and-bike trail and pave it with wood chips. Senior citizens complained that the unforgiving surface caused plantar fascitis. Where did Frank stand?

On this issue he stood wherever she wanted him to. He empowered Randi to cast a proxy vote on his behalf.

"There's a meeting at the Community Center," she said. "Won't you come with me?"

"I'm busy. Preoccupied." He left the impression that, night and day, he was pondering the pros and cons of marriage.

"Let me hear from you when the dust clears."

He couldn't guess when that might be. Like a two-bit amateur magician, Frank felt he had tossed a handful of glitter into the air to distract the audience only to have it blow back and blind him. The whole time he imagined he was pulling the strings, had he been somebody else's puppet? He couldn't decide what to make of Barlow. Or what Cal had made of him. One moment, Frank seemed to have backed himself into a corner. The next, he suspected that Cal had shouldered him to the wall.

That's what came of allowing a crook in paradise. A criminal felon, not a garden-variety corporate bandit. People mistook him for a solid citizen and dropped their guard.

Because Frank hated having been hoodwinked, he wondered whether Cal was being honest with him now. In the hall of mirrors they had mutually constructed, Pritchard retraced the bends and elbows of Barlow's astonishing story. Could his apparent candor about his record and his fear of being expelled from Eden amount to another scam? Would Frank vandalize his house, only to learn afterward that it was an elaborate double-cross?

Finally Cal rang him. "Where you been hiding?"

"In plain sight. On my patio."

"That thing we discussed, we have to review the nuts and bolts."

"I'm listening."

"Not on the phone. Someplace quiet."

"Another trip to the mangroves?"

"My ass is sore from last time. Meet me this evening at the mall parking lot. Look for a guy in a wheelchair."

Late that afternoon, the wind swung around out of the north and churned up whitecaps in the pool. The temperature fell fifteen degrees in an hour. The air still wasn't cold, it just felt like it was. Ariel stayed in the water swimming laps while Frank and Nicholas snuggled close to the TV, which crackled with the bloodcurdling warmth of fire-breathing dragons consuming Asian damsels. During commercials, Frank surfed to the Money Channel, where the crawl indicated that the market had risen 400 points, declined 600, then rebounded to finish the day dead even.

So much melodrama to maintain the status quo. What was it they used to say when football games ended in a tie? It was like kissing

your sister. What was so bad about that? Pritchard would have wel-
comed affection from almost any source. But he knew he had better
lighten up with Nicholas. If he kept cuddling the boy, Ariel might accuse him of child abuse.

He found himself lecturing about cold fronts, isobars, and mil-
libars. He regaled Nicholas with yarns about the weather back home
where he grew up—the lake-effect snow, the Alberta clippers, the
Chinook winds. A man his age had accumulated so much arcana, so
much wisdom, what was the good of letting it die with him? He was
eager to pass it along.

But there were the pitfalls to this information-sharing. When they
switched to Animal Planet, it showed an alarming program about
hyenas. The commentator's discussion of their mating habits and the
false penises of high-testosterone females provoked Nicholas to ask
how babies were born. Pritchard offered an abbreviated explanation
that silenced the boy for a few seconds. Then Nicholas asked, "What's
that stuff that shoots out of a whale's head?"

When Ariel pulled herself from the pool, Frank went and draped a towel
around her shoulders. In a daring move for him, he gave her a rubdown,
all aboveboard, like a coach with his star player. The frailty of her bones
felt like a wire armature until she slowly yielded to his hands.

"You must be freezing," he said, his own teeth chattering.

"I'm fine. Thank you. That helps."

"It does, doesn't it? I mean I've always benefited from your massages."

"Well, that's what they're for." Then she added, "We really need to
talk sometime, maybe when Nicholas is taking a nap."

"Yes, we do," was all he could think to say.

"Time to go home," she called to Nicholas.

. . .

After they left, the wind chased Frank indoors. He cut off the AC and advanced the heat register. From behind the baseboard, the woolly thump of warming pipes called to mind the raccoon ricocheting through the club's air ducts. Thus far, every attempt at trapping the coon had failed. There was talk that they would have to tent the building and hire fumigators. It appeared that the pet he had bought as a gift for an imaginary son was one that would keep on giving.

Adamantly as he had argued against it, Pritchard was now anxious to rush next door and start the destruction. His hands itched. The sword on the mantelpiece looked inviting. Why not let it rip? But he stuck to the plan and set out to meet Cal, tooling along toward the mall on a roundabout route past the beach. In the dunes between the ocean and the road, gardeners had planted sea oats and spartina grass, and the wind ruffled them like the stubble on a man who had had a hair transplant. Seaweed blew across the asphalt, trailing rubbery strands that resembled used condoms. These were the empty egg casings of whelks. With no one else around to witness it, Frank would have sworn that the sunset ignited the famous green flash. The first of his life.

He sped off, holding at bay the sadness that he feared would swim along in the wake of his exhilaration. It was like having Nicholas on his lap, constantly aware that the boy would soon leave and would, in any case, eventually grow up. Everything in life seemed to teeter on a knifeblade.

Barlow waited in his wheelchair beside the VW, battered by wind, his dark hair flailing his face. He wore a black leather jacket, and while this gave his upper torso the brawling menace of a Hell's Angel, his helpless legs were lost in baggy sweatpants.

Frank threw the Jag's door open into the teeth of a fifty-mile-an-hour gust. "Let's get inside."

"We're fine where we are. Tonight's the night," Cal told him. "I'll be at art class." He didn't mention that he was to be the model. "A group of us are going out for dinner afterward. One thing. My house has a burglar alarm. The cops'll smell something fishy if I leave it switched off. So stick to the pool and the patio area where the alarm doesn't cover. There's plenty to do out there."

Pritchard nodded.

"When you finish," Cal said, "go home and go to bed. By the time I call security, you should be asleep."

"I'll be in bed. I can't promise I'll be asleep."

"The police'll probably ask you questions. Don't complicate the situation. Just say you didn't see or hear a thing. And don't forget to wear gloves."

"Count on it."

"What's that they tell actors?" Rolling away under the arcade of royal palms, which the wind threatened to unscrew from the parking lot, Barlow shouted over his shoulder, "Break a leg!"

Back at the house, Frank squeezed into a pair of Dorothy's old rubber dishwashing gloves. Then he departed by the rear entrance, where wind splashed water over the patio. A tempest in a pool, if not a teapot. A hurricane that seemed to have been conjured out of inner chaos on a star-strewn night. Although no rain fell, ocean mist and humidity from the pool and fairway hazards moistened his skin. Palm fronds scratched at the mesh like fingernails. Spook-show acoustics.

At Barlow's patio door, he thrust a foot through the screen. It required so little effort to kick in that panel, it seemed logical to go ahead and poke holes in the others. The harder thing would have been to stop kicking, stop smashing whatever lay close to hand or foot.

He flipped over flowerpots, scattering dirt, and flung fake ceramic amphorae into the pool. Then he tossed in cushions, aluminum folding chairs, and a plastic card table. When the floating debris looked solid enough to walk across, he stove in a wicker cabana and knocked a plaster porpoise to pieces.

A suite of lawn furniture—four chairs and a circular table—appeared to have been woven out of green vines. But each piece was forged of cast iron and felt as though it had been bolted to the ground. Straining with all his might, he managed to drag the chairs one at a time to the pool and tip them in.

The table wouldn't budge no matter how much he heaved at it. Still, he wouldn't quit. Bending at the knees, he meant to turn the table on its side and roll it like a millstone into the water. He set his shoulder under it and struggled to stand up. He didn't hear a rip, but he felt it and was afraid that he had torn the seam of his trousers from the crotch to his bellybutton.

Duckwalking out from under the table, Pritchard again attempted to stand up. He could see that his pants weren't split, but his shirt collar felt as if it had been buttoned to his fly. When he forced himself upright, a loose thread—no, it was more like a noose—tightened around his throat and tugged his shoulder down toward his chest.

Defeated by the table, he hobbled home, his left arm dangling, dead to everything except pain. Forked lightning flashed from his elbows and shot sparks from his fingers. His right hand functioned, but poorly, very poorly, more like a claw than an appendage with an opposable thumb. When the door to his patio with its simple push-pull handle wouldn't submit to his jam-bang efforts, he kicked in a square of mesh and hunched through the hole.

On the glass sliding door to the house his rubber gloves could

gain no purchase. One good swift kick convinced him he'd frac-
ture his toe before he cracked the double-glazed pane. So he head-
butted it until something shook loose. The door opened a precious
few inches. Pritchard squished through with the agony of a forceps
delivery.

The flashing pain in his left arm was a classic symptom of a heart
attack. Could a slipped disk cause a coronary? Did pinched nerves
and lumbar trauma respond to a heat pad or a cold pack? He owned
neither and resolved the debate between fire and ice by cracking a
bag of frozen peas from the refrigerator and strapping it to his shoulder with a dish towel.

He reeled into the bedroom. Barlow had instructed him to sleep.
Or pretend to. That entailed climbing the slick percale sheets to the
summit of his Dux mattress. First, however, he had to undress, and his
clothes felt as if they had snagged on his skin. Unbuckling his belt
was as bad as throwing the switch on Old Sparky. Electrical charges
spiraled up his vertebrae and set his hair on fire. There was a sulfurous
smell. As his trousers fell to his ankles, he was afraid he had soiled
himself. But the wetness was splashed pool water.

Once in bed, he simulated a schoolboy's dimly remembered fire
drill. Stop, drop, and roll. In T-shirt and undershorts, with the frigid
peas bunched on his shoulder, he sought the fetal position, folding
his legs to his chest, clasping his hands between his knees.

Pritchard snuffed the bedside lamp, but was blinded by a glare behind his closed eyelids. On the night table, there was the airline sleep
mask Cal had recommended. Frank stretched the elastic band over
his aching hair, and let the mask fall against the bridge of his nose.
This almost smothered him. So he applied a Breathe Right, and air
scoured his sinuses and hit his brain like a blacksmith forging horse-
shoes with a ten-pound mallet. To mute the noise, he stuffed in the
earplugs that Barlow had also recommended.

He felt trapped in a web, one of those immense filament nets spun by a golden orb weaver. Suspended at its center, he waited for the spider to tightrope down the quivering wire and move in for the kill. The image recalled Dorothy's last days in intensive care. Trussed up in tubes, an oxygen mask over her nose and mouth, she had gazed at Frank with an expression of unfathomable yearning. He had assumed that she longed to live. Now he suspected that she may have been equally eager to die. Either way she wanted out of the place where pain had put her.

Through his earplugs there sifted the melody of harps. It wasn't the bittersweet anthem of heaven, nor the sound of a golden orb weaver plucking the chords of its web. This was worse. The front-door chimes. The cops were here.

Bumping down from the bed as if over the ice falls of Mount Everest, he touched his feet to the floor, bit his lip, and let his full weight settle. A seizure shot through him, then thunder and lightning. Shoving the sleep mask up to his forehead, he left the earplugs and Breathe Right and pea pack in place.

As he lurched along in a hermit crab's hideous fashion, the hall mirror, an antique whose silver backing had contracted smallpox, offered him a horror-show glimpse of himself. White-haired, white underpants, his throbbing eyeballs on stalks, his nostrils spread like the snout of a razorback in rut, his left shoulder hitched six inches higher than the right, his head Siamese-twinned with the defrosting bag of peas.

When he opened the front door, Ned said, "Jesus Christ, what's wrong with you?"

"I threw my back out swimming," he croaked.

"Sorry to wake you, pal," Barlow said. "But somebody trashed my patio and tossed everything into the pool."

"Looks like the prowler planned to hit you next," Andy Mingle said. "He punched through a panel of your patio screen. Something must have scared him off. Did you hear anything?"

"I wear these at night." Frank removed the earplugs. "Didn't hear a thing."

"Mind if we look around?" The burly investigator had on a hooded anorak. Wind riffled inside it, inflating his head like a balloon.

Pritchard glanced at Cal. They hadn't discussed this eventuality. Shifting unsteadily, he cleared the entrance for the three of them. Mingle hurried over to the patio door, and when he found it dilated the same six inches that Frank had slithered through, he whistled.

Crouched like Quasimodo, Pritchard caught up to him. "When I came in from the pool, I may have forgotten to close it. I was in pretty bad shape."

"You don't look so hot now," Cal said.

"I'll be fine once I'm back in bed."

"If we lift any latents from Mr. Barlow's place, we'll be here in the morning to dust for comparison prints." Mingle slammed the door shut with his shoe. As the air seeped out of his anorak, his head deflated. "Can I ask you a question, Mr. Pritchard?"

"Of course."

"Why are you wearing rubber gloves?"

Frank examined them as if he were just as mystified as Mingle. "Oh, these! I wear them to bed for . . . for my high blood pressure. Rubber gloves and support hose."

Mingle glanced at Frank's bare feet.

"Except tonight," Pritchard said, "I couldn't bend down to pull on my elastic socks."

"I've got the same problem," Ned said. "I take pills."

"Tell me about it," Cal chipped in. "One thing and another, I take a dozen pills a day. Tonight I'll add a dose of aspirin. What a headache. I'll be on the phone for hours with repairmen and insurance claims adjusters."

As Mingle roamed the house, Frank clomped along in his footsteps. At the master bedroom door, it occurred to him that his shirt, shoes, and trousers were inside on the floor, soaked in pool water. What could he do—claim he swam in his clothes?

"Wait a second," Frank said.

Impatience—or was it suspicion?—furrowed Mingle's ham-loaf face.

"I'd rather you didn't go in there." Pritchard scrambled for an excuse. By now, Ned and Barlow had joined them. "There's a friend spending the night."

"Maybe your friend heard or saw something," Mingle said.

"No. She was asleep. Same as me."

"Still, I'd like to talk to her."

"Hey, you don't think Frank's friend trashed my house, do you?" Cal's voice dripped sarcasm. "Not very damn likely. Those lawn chairs must weigh a hundred pounds apiece. She'd have to be a lady wrestler."

Ned laughed. Mingle didn't. "Thanks for your help, Mr. Pritchard. Call the gate if you need us."

Pritchard skulked down the hall past his Frankenstein reflection in the mirror. In the bathroom, he swallowed six ibuprofen and replugged his ears. From a shelf in the closet, he retrieved the soft cervical collar that Dorothy had worn when her neck ached. Peeling off the pea pack, he wrapped the foam rubber around his throat, attaching it with Velcro tabs. Perhaps because the collar bore the scent of his dead wife's perfume, it provided some relief from the pain.

In the solitude of his bed, Frank stopped, dropped, and rolled. Then lowering his sleep mask, he lay wide awake watching the aurora borealis blaze in his eyeballs. Perfect bookends, he thought—the green flash at dusk, followed by fireworks till dawn.

2

All night the wind rocked Ariel's trailer on its cinderblock founda-
tions and strummed the pines that caged the property. Next morning
as the storm ebbed to a breeze, she ate breakfast and did her stretches
and crunches in a crystalline silence that recalled days in South Africa
when, after blowing for a week, the Cape Doctor, a wind that reput-
edly cleansed the coast of germs, died down.

Nicholas woke up fussy. She hated having to clean and feed and
dress him when he was in a foul mood. He was getting too big for
these mauls and rucks. But once outside, the boy went quiet, and as
she strapped him into the Land Rover stroller, they both gaped at the
storm damage. The picnic table had been upended and the umbrella
had flown to the highest branches of the gumbo-limbo, where it
looked like something you'd see atop a cool green drink. Scooped dry
of water, the plastic wading pool was suction-cupped to the aluminum side of the trailer. Bright flags of trash fluttered from the rose-

bushes like prayer rags tied by true believers to shrubs in a Moslem graveyard.

Gooseflesh spackled her bare legs, quickening Ariel's stride. Her neighbors congregated for warmth around the outdoor grills they used for their weekend *braais*. But far from carping about the cold, they reveled in it, confident they would be basking in sunny warmth by the afternoon.

Nicholas sang as she wheeled him along. Individual words were indistinguishable, but she recognized the tune—"Graceland," that Paul Simon song she had sung to him so often it was now an earworm on his brain tape. In front of a pawnshop, the ATM of the poor, men loitered until the business day began. They all had on ball caps worn backwards, and in a fashion statement new to Ariel, several of them had reversed their sunglasses as if to shield light-sensitive eyes behind their heads.

On the causeway, few fishermen had braved the chill, and Ariel had room to sprint if she cared to. Still, she plodded along, her thoughts tugged this way and that. Questions hovered in her head like the gaudy parasails that hovered in the sky. The rubdown Mr. Pritchard gave her last night had got her wondering what was on his mind. For weeks he had seemed poised to make a statement or a move. She didn't think she was imagining this. She thought she knew what he was thinking. The question was what she'd do if he acted.

At the security gate the fellow with the hose made as if to wet her down. But it was too cold for that today. She shooed him off.

Maintenance crews in brigade strength busily cleaned the streets, which were in a disheveled state that Ariel found refreshing. At last the island looked lived in. On the hike-and-bike trail she dodged exotic debris—coconuts, boomerang-shaped seedpods, and sponges as bulbous as cauliflowers that had blown out of the ocean. As she swung in at Frank's driveway, a swarm of palmetto bugs lazed in the sun shaking off the night's low temperatures. They scattered like a wagon train fleeing Indians, but Nicholas's carriage crunched a path through the stampede.

She let herself in with her own key. It surprised her that Mr. Pritchard wasn't out on the patio. Even in bad weather, he huddled in front of the TV and smoked until the instant they arrived. Then he hid his cigarettes.

Nicholas unbuckled himself from the Land Rover.

"Watch TV in the living room," she told him.

"Where's Frank?" he asked.

"That's Mr. Pritchard to you."

"But where is he?"

"Probably eating breakfast with his friends."

To rinse off after her run, Ariel usually swam. But in the boss's absence, she decided to take a shower. During Dorothy's illness, the guest bathroom had been fitted with a walk-in stall large enough for her and a caregiver. Several days a week Ariel had seated Dorothy on the tile bench beneath the spray and shampooed what was left of her hair. She remembered the dying woman, groggy from drugs and chemo, surrendering to her hands and saying, "When Willow was a baby and I was breastfeeding her, I'd wake in the middle of the night, frantic. I'd claw at the covers, afraid she was smothering somewhere on the bed. Now I wake up and it's me who feels tiny and lost. You're so good to me."

The emotions this had whipped up in Ariel thrust her into a state of bewilderment. In a shifting of boundaries, the woman became her baby, and she had found it almost as urgent to tend to Dorothy as she did to her little boy. Then there was the care she felt Mr. Pritchard was due.

Prying off her shoes, stepping out of her shorts, and removing her sports bra, Ariel was in sensible white cotton underpants, adjusting the shower tap, when Frank staggered into the bathroom. Blinded by a sleep mask half shoved out of his eyes, yoked in a cervical collar, one arm dangling, the opposing shoulder cricked, hands gloved in latex rubber, he looked like a charade player's idea of a disaster victim. To complete the comic effect, he had plugs in his ears and a Breathe Right strip across his nose, one end of it fluttering like a moth wing.

Ariel did the worst thing imaginable. She laughed at him. Only as he turned to face her did she realize he was in pain and she was in her underpants, just like Mr. Pritchard was. She folded her arms across her chest and further covered herself with a brisk, professional demeanor. "I was dressing for work. I thought you were out."

"I couldn't handle the tub in the other bathroom," Frank said. "Thought a hot shower might help."

"What's wrong with you?"

"Hurt myself lifting something heavy."

"Let me have a look." She unfastened his foam collar and unplugged his ears. He winced. "Show me where it hurts," she said.

In no shape to do much demonstrating, he murmured, "My arm, my shoulder, my neck, my lower back."

"A right mess you've made of yourself."

Busying herself with Frank's body, she temporarily forgot her own. Quite a feat considering the extent of her exposed flesh. She removed his sleep mask, the Breathe Right, and the rubber gloves. After testing his fingers for feeling—they seemed to be functional—she kneaded his shoulder and the small of his back.

She knew he was self-conscious about his physique, and nothing she said could convince him of how much progress he had made. But it was there for anyone to see, and she was pleased by what they had accomplished. How could you not love a client who responded so well to your care? That there was more to be done didn't diminish her pride in him.

Few aspects of the human anatomy offended her. She admired

what worked, fretted over parts that didn't, and derived satisfaction from repairing them. Just two things made her gorge rise—neglected teeth and toenails. Without proper attention, a senior citizen's extremities sometimes appeared to switch positions so that the mouth was fanged with yellow toenails and the feet were snaggled with blackened teeth. Fortunately, Frank valued personal hygiene.

"Let's move into the shower," she said. "Warm water will help."

"I can do it on my own."

"No you can't." She slipped an arm around him, accepting his lopsided weight, and they entered the stall. "Are you able to lie down?" she asked.

"I'd rather not. I'll kneel." Raggedly expelling air, he creaked to his knees and curled forward as if praying at the bench.

Ariel aimed the spray at his lower back. It was a power shower, and she controlled the water pressure as well as the heat, and incrementally increased both. Once the tension loosened in his spine, she directed the nozzle at his shoulders. Soaping her hands, she skimmed them over the afflicted areas, lightly at first, barely smoothing her palms over the skin. Then as she dug her fingers in deep, she hit gnarled clumps, hard as gristle. He gasped, but said, "Don't stop." He gasped again and murmured, "That's good."

"Want to lie flat yet?"

"I'll try."

Grimacing as his vertebrae uncoupled with audible clicks, he stretched out on the bench on his stomach. His left shoulder looked frozen, and Ariel manipulated it with the heels of her hands, then her elbows. While she bore down harder and harder, the warm spray bore down on her, turning her cotton underpants pinkly transparent. Wet tresses of her hair metronomed back and forth. She tossed them aside, but they slid forward again, lightly painting Frank's spine.

"That's enough for now," she said.

As she dried him with dabs and pats of a towel, he said, "I'll do that." He sat up, embarrassed.

By what? she wondered. His pain? His helplessness? Her presence here, witnessing both? Or was it her seminakedness? She grabbed a second towel and swaddled herself in it.

Frank's eyes were fixed on the floor. Ariel urged him to stand up. He stayed seated and leaned his head against her flat stomach. Burying his face in the nap of her towel, he locked his good arm around her thighs and held tight. She heard him breathing. She felt the warmth of his breath.

"Does it hurt too much for you to stand?" she asked.

"No, I can bear it."

"I mean, is it too painful for you to stand up?"

"No." Promptly—too promptly—he pitched to his feet.

"You ought to be in bed," she said.

"I'm fine," he insisted. "That talk you mentioned last night, we need to—"

"It's better for you to be lying down."

Hip to hip, her arm around his waist, they swayed out of the shower stall along the corridor to the master bedroom. Ariel felt moisture from her drenched underpants purl down her legs.

His clothes from last night were still beside the bed, a damp coiled anaconda. As he slithered between the sheets, he looked snakelike too, but a snake with a broken back.

"I'll be with you in a second," she told him. "I have to check on Nicholas."

Hugging the towel, she hurried to the living room, where the boy was watching *Jerry Springer,* today's program featuring lesbian lovers, turkey basters, and childbirth. "Mr. Pritchard's sick. Mummy has to help him," she said.

After changing the TV to the History Channel, she retraced her wet footprints down the hall, refusing to think in specifics how she would help Mr. Pritchard. As she passed the guest bathroom, she saw her own clothes—sports bra, jogging shoes, and shorts—on the floor. It would have been simple to stop and put them on. She didn't do that. She reached up under the towel, pulled down her sopping underpants, and dropped them beside the pile.

In the bedroom, she said, "I agree that we need to have a serious talk."

In response, Frank raised his good arm, like a child begging to be picked up. Or maybe not, she thought. No, that wasn't it. He wanted her to lie down beside him. She let the towel fall and crawled into bed cautiously so as not to jostle him. At that distance, really no distance, she felt and smelled and tasted a man whose age was irrelevant. Up close, his face, essentially just his eyes, revealed no imperfections, only deep longing. Her hands, which she believed already knew his body, found his shape changing. And his hands recollected sensations that she had forgotten for ages.

He was good to her. That was the basic truth. He was good to her and for her, and had been for a long time. He cared about Nicholas, and he would let her care for him.

"Tell me if I hurt you," she said.

"Shouldn't that be my line?"

She liked it that he could joke, but didn't imply for an instant that he was anything except dead serious. She liked how he kissed—hungrily, but with no sense that he was devouring her. He proceeded with deliberation, not too slow, not too fast, never as though he had lost track of where he was going, more as if to make sure that they both savored every step.

Supported by her hands and knees, she was poised above him, touching him with her mouth and mound, nothing else. For a slippery second, he was inside her. Then she heard a key jammed into the front door. Ariel felt the jab in her belly. As the lock untumbled, so did her insides. Frank groped with his good hand. Whether to grab her or push her away, she didn't wait to learn. Ariel vaulted off the bed.

"Halloo," hollered Randi's unmistakable voice.

"Hi," Nicholas hailed her from the living room.

Randi stopped to speak to the boy. Their prattle was audible, but impossible to follow. Ariel yanked the covers up to Pritchard's neck. He looked misery-stricken. As for her, she was miserable and stricken and verging on panic. Rewrapping the towel around herself, she shot a glance from the door down the empty corridor. Then she flashed into the bathroom, stepped into her jogging shorts, forced on her shoes, and flexed her arms behind her back to hook her sports bra. She had forgotten the wet wad of her underpants and had to take off her shorts again. The underpants were still soaked. She wrung them out at the sink and considered gunning them with the hair dryer. But there was no time. She wore them wet, with the jogging shorts on top.

In the mirror, she looked like what she was—a woman who had been caught fucking. Her eyes had a shifty glint. Her hair roiled in Medusan wires. There was nothing to be done about any of it.

Outside the bathroom, she bumped into Randi, who was sashaying down the hall, jinking her key ring like a shaman exorcising ghosts from her path. On this chilly morning, she wore wool slacks and a beige cable-knit jumper. "Late for volleyball practice?" she asked.

Ariel suppressed the urge to say, Sod off. "Mr. Pritchard hurt himself. I did what I could for him. Now he needs rest."

Randi pursed her mouth, crimping her upper lip. It was as notched as a gun barrel. Time had gouged its eradicable calculations, and the sun had done the rest. "I'll just look in on him for a quick hello."

"I'd better get back to Nicholas."

"Yes, why don't you? What an adorable little guy."

Frank lay as Ariel had left him, on his back. Eyes screwed shut, he feigned sleep, praying that Randi would evaporate and Ariel would reappear. He felt amputated without her. His cramps and spasms couldn't compare with this aching absence.

"Honey," Randi said. "Honey, are you awake?"

He blinked. "I was asleep."

"I needed to make sure you're okay. Cal phoned to tell me about the break-in and mentioned you had strained a muscle."

"Hmmm," was all he managed.

She sat on the edge of the bed. "Isn't Miss Skinny Butt doing her job? I mean, what's the point of a personal trainer if you end up a wreck?"

"It's not her fault. I was swimming extra laps alone."

"Still, I have to question her qualifications and her common sense. What kind of physiotherapist treats a patient in her shorts and sports bra?"

"It was an emergency. She rushed in when she realized I needed help."

Randi lifted the sheet. "Rushed in before you got dressed?"

"I can barely move much less dress myself. I'm damn lucky she showed up."

"And me?" She released the sheet. It fell over him like molten lava. "Are you lucky I showed up?"

"What is this? The third degree?"

"No. It's your lover who's been waiting for days to find out whether we're getting married."

"I told you I've been thinking." He lowered his voice, hoping Ariel wouldn't hear.

"Why not do more than think? Why not discuss the subject face to face like grown-ups?"

"Because I have a pinched nerve and a herniated disk," he whispered.

"So that's why you didn't call me this week? You knew in advance that you were going to wind up in bed with a backache and Miss Hotpants?"

"Chrissake, Randi, you sound like a jealous teenager picking a fight with her prom date."

"Wouldn't you be jealous if you caught me with another man?"

The question caused an electrical short in his sinews. Had Randi seen Ariel in bed with him? "I wouldn't mind," he lied, "if you were injured and the man was a trained professional."

"Trained professional, my foot! Do you expect me to believe she was here last night innocently licking your wounds?"

Suddenly he saw, as they say, where she was coming from and where this was headed.

"How do you think I felt," Randi said, "when Cal thought I already knew about your accident. He thought I knew—I had to worm it out of him—because he presumed I was the woman in your bedroom last night."

"I trust you told him the truth."

"It's none of your business what I told him. Not after what you've done."

"I haven't done anything. Nobody was in my bedroom."

"That's not what you said then."

"It was late and I was in agony. I wanted to get those security boobs out of my house. If you don't believe me, ask Ariel."

"I don't want to talk to that woman again in my life. Oh, Frank." She coughed up sobs that caught in her throat like fishhooks. "I'd like to take care of you. Why won't you let me?"

"There, there." He patted her leg. The front door slammed. He felt the concussion in every joint. "She must be going over to Cal's. If I was having a fling with her, do you think I'd let her touch him?"

"Why not?" Indignant, Randi dried her eyes on the sheet. "The poor man's harmless."

Pritchard grinned, glad to shift the attention to Barlow. "You'd be surprised what he's capable of."

"I'm never surprised by men and what bastards they can be. Be honest with me, Frank."

"I swear to God Ariel wasn't here last night."

"No, not that. Tell me whether you're still thinking about marriage."

"It's on my mind all the time."

"When will you let me know?"

"Soon as I'm back on my feet."

"That's all I ask, Frank. That you tell me before it's too late."

"Too late for what?"

"Neither of us is getting younger. How much time do you think you have left?"

She couldn't have struck a more discordant note. She might as well have raked her fingernails over his back. Yes, time was unspooling at warp speed. Nothing could stop it. Only Ariel might slow it down and, along with Nicholas, make its passage bearable.

Randi kissed Frank's forehead, dealing him a jolt that spread and played riffs on the xylophone of his spinal column. After she left, he dialed Cal's number to speak to Ariel. But there was no answer. He lumbered out of bed, looking for Nicholas.

Everyone had vanished.

3

How much time do you think you have left? Randi's words clanged like a brass clapper in the bell of his head. More a conundrum than a question. It was like asking, How long is a piece of string? A couple of months ago, Frank would have said, The shorter the better. He had reached the end of his rope and was summoning the courage to let go. But then he decided to settle a few scores, and that had sent him clambering hand over hand back up the rope.

Now all that mattered was hanging on. Hanging on and having Ariel with him. Not that this would defeat death. Like the eye spider, it would always loom at the edge of his peripheral vision—until at last it crowded to the very center and blocked out everything else. What was it Adrian said at the Breakfast Club? If you can't cure it, you gotta endure it.

As the hours unraveled, Randi played no part in his reveries about time, that malleable dimension that quirkily expanded and contracted in concert with the fluctuations of the human heart. No, Randi didn't figure on the clock face that glared at him from the bed-side table. In the chronology Pritchard confronted, she represented the past tense, a disturbance in his slipstream, an ellipsis. He couldn't conceive of what had ever compelled him to cross the fairway to her townhouse. She and he didn't inhabit the same temporal plane. She was digital, he was analogue.

Ariel was tidal, lunar, oceanic. He longed to merge with her. The irony was how little there was of her to melt into. Because of her lean-ness, high coloring, and thin skin, light seemed to stream through her. Mercurial and evanescent, she was more like air than flesh, a zephyr he yearned to ride.

As day dwindled into night, Frank alternately slept and stared at the clock. He didn't bother with the eye mask, the earplugs, or a Breathe Right strip, but he wore the cervical collar. By morning the worst of his pain had receded, and he tottered through the alien won-derland of his house, eager for Ariel and Nicholas to arrive.

Juggling a glass of orange juice and a cup of coffee, he stepped onto the patio. A breeze out of the south bore the scent of suntan oil, and Caribbean spices. He might have flicked on TV and checked the Asian and European markets, but he left it off and sat there smoking and listening to the loose mesh panel luff like a sail.

Tentatively, as though testing his painful shoulder, he permitted himself to speculate about the panther. By now it might be dead. Where would they locate its corpse? He surveyed the sky for carrion birds. None in sight. That was a relief. Still, it didn't guarantee that a gator hadn't dragged its carcass into a pond. If the big cat sank with-out a trace, nobody would believe Frank had seen it. In the clear light of day he had trouble believing it himself.

No matter how he turned the mystery in his mind, he couldn't fathom how the panther had reached Eden. He knew they swam. But at its nearest point, the island was half a mile from the mainland, and it was difficult to visualize the swaybacked, decrepit cat paddling through the Atlantic. Had it miraculously managed to cross the causeway, sneaking by the security guards at either end? Or had it inhabited Eden forever, slinking around the mangroves, migrating in darkness from one golf course oasis to the next, surviving on a diet of lizards and frogs, house cats and pet dogs? Only in old age, as disease slowed it down, had there been those scarcely credible sightings.

After a few hours Frank heard Cal flop into his pool. If he hadn't been waiting for Ariel, he might have gone next door and joined his friend. Not that he was in any shape to race. Still it would have been some solace to sit in the sun and shoot the bull.

Instead, Frank negotiated the ladder into the shallow end of his own pool. Cold water wrapped around his legs, tight as the support hose he claimed to wear for high blood pressure. He released himself onto the sluggish current of the filtration system, floating on his back. With the susurrus of his breath in his ears, he felt just being alive was a gift, a joy, like having Ariel suspended above him, flawless as the blue Florida sky that arched overhead.

Frank did a few desultory laps. Without arms to oar him along, he understood something of what Barlow endured without legs. To stay afloat didn't require much effort, but once you wanted to go somewhere, it took all you had to get there. He thought of Cal being scraped off the prison floor, starting over as an infant. Worse than that, an infant in a wheelchair aware of what he had lost and that he'd never get well again. He had to hand it to Barlow. Had, grudgingly, to concede that he was the better man.

As he was hauling himself from the water, the front-door chimes sounded and he hobbled into the house, convinced that it had to be Ariel. She hadn't used her key for fear that Randi was around. She wanted to give him fair warning. She was always so considerate.

But he opened the front door to find Barlow, dressed now, studying the cinders at the bottom of the light fixture.

"You know, you're right, Frank. We really should do something to
save the anoles."

"What do you suggest?"

"I did some research. Seems these brown anoles aren't completely
blameless creatures. They invaded from the Bahamas and killed off
the indigenous green anoles. Another race war. We might start by
bringing back the original lizards."

This kind of arcana was ordinarily catnip to Pritchard, but at the
moment he was in no condition to appreciate it. He invited Cal in. Barlow gestured for him to come out. The two of them proceeded down
the driveway where an army of ants was dismantling the palmetto bugs
that had been run over. The scene resembled a junkyard of tiny
wrecked cars, foreign roadsters, being cannibalized for spare parts.

"Thanks for your help," Cal said. "The heat's off now."

"I'm shocked they bought my story. Mingle seemed awfully suspicious."

"What do you expect when you're wearing rubber gloves—the
accessory of choice of a B-and-E man?"

"I was in such pain, I forgot I had them on."

"That's what did the trick. Your pain. Gimped up like you were,
nobody would believe you moved those chairs."

"It was the table that almost killed me."

"Why'd you bother with it? You already made your point. But
that's you, isn't it, Frank? You're a guy that can't quit overdoing it.
Sorry you crippled yourself, but now that your night job's kaput,
you'll have time to recover."

"How much time do you think I have left?"

"Jesus, pal, what are you saying? If you're feeling that bad, let's run
you over to the Doc-in-the-Box."

"It's not my health. It's Ariel. I can't get her out of my mind. Yesterday we sort of . . . sort of wound up in bed together."

"Sort of?" Cal's bronze sculpted visage was a leering Olmec mask.

"It didn't last long."

"Length, most ladies'll tell you, doesn't matter."

"This is no joke."

"Hey, it happens to all of us. The first time's tricky under the best of circumstances. But you know the saying—you get thrown by a horse, you gotta climb right back on."

"I didn't get thrown. It was worse. Randi broke in on us."

"She caught you in the sack with Ariel?"

"No, but it was a close call. Ariel got upset and left. I haven't seen or heard from her since. She's never been this late."

"Is it just me?" Barlow clapped a hand to his ear as if it were clogged with water. "Am I old-fashioned? I thought the man was supposed to get the stick on the ball. She's waiting for you to phone. She's the woman you love, not an employee. Give her a jingle. Better yet, go see her."

"You sure?" Frank was palpably willing to be persuaded.

"Sure I'm sure." He started to cuff Pritchard's bad shoulder but caught himself. "Lemme know how it goes. And thanks for the other night." With that, he spun off down the driveway.

Frank waded back through the carnage of palmetto bugs, treading daintily over desiccated shells and segmented legs. By nature and training a can-do guy, not normally a procrastinator, he wanted to call Ariel right away. But he couldn't deal with it on an empty stomach. So he fixed a bowl of cottage cheese with pineapple chunks. Richard Nixon, according to political lore, ate cottage cheese smothered in catsup every day for lunch. Though he had loathed the man, Frank shared Nixon's liking for an unvarying diet, one devoid of strong tastes or complicated textures. It left you at liberty to contemplate the big picture, not the petty concerns of your digestive tract.

But given the size and complexity of the big picture, it took the larger part of the afternoon to achieve an Olympian view. And even then the prospect of speaking to Ariel filled him with all the acne-ridden insecurities of adolescence. He who had negotiated with Yeltsin and various ayatollahs, who had had face time with Reagan, Kissinger, Lady Thatcher, Nelson Mandela, and Bill Clinton, felt that his life depended on the sufferance of a single mother in a trailer in the pine barrens of Florida.

Finally, leaning his elbows on the drainboard to relieve the pressure on his spine, he dialed her on the wall phone in the kitchen. Nicholas answered the first ring. Frank asked to speak to his mother about something atrocious.

"No, dee-licious," Nicholas said, playing their old game.

"I don't think she'd agree. Will you pass her the phone?"

The boy dropped it on the floor. The farthest corner of the trailer was no more than three steps distant, but Ariel picked up the receiver laboring for breath, as if on the last mile of a marathon. Maybe he had interrupted her circuit training. "Six double-ought, treble-four one," she said.

It took him an instant to recognize that this wasn't an obscure South African oath. It was her telephone number. "Are you all right?" he asked. "When you didn't show up today, I was afraid, you know, that you might not be all right."

"Hang on a minute. I'm going to my room for privacy." She pronounced it priv-a-see. "What were you saying?"

Her accent with its curious stresses and cadences caused him to question whether they spoke a common language. And her self-containment made him wonder whether she had truly been in his bed. "I was worried when you didn't show up this morning," he said. "I miss you. I miss Nicholas. I'd like to drive over and pick you up."

She drew a deep breath. "That's not a good idea, Mr. Pritchard."

Her use of his surname sank a blade between his shoulders. "I need you," he said.

"I'll recommend another physio."

"I don't want a different one. I want you."

"Oh, Mr. Pritchard"—her poise evaporated. "—I'm so ashamed. What I did violated—"

"We did. The two of us together."

"—violated every ethical canon. There's a line between a patient and a therapist, and I crossed it. I deserve to lose my license."

"We," he tried again.

"Every caregiver has the same lesson drummed into her. You can't help a patient unless you respect proper boundaries."

"I won't tell if you won't."

"That's not the issue. We can't fool ourselves. After what happened, how are we supposed to reestablish a healing relationship?"

"Simple. Strap Nicholas in the stroller and jog on over. Or let me get you."

"You're in pain. You're in no position to make an informed decision."

"My pain is nothing compared to what it'll be if you don't come back."

"I'll send a substitute." She sounded close to tears. "I'm no good to you."

"Will you please, for Chrissake, cut out the apologies and speak to me as a person, not a client. If I hurt you or scared you, I'm sorry."

"I'm the one who should be sorry. You're the one that deserves compensation. I could be sued."

"Not by me. I don't intend to talk to another lawyer as long as I live." Mention of the length of his life provoked a twinge. "I need you," he repeated. "Give me a chance to make it up to you."

"I can't stay on the line. We'll speak after we both calm down."

"I'm calm," he vehemently protested.

"I'm going to ring off." Then to complete his torment, she added, "Mr. Pritchard."

Frank leaned against the drainboard for a long time. He feared he might throw up his cottage cheese and pineapple chunks. At the corner of his eye, spider legs twitched. He paid them no mind until he realized the hairy appendages weren't eye floaters. They were the feelers of a palmetto bug, peeking through the flaps of the garbage disposal. Any other time he would have regarded this as an appalling violation of his personal space and annihilated the intruder with scalding tap water. But he refused to add even an insect's death to the sum of the world's suffering.

As for his own suffering, he wouldn't accept it. He intended to do something about it. Pushing away from the drainboard, he wondered whether to wear the cervical collar. No, such a blatant play for sympathy was contemptible. So what if his neck felt like a broken dial on a dishwasher, and his head ratcheted from one setting to the next with a resonant click at each slot? He could still drive.

At the road to Tahiti Townhouses, the Jag threatened to turn of its own accord. There lay the avoidance route. Frank sped past it to the security gate.

Down on the beach, the man with the metal detector maintained his lonely vigil, sweeping the sand for nonexistent treasure. At his feet, jellyfish had dried into strands of tinsel. Overhead, a jet tugged a white thread across the evening sky. It didn't detract from the view. Rather, it stitched the otherwise formless heavens together and gave the fading sun something to glow against.

The poured-concrete slabs on the causeway jolted his tires and unleashed lightning up his spine. The ocean, a polished slab of turquoise flecked with silver and gold, offered some diversion from the discomfort. During the last seconds of daylight, neon burst on, and blinking signs across the mainland spelled out praise for our boys in blue, brown, and khaki, heroes every one of them.

On side streets, the neon glow faded to a purplish gloaming. Outdoor grills scented the air. The aroma of hot dogs and hamburgers in olfactory conflict with fried plantains and piccadillo, cumin and coriander, fish marinades and spiced meats. The unfamiliarity of the smells, the foreign faces, the full spectrum of flesh tints had the simultaneous effect of making Frank feel vividly alive and very tired.

The shape of Ariel's trailer, with its outsized front window, resembled the microwave in his kitchen, a high-tech burn box. What would it be like to live there, eating picnic meals under the umbrella, bathing Nicholas in the wading pool? Check out of paradise until the afterlife and sink his roots into these plebeian pines?

A stickler for preparation during his professional career, dependent on briefers and speechwriters, Pritchard had seldom uttered an extemporaneous sentence when something crucial was at stake. Now he was depending on improvisation and the earnestness of his good intentions to compensate for the absence of a script.

The trailer door resounded under his knuckles like a barrel—the kind a fool would ride over Niagara Falls.

"Come in," Ariel called.

The trailer floor wobbled under his footsteps. Or was that his knees? "You leave the door unlocked after dark?"

"Why not?" After her anguish on the telephone, she appeared serene and not at all surprised to see him. Had she known he would come? Counted on it? She sat on the couch with Nicholas, who was in a pair of footed pajamas. A book lay open on his lap. Ariel wore a T-shirt with a Puma logo and a pair of bicycle shorts.

"A stranger could walk in," he said.

"I know my neighbors. Anyway, I recognized your car when you drove up. We don't see many Jaguars on this street."

The trailer was as neatly outfitted as a ship's cabin. Seashells ranked by size on shelves. Photographs magnetized to the refrigerator. A few books, most of them about running. If Nicholas had any toys, he stashed them out of sight. "You need somebody to look after you," Frank said.

She smiled. The laugh lines deepened around her eyes and mouth. He remembered thinking that she would taste like a vanilla milkshake. But her strawberry-blond hair, free of its ponytail, suggested that there would be a fruity after-flavor. "I've gotten very good," she said, "at taking care of myself."

"What happened to Nicholas's hair?" The boy's bowl cut had been shorn to a burr.

"It grew so long," Ariel said, "kids started to make fun of him."

"They called me a girl," Nicholas protested.

"Now there's no mistaking him for a big mun." She brushed a hand over his bristly scalp.

"Mind if I sit down?" Frank edged toward the dinette set.

"Not at all. How are you feeling?"

"Fragile," he confessed. "I need a personal trainer. I'd like to discuss terms with you."

Because of her freckles it was difficult to judge whether she flushed in anger or blushed. "We've been through that," she said.

"I don't expect you to come back just for me. There's Nicholas to consider. You like it at my house, don't you?" he appealed to the boy.

"Yeah, I like the pool and the television."

"In a couple of years we'll have you out on the golf course and the tennis court."

"Really?"

"You can count on it."

Ariel glared poisonously at Frank for not playing fair. "Time for bed," she told Nicholas.

"We haven't finished reading."

"Look at the book in your room. Then lights out."

Scooting around on his knees, he kissed his mother. He climbed down from the couch, and in a move that Pritchard couldn't have choreographed to his greater advantage, Nicholas kissed him too. Then he skidded into his room and slammed the door.

"What a wonderful fella." Frank laid it on thick.

"He has his moments." She drew her bare feet up under her rump.

"Did you run today?" he asked.

"Don't let's talk bollocks, Mr. Pritchard. Say what you're here to say."

"Will you at least call me Frank?"

"Sure. Since I don't work for you any longer, I'll do that."

"Okay, do it."

"Frank," she said.

"Thank you." He rubbed his thighs, the reflex gesture that erased his trouser creases. "You can probably guess what I'm here for."

"And you could guess what I'll say."

"You haven't heard the question."

"I don't need to. I only need to know the right answer. I can't work for you again."

"That's fine, because I don't want you to. I want you to move in with me."

Ariel's hand fell from where it fretted with her hair. Her pretty mouth popped open. "I'm gobsmacked."

"You're what?"

"Flabbergasted."

"Wasn't it obvious how I felt about you?"

"I had a hunch. Still, this is awfully sudden."

"What about your feelings?"

Again her freckled face darkened. She paused for what struck Pritchard as an agonizingly long time. "Well, we have been through a lot together."

"Then why not stay together?"

"Will you please quit fidgeting with your pants? Your shoulders are tensing up. I can see that from here."

Frank let his hands hang between his knees.

"I won't lie," she said, "and claim you don't matter to me. But you're injured now. Once you're better, you'll think this over and—"

"I won't change my mind. I love you. Do you think you could love me?"

"It's not as simple as that, Frank. I'm forty. Not a romantic kid. There are practical considerations. What about Nicholas? Will they let him live on Eden?"

"If they won't, I'll up stakes and leave. I'll buy another house. We could move to South Africa. We could go anywhere."

"What about your daughter? What'll Willow say?"

"I hope she'll be happy for me. Maybe we'll live in Europe and I'll get to see her more often."

"What about your friends?"

"I don't care what they think."

"Not now, you don't. But later, that's when you'll have doubts."

"Sounds to me like you're the one with doubts."

"Sure, I have them. How could I not? There are so many differences between us."

"You mean my age?"

"That's one difference. If we lived together, we might learn there are a lot more."

"Would it help if I said I wanted to marry you?"

"That might frighten me."

"I don't expect you to make up your mind and move in tonight. We can take this in stages."

In his day Frank had been a superb closer. Intuiting acquiescence, recognizing the precise time to move in, he switched from the chair to the couch, as close to Ariel as Nicholas had been. But before he could speak, she asked, "What about Randi?"

He frowned as if deeply confused.

"Don't pretend you don't understand," Ariel said. "She has a key to your house."

"So do you. She's an old friend from when Dorothy and I first settled on Eden."

"She's more than that."

"Nothing compared to what you are. I've made my choice. It's up to you."

She unfolded her legs and crossed her arms. It seemed some part of her had to be wound tight at all times. Frank thought she studied him as she might size up a prospective physiotherapy client. Did she recognize his strengths as well as his flaws? He wanted to highlight his good qualities but feared sounding like a salesman promoting a product. He didn't regard himself as a great bargain, just wanted her to know what she could count on in a friendly merger.

"You wouldn't have to be responsible for my personal training and massages," he said. "I'll hire somebody else for that."

This amused her. "I'm not sure I'd trust anyone else."

"If it's me you don't trust, we can hire a masseur."

"That might be worse," she teased him, and she leaned her head against his chest.

Frank hugged her. "Last winter I wondered whether the world was dying or I was. Now I know it's me. I have a lot of money and not much time. It would please me that you and Nicholas have plenty of both."

She laid a finger to his lips. "I don't need to know everything at once. Let me get used to the idea first."

"So you'll think it over?"

"I will. And you do the same. I meant what I said about Randi. I'd rather not have her around. To be walked in on like that once in a life-time is quite enough."

"I'll get my key back from her. How do you think Nicholas will take the news?"

"He likes you. He'll be happy."

"I was afraid he might complain about sitting on my lap. Or that you would."

"I've never sat on your lap."

"I mean you might not like having him sit there."

"I had my eyes on you to be sure you kept your hands to yourself."

"I do like little boys," he said. "But it's women, it's you, I love."

When he kissed her, Ariel was light as a hummingbird and had a moist darting tongue.

"Mummy, I'm tired," Nicholas called through the closed door. "Please tuck me in and turn off the light."

"I'd better go," Frank said, half hoping she would insist that he stay. But he knew they would have no privacy here, and he had un-finished business on Eden.

In his dreamy preoccupation, he glided along Gumbo-Limbo Lane and through the gaudy crescendo of the commercial grid without switching on his headlights. The guards at the first gate shouted, but he wasn't listening. A full moon spangled the Atlantic and illuminated the causeway. The water's phosphorescence seemed to warm his in-nards, and the night flowed through him as sensuously as a silk scarf.

At the second gate, the guy with the hose splashed the Jag and brought Frank to his senses. Punching on the low beams, he advanced onto the island at a jogger's pace and realized that the next phase—retrieving his key from Randi and returning hers—would be no picnic. He could have driven directly to her townhouse, but he thought it wiser to gird himself for battle. The cervical collar, which he had rejected as mortifying sissiness for a visit to Ariel, struck him as good sense now. Back at his house, he strapped it on and applied a Breathe Right to guarantee an ample supply of oxygen. He considered wearing earplugs, but resigned himself to being loudly upbraided.

The spontaneity, the extemporized emoting, that had marked his proposal to Ariel wouldn't sway Randi. He needed a script and half an hour's rehearsal. Roughing out some dialogue, he hiked a circuitous route across the fairway—and this suggested fairness as his theme. Their relationship simply wasn't fair to a vital woman in her middle-age prime. She didn't deserve to be saddled with a sixty-six-year-old man. While selfishly he had enjoyed the affair, he refused to exploit her generous spirit any longer and wanted to wish her every good luck at finding an age-appropriate partner.

The breeze, Frank couldn't help noticing, carried a whiff of putrescence. This might have been all in his head—the stink of the self-serving alibi he was concocting. But no, the air tasted of . . . what? Decay? Carrion? He feared that he smelled the panther.

Drawn by the scent, he detoured to one of the hardwood hummocks that flourished amid the golf course's manicured grass. Palmetto, jacaranda, and droopy-rooted banyans described the silhouette of a desert island on an undulating green sea, a canopy of foliage where a castaway sailor might survive. But it was death, not survival, that Pritchard believed he inhaled through flared nostrils. He dreaded finding a gutted sack of maggoty fur. Still, he didn't turn back. He felt obliged to face it, just as he would have to face Randi.

He crawled on hands and knees into a tunnel of oleanders. Its depth shocked him, as did the light at the end of it. The tunnel opened onto a womblike space silvered by the moon and stars. A pathetic mewling sound alerted him to the possibility that the big cat wasn't dead yet. In its terminal throes, it might slash at him, might even pounce, determined to draw blood with its last breath. Still, Frank wormed forward.

Suddenly there it was in front of him. A matted pile of khaki-colored fur, a spill of blood at the rear end. The panther lay on its side, its spine arched, its flanks shuddering. As its legs stiffened, formidable claws distended in scimitar curves.

Its death rattle raised the hair on Frank's arms. A fleeting flashback of Dorothy's deathbed brought tears to his eyes. He was about to sob—until he saw two kittens climb up the panther's rib cage and peer blindly at him. Tiny tufted creatures with camouflage speckling, they mewed and burrowed in their mother's pelt for milk. Between contractions, the cat swung its great head around. White fur muzzled its nose and mouth, and masked its agate-shaped eyes. It gave a single deep-throated growl, perhaps in warning, perhaps in pain at delivering the afterbirth.

Whatever, Pritchard backed away slowly, sliding from the passage feet first. Slick with leaf mulch and mud, he forgot his aches and pains, and sprinted off to tell Randi that the panther wasn't dying.

4

"Why won't you watch *The Sopranos* with me?" Randi asked.

"I dunno. Hard to explain." Cal was sprawled on her king-size bed, propped against the padded headboard. His wheelchair stood next to the night table on her side. Somehow in the gymnastic tussle of sex they had reversed positions with neither of them noticing it until now.

"Is it because you're Italian?" she asked. "You think it's defamatory? An ethnic slur?"

"Who says I'm Italian?"

"Well, aren't you? You look it."

"Yeah, I guess I got ancestors from the old country."

"I can imagine *The Sopranos* might offend you."

He combed his fingers through his rug of chest hair. Randi moved his hand to her bare rump. Because unlike her first husband he didn't shed, she could overlook his hairiness as long as he didn't groom himself in her presence.

"It doesn't offend me," he said. "It doesn't do one thing or another for me. I'd just rather watch the *Ally McBeal* rerun."

"Why? Do you like anorexic women? Maybe you've got a letch for Ariel. This is shattering to my ego."

"No, baby. I'm a meat-and-potatoes guy." He slipped a finger between her legs. "Meat and potatoes and pussy gravy."

For the most part, Randi tolerated his earthiness, but she had her limits. Somewhere between "down there," which she favored, and "pussy," there had to be an expression they could compromise on. They needed to discuss this and negotiate an acceptable vocabulary. But not now. Not here.

"Don't you think James Gandolfini is a perfect Mafia family man?" she asked.

"What makes me an expert on the mob?"

"I thought growing up in New Jersey you maybe ran across the type."

"Princeton's in New Jersey. Why not ask me about Russell Crowe in *A Beautiful Mind?*"

"Okay, let's talk about something else."

"I'll tell you one thing about the Mafia, I don't feature any of them blabbing to a shrink."

"That's something they'd keep quiet, isn't it?"

"Yeah, real quiet. Dead quiet."

As he spoke, his hand was exploring her with a skill, a tenderness, that astonished Randi. Everyplace she touched him, he was hard muscle and bone. Yet when he touched her, his fingers felt creamy smooth, nearly as pleasing as his pliable tongue.

"I'll tell you another thing," he said, smiling now. "I was as mad as Tony Soprano when I thought you were spending the night with Frank."

"You know I wasn't."

"I believe you. But it hurt then," he admitted, and he sounded amazed to do so. "It hurt me bad."

After a moment, she asked, "Do you think you'd ever like to take a cruise with me?"

"A cruise?" His voice was solar systems distant as his fingertips pressed closer.

"A luxury liner to the fjords of Antarctica."

"Wouldn't that be cold?"

"Yes, but we'd curl up in a warm cozy bunk in our cabin."

"Sounds nice. But I don't think I have that kind of dough."

"What if it was my treat?"

"Baby, you're too good to me. You'll spoil me." With his free hand, he brought her face to his for a kiss.

"Do you ever think about remarrying?" she asked.

"Is this a proposal?" he joked.

"I'm serious."

"Don't get upset. You caught me off guard is all."

She sat up. Her tongue skimmed her front teeth as though an idea she was searching for might be stuck between them. "I didn't believe I'd ever feel like this again, but I'm ready to spend the rest of my life with you."

"What a sweet thing to say."

"I'm not just saying it."

"I feel the same way about you. But what about the problems?"

"You mean because you're younger than me?"

"I mean I'm in a wheelchair. And I don't have a job or a million bucks in the bank."

"The wheelchair hasn't bothered us so far. And . . ." It took her a moment to get this admission out. ". . . and I have enough money for both of us."

"How do you figure Frank'll react?"

"What's he got to do with it?"

"You tell me."

"I already told you he's a friend. Someone I knew through Dorothy. Nothing more."

"Easy there. I'm just saying the guy's got a key to your house, and I've seen how he looks at you."

"I'm not responsible for the way men look at me. Only the way I look."

"And you look great. I needed to make sure I wasn't breaking something up between you two."

"What you'll break is my heart if you keep harping about Frank. Let's forget him."

"It's hard for me to do that when he's all crippled up with pain."

"Ariel'll take care of him," she said.

"Yeah, I hope so."

"And I'll take care of you."

She lowered her head down the length of his muscled torso. She had begun to like this, especially since he always returned the favor. She no longer even closed her eyes. Kneeling between his knees, she watched him watching her over the stepped ledges of his stomach.

Sometimes Randi Dickson amazed herself. The distance she had traveled, the new her that had evolved in the last few months. The old mantra "This isn't me" seldom entered her mind. She loved the complex, occasionally contradictory woman she had become. Multi-dimensional. Multiorgasmic. And paradoxically all thanks to a man paralyzed from the waist down. Whereas before she believed Frank and Cal might add up to a satisfactory whole, Cal alone seemed sufficient. Why not marry him? Why not?

He flinched. His legs jumped in involuntary spasms. It thrilled Randi to think that sex with her might be regenerative. If they did it often enough and well enough, maybe he'd walk again.

A second flinch, and he palmed the top of her head and groaned. Fearful she was about to get a gullet full of gism, she cinched her mouth, deepening the grooves into a dainty starfish of distaste. Barlow's eyes, she noticed, hadn't glazed over as they did when he abandoned himself to the blue fallout from his pill. He was staring at something behind her.

"What the hell is this?" a male voice boomed.

Randi craned around, the second female in the past fifteen minutes to glance up from her fundamental privacy and confront Frank Pritchard. He hung disjointed at the foot of the bed like a scarecrow that had been crucified in a cornfield. The cervical collar was askew. The twin tabs of the Breathe Right strip had scrolled into quivering scorpion tails. Grass stains streaked his trousers, and a bib of leaf mulch clung to his shirtfront.

"You told me you didn't do this," he shouted. "You said it wasn't you."

"Frank, Frank. Calm down," Cal had the presence of mind to say.

Randi rolled frantically to the edge of the bed, searching for words, searching for her nightgown, searching for a corner of the sheet to cover her nakedness. But there was nothing to hide behind, and the exculpatory phrases—This isn't what you think, I know how this must look—never reached her lips.

It fell to Cal to do the talking. "Why don't you wait in the other room, Frank? We'll get dressed, then discuss this like adults."

"Adults? Is that what you call yourselves? I'd call you a couple of deceiving cocksuckers."

"Slow down, pal. Don't say something you'll regret."

In his lap, Cal's pharmaceutically enhanced manhood described a pulsing question mark. The intrusion hadn't deflated him. It took its own good time, Randi knew, to go down. She wanted to hide his sex as well as hers. But what was she to do? Throw a pillow over him?

"Get out of my house," she told Frank.

"Glad to, soon as I have my key."

"She'll give it to you tomorrow," Cal said. "We'll talk then."

"The hell with talking. The hell with tomorrow. This ends tonight!"

"Fine by me," Randi snapped. "Go and good riddance."

"I come by to tell you about the panther. It's not dying, it's having babies. And this is the thanks I get. You're worse than a two-bit whore."

"Hey, Frank, no name-calling," Barlow cautioned him. "You're not, you catch my drift, an entirely innocent party."

"Get out," Randi shouted. "This is my house, my bed, my body, and I'll do what I want with them."

"I'm not leaving until I have my key."

"Everybody chill for a second," Cal said. "Don't go nuts on me, you two. We're all friends."

On the strength of his arms, Barlow was paddling to the center of the bed when Randi heard a strange voice repeat Frank's question, "What the hell is this?"

In the bedroom door, a man in a dark suit and buzz-cut hair looked on, astonished by the scene in front of him—the naked couple, the white-haired gent slathered in mud and leaf mulch. Randi realized she had seen him before, that day at the tennis court. Only then did it register that he was holding a gun.

"What the fuck are you doing here, Delk?"

"You know this person?" Randi asked Cal. Then to Delk, "How did you get into my house?"

"The door was wide open, lady." He advanced into the room, gesturing with the gun for Frank to move over near the other two.

"Who are you?" she asked.

"He's a private investigator," Frank said. "I bumped into him one night at the marina. But this is going too far. You have no right to invade people's homes."

"What's the problem?" Delk was grinning. "Am I breaking up a threesome?"

Randi couldn't bear to lie there while he examined her like a specimen. She climbed out of bed beside the wheelchair.

"Put down the gun, Delk," Cal said. "Or this time I'll report you."

"To who? The wrinklies guarding the gate?"

"Who is he?" Randi asked again.

"A federal agent," Cal told her.

"Not exactly," Delk said.

"I'll explain everything later."

"I'd like to hear that explanation." Delk was enjoying himself.

"Whatever we have to discuss," Cal said, "let's do it alone. These people don't need to know."

"Does this have something to do with your previous life?" Pritchard asked Cal.

"Bingo! Give Pops a cigar," Delk said.

"I've had about enough of this." Frank turned on Delk. "You're on private property and you're not welcome. Mr. Barlow and his attorney will be happy to deal with you in the morning."

"There isn't going to be any morning, Pops. Just a short, sweet message from Cal's old friends up north."

"How'd you find me?" Barlow was still in the middle of the bed, jacked up on his arms in what Randi's yoga guru called the cobra pose. "You'll never get away with this. Not in front of two witnesses."

"All this easy Florida living, boy, have you gone soft." With his free hand, Delk drew a second gun, a snub-nose .38, from an ankle holster. "There aren't going to be any witnesses. Just a tragic love triangle."

Lionhearted, Pritchard roared and leapt at him. The snub-nose bucked in Delk's hand, making no more noise than a firecracker, a ladyfinger. There was a plume of smoke, the stench of sulfur, a stunned look on Cal's face, and one of deep shock on Frank's. He clasped his hands to his belly, and his shirtfront shed leaves like a red maple in autumn. As Frank sagged to the floor, Randi fell into the wheelchair as if she too had been shot.

"Oh, fuck me," Cal moaned.

"That all you got to say for yourself?" Delk aimed the other gun at him. "No last-minute greeting for the guys?"

"Wait!" Randi screamed. She had a hand between her legs.

"Too late to hide your pussy, lady. I already saw it. I got half a mind to give you a good stiff one before I . . ."

Randi pulled the Beretta from under the seat cushion, and in the same motion, squeezed the trigger. Her first shot flew wild. The second hit Delk in the dead center of his forehead, and he went down.

She sat there shrieking as Cal slithered onto the floor with Frank and Delk. Then suddenly she was on her feet running, still shrieking. But Cal tackled her before she reached the bedroom door.

"For God's sake, get a grip." He pinned her down and gingerly disentangled the Beretta from her fingers. "I need your help."

"Save the panther," Frank babbled.

"He's delirious," she cried. "He's dying."

"He'll be okay if we hurry. Everything'll be okay if you listen to me."

The calmness of his voice had the curious effect of feeding her hysteria. "Let me go. Letmego," she hollered.

"The panther's not dying," Pritchard mumbled.

Cal tightened his grasp. Frank's blood helped glue her bare flesh to the tiles. "Pay attention," he said. "There's no time. You gotta get this straight. I can't be here when the cops show up. You have to tell them what happened."

She shook her head and writhed.

"Not exactly what happened," Cal corrected himself. "Tell them

Frank stopped by for one of his late-night talks. The prowler broke in and shot him, and you shot the prowler." The unflustered pitch of his voice was like an astronaut's, one of those doomed, dead-calm flyers plummeting toward earth.

"You call the police and tell them," Randi said.

"Not me, baby. I been to jail and I'm not going back."

This made no more sense to her than Frank's gibberish about a panther. "Why would you go to jail? You're a witness."

"I'm a lot more than that. The *Reader's Digest* version, I've got a record. The cops catch me anywhere around a gun, they'll slap me behind bars."

It hit her that he might be in shock and every bit as unhinged as she was. But then he explained, "I'm in the Witness Protection Program. If I'd like to go on living, I need to stay in it. And I can't do that if I hang around holding your hand."

"What about Frank? What if he tells the truth?"

"He won't. He knows there's nothing in it for him. Don't you, Frank?"

". . . not dying," Pritchard repeated. Blood was dribbling between the fingers clamped over his wound.

"He has his own secrets," Cal told Randi. "His own interests to protect. Once they patch him up, he'll back your story."

"But if he dies . . ."

"He's gonna live. Can I let you up now? You won't flip out and run?"

She nodded that she wouldn't.

"Bring me my wheelchair. Don't drag the tires through the blood."

Randi felt as spectral as a figure in a nightmare, a naked woman shoving an empty wheelchair toward a naked crippled man, while a second man twitched in a pool of gore and leaves, gabbling about a panther. The stickiness between her thighs, the egg-yolk aftertaste in her mouth, added to the unreality. Then there was the third man, with a hole in his forehead the size of a fingertip and a hole in the back of his skull the size of a fist. Delk had a death grip on both pistols.

Cal wiped down the Beretta with the sheet and held it out to her. "Take it by the butt," he said. "Not the barrel. We need your prints on it. Not mine. Now put some clothes on. And lemme have my stuff."

Agile as an arboreal creature, he scooted up onto the bed and studied the floor. With the sheet, he reached down and swabbed away his leg prints and handprints. Frank's monologue had subsided to disconnected syllables. His upper body was agitated, jerking from side to side. But his legs were motionless.

Randi handed Cal his T-shirt and baggy pants, and he fumbled them on. "They'll ask where you got the Beretta," he said. "Swear it was a gift from an ex-husband or boyfriend."

"Oh, Cal, when will I see you again?"

"Soon, real soon. Gimme a few minutes to get out of the garage. Then phone security. You feel like falling to pieces, do it in front of them."

As he was rolling down the hallway, she called after him, "I love you."

"Me too, baby," was all he had time to say.

5

He freewheeled to the bottom of the driveway before he realized he had left a perfect set of tracks in the fallen bougainvillea blossoms. Reversing up the pavement, he trailed a hand through the petals to disguise his retreat. Then he peeled out, building speed for hundreds of yards in a sprint that made his lungs scream. Perspiration flew from his face and backswept hair, but his mind stayed slow and dry. He was going to get away. There was no proof, nothing to connect him to the shootings.

Still, fast as he traveled, disgust soon overtook him. This rancid scheming and skin-saving were too much like his old life. He was ashamed to have abandoned Frank and Randi. What kind of creep had he become? He used to be a stand-up guy.

As he surged onto the golf course, he tasted tears diluted with sweat. He was crying. Cal Barlow who had toughed it out when he learned he was paralyzed, and when his wife passed on the Witness

Protection Program and snatched his son from him—suddenly he was as rheumy-eyed as a spaniel. Because although he was in the clear, he felt dirty. A crook again and alone. Whatever Frank's fate, he feared that he had lost his friend. Pritchard might pull through with luck and prompt medical attention. But in a few days he'd probably wish he were dead. Then he'd wish Cal was dead too.

Grinding uphill, he gained the island's highest elevation, a berm twelve feet tall. It commanded the Florida flatlands like an overlook in the Alps. Sluggish air swam up from the mangrove swamps, smelling of life and death and infinite gradations in between. As Barlow dredged it down, he didn't have it in him to pray for himself. Pritchard had a hard road ahead, and Cal couldn't make up his mind whether to wish that his friend lived or died. But he did manage one fervent prayer—that Frank had indeed seen the panther before his life broke in half.

From where he sat, he heard sirens and noticed the flashing lights of an ambulance and squad cars. It was up to Randi now. If he had kept going over the story with her, she'd have sounded rehearsed, and the cops would have been suspicious. Better for her to be frantic. As long as she stuck to the general outline, things would work out, he found himself thinking, hoping.

Then he recalled what Delk had said—how soft Cal had gone. Anybody halfway wised up would have recognized that no matter what Randi told the cops, things weren't ever going to be the way they had been. Cal's cover was blown. The mob knew where he lived and what his name was. He couldn't stick around here.

He was headed for his house when it dawned on him he shouldn't go there either. Whoever had hired Delk might be waiting for him. Cal had his doubts whether it was even safe to retrieve his car from the mall parking lot, but since he didn't see himself making a break for the mainland in his wheelchair, he had no choice.

Reduced to a skeleton crew, the security guards were busy gossiping about the shooting and waved him onto the causeway. Once on the other side, he was torn between hiding and fleeing. With eighty bucks in his pocket and a wallet full of now worthless IDs, he didn't figure to get far and he had no safe place to lie low.

He wound up at a corner table at Bare Assets, nursing a drink and ignoring the girls. He needed a plan. He needed to think. As a last resort, he decided, he could contact the feds. The question was how much to tell them and when. If he called now, they'd suspect he had been there when Delk got popped and try to pin it on him. The mental meltdown he was in, he couldn't afford to be interrogated until he calmed down.

Even assuming they bought his story, the feds were bound to relocate Cal, and he wasn't ready to cut himself off yet. There was Frank to consider. And there was Randi. They both deserved an explanation.

I love you, she had said. These days you heard that from people no better than acquaintances. Love you! had replaced hello and goodbye. It was a casual greeting in the street, the end punctuation to a telephone call. But Cal wanted to believe her and wanted to believe he loved her too.

When Bare Assets shut for the night, he drove from that gloomy hormonal den to the glare of a twenty-four-hour-a-day truck stop. Almost as crowded and raucous as the lap-dance joint, the place twanged with country-western music and the laments of long-haul drivers stoked on coffee and speed. "I'm just a bug on the windshield of life," the jukebox wailed, and Cal found himself missing Randi.

One more thing he missed. He missed the Beretta. He felt naked without it. Already unlegged, he was now unarmed. A helpless hunk of meat. So at daybreak he set off to buy a weapon. He knew to avoid gun stores and pawnshops, where he'd have to fill out forms in triplicate and leave a thumbprint. The wrong side of the tracks, deep in narrow lanes leading to the 'Glades, seemed a smarter bet. He soon bumped into a meth freak open to any sort of business proposition. The guy offered him a High Standard .44 Mag Crusader for a hundred bucks.

At that price, Cal guessed the piece had to be hot enough to singe his fingers. And it had the heft of a cannon. When he tucked it under his cushion, it would be like sitting on Big Bertha. Hemorrhoids was the least it threatened. Hadn't he learned anything last time?

He told the freak he would access an ATM and be back in a jiffy. But he was lying. He wasn't coming back, and cranked up like that, the guy wasn't about to wait around with his thumb in his ear.

Out on the highway, Cal tuned in the radio, which interrupted that hour's fourgasm with a news update about last night's shoot-out in Eden. The dead man, suspected of being the prowler responsible for recent incidents on the island, had been identified as a career criminal with a long rap sheet of arrests for extortion, assault with a dangerous weapon, and attempted murder. Currently on parole for manslaughter, he was carrying identification with a New Jersey address.

At the rate events were unraveling, Cal realized it wouldn't take long to tie Delk to his former friends. Then the feds wouldn't wait until Cal phoned them. They'd swoop down and take custody of him. He was running out of time and space and options.

Near the causeway he spotted Ariel pushing the buggy and her little boy. She recognized his VW and flagged him down. Sniffing back tears, she told him, "Frank's been shot."

"Are you on your way there?"

"I've been. There's nothing more I can do. They flew him to Miami."

"How is he?"

"In critical condition, but he's expected to live. They're afraid there's spinal damage."

Barlow's head dropped. As he slumped over the steering wheel, the VW would have rocketed down the road if it hadn't been in neutral. He recalled his own months in rehab—the obliterating pain, the ceaseless pumping of ventilators for quads who couldn't breathe, the nurses flipping you like a burger in a bun.

"Are you okay?" she asked.

He nodded. "Is there anything I can do? Any way to help?"

"Not now. Not yet. Maybe in the days ahead."

"I won't be here," he told her, and he proceeded to spill his guts right there on the roadside. She'd find out soon enough, but Cal wanted her to hear the story from him and hoped there was a chance she would appreciate why he had to disappear. Then eventually, maybe Frank would forgive him.

"I know this is a lot to swallow at once," he said. "But I may not see you again. I'll stay in touch. I'd be grateful it if you'd let me know how Frank's doing."

"What about Randi?" she asked.

"What about her?"

"This morning she told me a lot of what you've just said. Of course, she was stressed out and not always making sense. But she seems to think you two are going to get married."

Cal straightened behind the steering wheel and turned his deeply tanned face to Ariel. "She doesn't understand what that would mean for her."

"I don't know about that. Before you go, don't you think you ought to let her say whether she does or not?"

"Where is she?"

"The police are at her place. She's at Freddy's apartment. "I'm sure she'd like to talk to you."

"Thanks, Ariel. I'll call."

He slipped the VW into gear and pressed the steering wheel, accelerating toward the island, wondering how to convince Randi that the Witness Protection Program would be like a long luxury cruise.

6

On Eden, whenever things went awry, which they do in even the most ingeniously designed machine for living, fail-safe systems and backup procedures kicked into operation. Despite the island's singular lack of success at capturing the marauder who had rioted like a virus through the populace, there were resident experts in problem solving and public relations. So when word spread that Frank Pritchard had been shot, competent individuals assumed control.

By the time the state troopers arrived, paramedics had stabilized Frank on the bedroom floor, and Randi Dickson's personal physician had administered a strong sedative to his distraught patient. Her attorney was on the scene, shouting instructions that all questions should be addressed to him. His client, he said, was in no state to comment. His own comment was No Comment.

Notified of the emergency at his office up north, Bob Emery put the fleet of corporate aircraft at the disposal of the much-beloved former CEO. A helicopter transported Frank to a hospital in Miami where doctors at the Trauma Center were combat-qualified in treating gunshot wounds. A news release described him as "receiving state-of-the-art care."

For days, Randi's townhouse was gift-wrapped in yellow crime-scene tape. Detectives and forensic experts bustled in and out, sifting the evidence. Then after more information about Delk's identity was established, the FBI got involved in the investigation. They questioned Randi and, once he was in condition to talk, Frank Pritchard. In an off-the-record interrogation Cal confessed that he had been having an affair with Randi and was the likely target of the hit. He hadn't been there that night, he swore, and Frank had taken a bullet by mistake.

While the cops were satisfied with this story, scurrilous rumors circulated. Edenites whispered that Randi was known to have a taste for kinky sex, and she and Pritchard must have let things swerve out of control when they invited a stranger in for a threesome. Since Frank had been wearing a Breathe Right and a cervical collar, there was gossip that they had been experimenting with erotic games involving asphyxiation.

Had Randi heard this tittle-tattle, life on the island would have been unlivable for her. But by now she was gone. Nobody knew where. This too prompted rumors.

By contrast, Cal Barlow's disappearance went largely unremarked. Only members of the Breakfast Club wondered—when, that is, they weren't fretting about Frank Pritchard—where the young handicapped fellow was. But then everybody on Eden dispersed for the summer to the cool weather of New England, Upper Michigan, and the Rocky Mountains, and the events of that season faded into obscurity along with all the snowbirds in Assisted Living who hadn't survived the winter.

The Witness Protection Program relocated Cal and Randi to Texas, where, under new identities, they owned a condo in the hills outside Austin. But they seldom resided there or anywhere else for long. Randi's money allowed them to travel for months on end. Once she had had her fill of cruises—they sailed to the Arctic, the Antarctic, up the Amazon, down the Nile, and over to the Galápagos—they started spending time wherever rich people felt safe. Because of all the airports they passed through and international borders they crossed, Barlow knew better than to buy a new gun.

Otherwise, whether in Monte Carlo or Marrakech, Phuket or Zanzibar, his day-to-day existence remained much the same. He took his pills and he took care of himself. To keep from going pear-shaped, he swam, lifted weights, and set out on aerobically draining spins in his wheelchair. He also continued to play tennis until he could no longer tell the difference between the yellow ball and a molting canary.

At Randi's insistence, he consulted an optometrist, who determined that he needed glasses. That or laser surgery. Barlow blurted, "No thank you very fucking much." He wasn't about to have somebody cut his eyeballs. At which the doctor accused him of being a horse-and-buggy guy, a fuddy-duddy who rejected scientific progress. Still, Cal ordered glasses—a pair with tortoiseshell rims reminiscent of Christopher Reeve, pre–broken neck, in his role as the mild-mannered Clark Kent.

Through the *International Herald Tribune* and via the Internet, he stayed in touch with events in south Florida and learned that a panther had been sighted on Key Largo. Animal lovers and environmentalists worried what this might portend. A bloody duel between endangered species? Big cat versus Key deer, those shy three-foot-tall Bambis? You had to pity the deer, but Barlow's money was on the panther—when, that is, he could bring himself to believe it existed.

He also stayed in touch with Ariel, phoning every now and then to ask about Frank. He couldn't let her have his new name or a contact number. But from public phones in foreign post offices, aboard ships, and through satellite hookups in isolated villages, he managed to chart his friend's progress. Or rather, nonprogress.

"Frank's in sad shape," Ariel told him, "Barely looks at anybody. Hardly speaks. Initiates nothing. Answers every question with a monosyllable."

"That could be the painkillers," Cal suggested. "Once he finishes rehab and is back in his own house and on reduced meds, he'll be his old self again."

"I hope so," she said.

But back at home, Pritchard didn't improve. "He's capable of a far better recovery," Arial told Cal. "His spinal column was damaged but wasn't severed. If he worked harder, he could regain a lot of mobility. He might be able to walk with sticks."

"Sticks?"

"Canes. Crutches. Whatever you call them. But he seems to have some kind of psychological block."

"What are you talking about?"

"I'm just repeating what I've been told. They say he may be punishing himself and prefers to be crippled."

"That sounds like bullshit."

"Why don't you tell Frank that?"

"Be glad to. Put him on."

"He won't take the phone. Not from you."

"What can I do if he won't talk to me?"

"Come see him. I know he misses you."

"He said that?"

"Not in so many words. But I'm around him all day, every day, and I can tell."

"If you can read his mind, you know he doesn't want me there. You'll have to handle it."

"I've tried. So has Willow. She was here for weeks. He won't listen to us."

"Why would he listen to me?"

"Because you've been through the same thing. Because he admires you."

"Jesus, that's a laugh," Cal wailed long-distance. "I bet he blames me for everything."

"Well—" She let a long moment pass. "You must feel some responsibility. I understand why you're afraid."

"I'm not afraid. It's just . . ."

"Just what? Do you think I'd trick you into coming back and betray you? Set you up?"

"No, I don't guess you would."

"It's up to you. You know where we are."

He didn't call again. Nor did he discuss the matter with Randi, who had no idea he was in contact with Ariel. The longer he dithered, the more he feared he'd lose his nerve. Then too he feared what Frank might lose with the passage of time. Only in soap operas did people stay the same. In life, they ping-ponged off every angled surface, and each bounce could be the one that landed a guy on hard ground or in the drink.

The next time Randi and he were in Miami laying over for a few days before flying to Madrid, Barlow hired a cabbie to drive him to Eden. They stopped twice on the way. Cal's stomach was a wreck and he ruined a handicapped stall at McDonald's. Ariel was wrong about his feeling responsible. He felt something worse and, for him, far stranger. He felt guilty.

On the causeway, clipping past the fishermen on the catwalk, he suffered another crisis of acute nausea and was tempted to toss his cookies over the guardrail. But at the security gate, he rolled down the taxi window and took some of the hose spray in his face. That helped.

In front of Frank's house, a new minivan with an electronic ramp for wheelchair access was parked under the porte cochere. Nicholas answered the door, receiving him with the solemnity of a midget butler. "I guess you're here to visit."

"You guessed right."

Ariel flitted into view, barefoot, her hair loose to the shoulders. In a T-shirt tucked into jogging shorts, she looked like she had packed on a few pounds, and her freckles had dulled from indoor living. "I'm so happy to see you," she said. "Frank will be too."

"I wouldn't count on that. Where is he?"

"Out by the pool."

She beckoned him into the house. A non-load-bearing wall had been knocked down to enlarge the living room into a paraplegic ward, complete with all the gadgets Barlow remembered from rehab. An examining table, pulleys and weights, parallel bars, a whirlpool and a tilt board. Even that padded gizmo for flipping patients.

"Are you his therapist?" Cal asked. "Or do you have help?"

"No. It's just me. He won't let anyone else touch him."

"He's lucky to have you."

"Well, it's not like he lets me do a lot of heavy lifting. He can be a right stubborn bastard. But I figure if the equipment is around, he might use it sooner or later."

While Nicholas wandered off, Cal and Ariel lingered in the paraplegic ward.

"And you'll always be here?" he asked. "Sooner or later?"

"He wants me to be. He asked me to marry him."

"Like I said, he's lucky to have you."

"I'm lucky to have him too. But I haven't agreed to go through with it."

"I can see why you'd have second thoughts."

"It's not what you think. It's a matter of leverage. I told him I won't marry him until he gets serious about rehab." After a moment, she added, "The night he was shot, he had gone to Randi's to tell her about us. For my own self-respect, I want you to know Frank proposed to me before he needed a full-time physio."

"He told me a long time ago that he loved you," Cal assured her.

"The question is whether he loves me enough to let me help him." She dashed a hand at her eyes, blotting two stray tears. "Sorry," she said. "Girly talk's been off the menu lately."

"You don't mind, I'll take my medicine and say hello to Frank."

"Be patient with him." She stepped aside as he passed down the hall.

Wearing his magician's robe, the one decorated with astrological signs, Pritchard slumped in a wheelchair as luxurious as a brand-new Lexus. Battery-powered, upholstered in sheepskin, with a pneumatic cushion that equalized pressure, this was, Cal recognized, an Independence iBot 300 Mobility System. Steered by a joystick, it could climb stairs, power through sand and gravel, and raise the sitter to a standing position.

A breeze had brushed Frank's hair into a coxcomb. His listless eyes gazed at the pool; rippling water alone gave the illusion of life to his pupils. Although he must have heard Cal wheel up beside him, he barely acknowledged his presence. He treated Cal like noise, lifting his shoulders and lowering his head to block it out.

"Hey, pal." He bumped Frank's chair with his own—a guy in a hot rod nudging a gas-guzzling sedan.

"Don't 'Hey, pal' me." Pritchard spoke in a monotone. "You have some nerve showing your face here."

"How do you know? You haven't looked at my face."

"I know what shit looks like. I've scraped enough of it off my shoes in my day."

"You oughta watch where you step. Chrissake, Frank, straighten up and look at me."

Grudgingly, he turned Cal's way, his eyes cold and hard as seed pearls. "What's with the glasses? Afraid I'll take a poke at you?"

Cal folded the tortoiseshell rims into a side pouch of his chair. "It'll make you feel better, swing away."

Frank shifted his eyes back to the quicksilver of the pool.

"I suppose you blame everything on me," Cal said.

"Who else?"

"It was you—correct me if I'm wrong—busted into Randi's bedroom without knocking. It was you left the front door open."

"I didn't bust in." He uttered each syllable as if passing a stone. "I had a key."

"But why didn't you leave when you saw what was what? You didn't even go when she asked you to."

"I was in shock. I didn't expect to find my friend being blown by my mistress."

"Is that what she was? Your mistress?"

"What she was—what she is—is a cheat. What you are is a crook."

"Ex-crook. Ex-con."

"Ex-friend. Ex-person as far as I'm concerned."

"Jesus, don't you understand? She saved your life. Saved mine too."

"Am I supposed to be grateful?" Frank demanded. "I hate being deceived."

"Hey, you deceived plenty of people. Now you're deceiving yourself. Think it over. Say you came that night to Randi's and I wasn't there. The Beretta wouldn't have been there either, and Delk would have killed you both."

"This is idiocy. I'm talking to a moron. If you weren't with Randi, Delk wouldn't have come there to shoot you and wouldn't have got me instead."

Barlow couldn't deny this.

"Go away, Cal—or whatever you call yourself these days—and leave me alone."

"So you can sit here feeling sorry for yourself? Like you didn't play any part in what went down? I'm not saying—if that's what you think I'm saying—that I don't bear some blame. But there's enough to go around for everybody. Admit it. What Randi and I did wasn't any different from what you were doing."

"Randi never did to me what she was doing to you."

"I'm talking about you and Ariel. You were two-timing Randi."

"That was once." Frank's voice cracked. "For a minute."

"But you'd been wanting to, meaning to for months. I'd never have been there that night if you hadn't told me you were going to tell Ariel you loved her. What the hell, you were about to dump Randi. Be honest, you came to her place to give her the kiss-off."

"Are you claiming she wasn't cleaning your pipes before that?"

"What's the big deal about timing? The bottom line is I didn't do this to you. Randi didn't do it either. I had my way, you'd never have known about us until you hooked up with Ariel and I was ready to discuss my intentions."

"Your intentions!" Frank snorted. "Your intention was to go on fucking Randi."

"No, that was your intention. That's what you did all that winter. You got your rocks off playing Dark Avenger, then ran to Randi and got them off again. I had something more permanent in mind."

"She'd never have married you. She'd never marry any man unless he had money."

"You're wrong. People change. Even you did for a while. Randi and I are married and in the program together."

Frank steeled himself to show no reaction. The wind died, and his coxcomb drooped. "Congratulations," he deadpanned. "Tell me your pattern and I'll send silver."

"This is stupid," Cal said. "We're fighting for nothing. You told me you didn't want to marry Randi. You're with the woman you love."

"Yeah, and a lot of good I am to her."

"That's up to you."

"Oh, please, spare me the sermon. It sounds too much like a pitch to a sucker. Something from one of your bust-out schemes."

"I didn't give pitches. I showed people the numbers and let them make up their own minds."

"Then do me a favor and let me make up mine. Don't feed me a lot of happy horseshit about how much I have to live for."

"I won't kid you, Frank. You won't ever be what you were. But there's things that help day to day. Stuff you could do for yourself and have a better life."

"What? Pills? Drooling over the lap dancers out on the highway?"

"I'm talking about rehab. I'm talking about letting Ariel help you."

"Help me do what? Hobble around on crutches?"

"Sounds pretty damn good to me. You could go to the Breakfast Club. Take boat trips and snorkel at the reef. Go kayaking with Nicholas and Ariel. What the hell, you could play tennis like me now that you don't have to worry about back pain."

"Not interested," Pritchard said.

"What about the panther?"

This perked him up a bit.

"You could search for it," Cal said. "Make sure nobody else finds it and hurts the kittens. But you can't do that sitting on a high-tech toilet seat. The panther would hear you a mile away. You need a chair like mine, and some shoulder and arm muscle to push it. Swimming would shape you up."

Frank shook his head. "No, I'd rather—"

"Rather what? Shrivel up and die?"

"Sometimes that doesn't seem like such a bad idea."

"But you won't do it. If you were going to, you'd have done it by now. Nah, you'll sit in that sofa-size chair, too chicken to do anything except whinge." He used Ariel's word, the one that sounded like a combination of "whine" and "cringe."

"What do you suggest I do?"

"Jump in the pool."

"You need legs to jump."

"Then just let yourself fall."

The water's sun-dazzled surface cast a jeweled spell over Pritchard's face. He stared at it, and let it stare at him. Then lowering his head, he jerked forward and thrust out his arms. Tipping out of the chair, his dead weight sank into the pool and he lay motionless on the bottom. Variegated as coral, he appeared to undergo a change into something rich and mysterious as his loose-flowing robe spread out in the signs of the zodiac.

Barlow feared that the fall had knocked Frank unconscious. Or maybe he had mistaken what Cal meant when he urged him to jump. Was he drowning himself? But then Pritchard slowly floated to the surface, and shedding his magician's robe as he rose, he set off in a laborious crawl, milling the water with his arms. After a second, Cal stripped off his shirt and trousers and dived in to join him. They didn't race. They advanced side by side in what Ariel would have called social swimming.